COUNTENANCE OF MAN

COUNTENANCE OF MAN

Matthew Nuth

Columbus, Ohio

This book is a work of fiction. The names, characters and events in this book are the products of the author's imagination or are used fictitiously. Any similarity to real persons living or dead is coincidental and not intended by the author.

Countenance of Man

Published by Gatekeeper Press
2167 Stringtown Rd, Suite 109
Columbus, OH 43123-2989
www.GatekeeperPress.com

Copyright © 2018 by Matthew Nuth

All rights reserved. Neither this book, nor any parts within it may be sold or reproduced in any form or by any electronic or mechanical means, including information storage and retrieval systems without permission in writing from the author. The only exception is by a reviewer, who may quote short excerpts in a review.

ISBN (hardcover): 9781642373424
ISBN (paperback): 9781642373158
eISBN: 9781642373165

Printed in the United States of America

I peered over the edge to look down,
Rocks and branches coated as with fine powder,
Just beyond the reach of my fingers.
Water chilling my arms,

I swirled my extended hand 'round
Expecting to disturb the sediment of everything under
But, finding no impact to linger,
Leaving the dusty blanket without harm.

I reached in farther to touch a stone
Seeking to retrieve this for personal collection,
To feel the cool, smooth surface,
Only to find that rock farther than expected.

Failing to reach is not my problem alone
For the shallow was only a perception.
So, my stone remained beyond purchase
My understanding of depth corrected.

Chapter 1

It had been a long time since my memory had been jogged back to my early days in Fort Collins. I can remember my dad banging down the hallway, hollering "time to get up" to start each day. On weekends, I would roll over, bury my head under the pillow, and hope that just this once he would let me sleep in . . . but, just like a snooze alarm, five to ten minutes later, here he'd come again. Persistence really should have been his name. He would not give up until I would swing my feet out of bed onto the cold wood floor and shuffle off to the bathroom.

Back then I thought his waking me early was his personal way of joking with me, while gently instilling a personal habit even though it wasn't as if I really had anything important I had to do on Saturday mornings. After all, I was too young to find a job and too old to watch Saturday morning cartoons on the television. All I would do on a normal sunny, summer Saturday would be mow our small lawn and then run down to the park to play baseball with my friends. Dad knew this aggressive schedule really didn't require me to be up at seven in the morning, but he took great pleasure in getting me going early.

All in all, I have to admit it was probably a good thing my paternal alarm clock worked so diligently. It was nice to have my limited chores done before the sun had reached its apex in the sky. My friends and I pretty much had the day to ourselves; to exercise our independence, to enjoy our day with the only requirement of being home in time for dinner. It was a simple time; a time when our major daily concern had been whether or not we would have enough kids show up at the park to field two teams for weekly baseball games.

Looking at Dad now made me long for those days. Gone was the mischievous smile and vibrant eyes. They were now replaced with a mouth that had somehow shrunken and pulled back tightly against the few teeth he had left. There was no hint of movement from his lips when I had walked in; it had remained slightly agape . . . and so dry it hurt me to look at it. His eyes . . . well there had been that brief moment of recognition and brightness when I first saw him, but it had faded as quickly as it had come. They had returned to a place that only he knew, certainly not this room.

I had not been back to Fort Collins very often to see Dad these past few years. Certainly, not as much as I would have wished; it's funny how quickly time flies. I can remember my wife suggesting that we needed to make time to visit since it had been so long since we had made the 1,100-mile journey from San Diego to reconnect. Weeks turned into months. Months turned into years. Maybe, I'm not such a great son. This time, however, it had really only been a few weeks since our last visit, but the change had been so sudden that I was shocked.

The bedroom no longer resembled the place my wife and I had stayed in the few times we had visited. The four-poster, double bed that we had spent years joking about how hard and uncomfortable it was had been temporarily dismantled and leaned against the far wall to make room for an adjustable hospital variety.

This new bed may not have been torturing its occupant; even

so, the occupant appeared more tortured than any soul I have ever seen. The bed stand was cluttered with items foreign to this previously homey room. They were the items necessary for preparing for death, not life. There were the sanitary wipes, the antibiotic cream, the towels, and the pain medication, a small bottle of liquid opiate administered drop by drop. Dad's pain became evident anytime he was moved; it was the only time his face broke with emotion. Paul Simmons was dying.

His hands held a beaten, dark blue, leather-bound book, its covers cracked with age and use. The pages had become bent over the years to a point that it no longer closed completely without the assistance of a heavy rubber band binding it closed, just as Dad's mind had become. Mom said she thought it was a journal of some sort, but really could not be sure since Dad had kept the contents to himself over the years. As far as she knew, no one other than Dad had ever seen the pages.

Chapter 2

WHAT A DAY this would be. Paul had much to do before heading off to school; he had set his clock to ring at 4:00 am. He had promised his father he would set up the shop for the awning production this morning. A batch of new material had arrived yesterday and he should have dropped by after school to unbox and log it into stock. He had had so much schoolwork to get to, he had to put off the family work that should have been done yesterday until now.

Slipping out from underneath his woolen blanket, Paul could feel the cold grip of the Colorado morning take his breath away. He sat on the edge of his bed, shivering, trying to motivate himself to stand up and start the day. He could hear the bustling noises of a fully awakened household two flights of stairs below him; Mother was already up making him breakfast and a sandwich for his school lunch. Paul could not remember a time that he had not awoken to that noise; sometimes he wondered if she ever slept. Paul rocked out of bed shaking the sleep from his eyes and began to shuffle to the steps and down to the bathroom. His thin arms wrapped around his body's bare torso to keep warm and to try in vain to control his shivering.

He had loved the idea of moving up from the second floor to the finished attic last summer. It provided him a room all to himself; something that neither he nor his younger brother, William, had ever experienced. The room was absolutely great that first summer; the windows looked out both the front and the back the house and, when opened, provided for a fresh breeze keeping the space cool and comfortable. The space was huge, representing an entire floor of the house. The high-pitched ceiling had only added to the uniqueness of the room. Of course, there were some downsides to the move; first his brother wanted to continuously encroach on his privacy, secondly, he ended up sharing the space with Mom's seasonal decoration storage, and lastly, it got really cold on winter mornings. This morning was one of those cold winter mornings; the bare wood floor chilled his feet as he made his way to a hot shower that seemed to promise the only hope of defeating his shivering.

In the bathroom, he completed his morning ritual. He rubbed his face to feel the imaginary beard stubble growing. This year Paul had begun shaving once a week even though his facial hair was more akin to the fine fuzz you expected to see on a grandmother's face than the face of an adult male . . . but in Paul's mind these were whiskers; as rough and vibrant as any man's. Perhaps the whiskers would turn dark . . . next year. He rubbed his face once again and decided it wasn't necessary to shave today; he could pass on using the shaving cup and soap Dad had given him two years ago for his 15th birthday. He turned on the shower, yanking his arm out as quickly as possible hoping to avoid getting splashed by the frigid water. He would let the water heat up while he brushed his teeth, as he did every morning. After the shower, he slipped on a pair of straight-legged, narrow jeans, a long-sleeved flannel shirt and then pulled on his well-worn, brown, lace-up work shoes and bounded down the last flight of stairs to the main floor of the house to eat breakfast.

Paul loved everything about this house, but the main floor was special to him. Although it wasn't particularly large, it was a place to for family and friends to get together. The steps ended at a small foyer off which there was a seldom used sitting room to the left, a living room/dining room to the right. Across the foyer from the steps was a simply carved, oak front door with colorful leaded glass leading to a covered porch, facing the street.

As with every morning, Paul exited the foyer on the right to walk through the living room and dining area to the rear of the house, to the ever-bustling kitchen.

Dad was already up by now, sitting at the table in his faded bath robe reading the paper. Early morning was Dad's time. He seemed to be oblivious to Paul, completely focused on the news from around the world and from down the street. It was if his day couldn't really start without this news fix; it was his addiction . . . and the addiction had become more severe with the wars waging on in Europe and the Pacific. With each passing day, Dad had become more concerned and convinced that this war would touch him and his family, personally. Ever since the United States had been compelled to enter the fray, he had been filled with a sense of foreboding.

Without a single movement, Paul heard his father's voice emit from behind the paper, "Paul, it's about time you got up and running."

Paul made no comment but glanced over to his mother for support with a "you have to be kidding" look. For Christ's sake, William would not would not be moseying down the steps for another two hours. Unfortunately, Mom appeared too preoccupied with cooking eggs and bacon on the stove to come to his defense. Paul could only guess that if she had heard Dad's comment, she had no desire to get caught up in the discussion this morning.

Dad continued, "Yesterday, you promised to get the material ready for sewing on your way home from school."

"That's why I set my alarm so early. I'll take care of it before I go to school."

Dad, looked up from the paper, eye's raised to look over his reading glasses. "No need to, I took care of it last night. I didn't want to take a chance on not having the material laid out and ready for sewing when Lyle and Virginia show up." Lyle and Virginia Jones had worked for Dad as long as Paul could recall. They would show up at 8:00 in the morning, Monday through Friday, and sew awnings until the day's production plan was completed. It wasn't unusual to walk by the shop at 8:00 at night and still see them finishing up the day's work. Dad paid them through a share of the profits rather than paying them an hourly wage; it seemed to fit them just fine.

Paul plopped down at the table without muttering another word, and buried his eyes in the plate of hot, just-out-of-the-frying pan eggs, disappointed both in his Dad and himself. He couldn't help but think that he had let down Dad. It never failed, Dad had to have things done his way. If he wanted something done at a particular time, it had to done at that time. He was a stickler for schedules and process. He was methodical in everything he did. Who could argue; it had served the family well. Their awning shop had grown and seemed to be a healthy business, they lived in a nice home close to downtown, on the corner of the very middle-class Mathews Street and Mulberry Avenue, drove a reasonably new Plymouth, and they always had food on the table. Growing up in the Depression had certainly been a lot easier for Paul than it was for most of his friends. At least that's what Dad always said.

Since he was already up so early, Paul decided to walk to the awning shop to see if there was some chore or task he could complete to potentially make amends for his lack of reliability the day before. The shop was only a few blocks west of home, just off the main north-south road through town, College Avenue. He unlocked the front door and stepped into the darkened shop. He always felt somewhat at ease when opening the shop. Even though he didn't really like the work, it was somehow rewarding to look around his Dad's shop and considered it his too. He was at home here, it was a place and feeling that none of his friends knew. His Dad didn't work for someone else; his family owned a business. It was a strange feeling of pride and power; controller of one's destiny, so to speak.

The shop consisted of two rooms; a front sales area where miniature awning samples hung from the walls and back work area that had two long stainless steel-wrapped work tables with industrial sewing machines bolted to the ends plus a work bench designed for building awning frames.

Paul entered the store from the front. He hated entering the shop from the back; the work area was so dark until all the lights were on, it gave him the willies. In the front, he liked the way the morning sunlight would blaze through the two big show windows. The whole area seemed to explode with light as the sun came up. In fact, he would have to shield his eyes from the glare. No hidden ghosts or demons in the front room.

Even though the shop was "neat as a pin," as Dad would say, Paul grabbed a broom from behind the door and mindlessly started to sweep the faded green and white 12 by 12-inch square, checkered linoleum. He had completed this task so many times he had made a game out of it. The challenge was to see how much dust he could pile up in the process. It was a way of demonstrating some small achievement in that he was completing a task better than Dad. After finishing in the sales area, making sure the dust had been gathered into a small pile on the green floor square directly in front of the doorway leading to the workroom, he could now begin with the back. In the backroom, life looked different; all the lighting back here was a harsh fluorescent. It numbed the body and was as dead as the sunlight in the front room was alive and vibrant. It was no wonder that his Father elected to spend as little time as possible in this back area. Although he had originally kept the business's books and completed the majority of the office work from the work room, he had moved these tasks to home years ago. For the awning shop, however, this back area was remained the heart of the business; the center of production and installation. Paul was especially meticulous with his sweeping. The floor back here was a shiny lacquered hard wood. It had seen years of wear, and yet,it still shined like crazy if you kept it clean. You could see any dust from a standing vantage point even in the unnatural lighting.

On the south-side wall, steps led up to a semi-open attic area. This was where all supplies: framing materials, sewing materials, tools and replacement parts for the sewing machines were kept. The Canvas was stored in roll form, hung on the back wall of the main work area. Everything that was crucial for the awning manufacturing was kept in the store, except for installation materials and tools. For that, Dad had purchased new, a dull green 1937 GMC panel truck that he kept parked in the alley behind the store. The business had done well and Dad had been looking for options to extend beyond awnings. The panel truck was center to his plans to expand into home remodeling.

Awnings! Even though the business paid for everything Paul's family needed, it offered nothing of particular interest to him. It was a pedestrian vocation and offered little of the excitement cherished by a 17-year old. That said, Lyle and Virginia's pedestrian demeanor appeared perfectly well fitted for a role sewing, assembling and installing awnings. Although always nice to him, they had personalities that made the drab forest greens, browns and the occasional striped awnings look incredibly colorful and vibrant. Paul could not discern if they had been boring to start with so chose a boring vocation or if a boring vocation had rubbed off on them and muted their spirit.

Little did Paul understand that awnings held nothing of particular interest to Lyle, Virginia, or for his Father and his Mother, for that matter, other than it had provided them a means to pull themselves out of the poverty from the previous decade. Paul and his brother had been too young to understand the financial challenges his family faced when the stock market crashed tanking millions of jobs with it. The modest family wealth evaporated quickly, and by 1931, Paul's father had been forced to drop out of the mechanical engineering program at the Colorado Agricultural College to earn what little he could in Fort Collins to care for his young family. He had needed to potentially sacrifice a better future to keep the current together. Paul's father had always planned and desired to go back to school to become an engineer. The awning business was nothing more than a means to an end. Even at his middle age, quietly he had made plans to finally begin attending school at Colorado A&M next fall. In his case, it would always be next fall.

Likewise, the business held little excitement for Lyle and Virginia. The Depression had thrown them into a similar predicament as Paul's family. Lyle, Virginia, and Paul's father had been childhood friends. The Depression had made them part of an extended family. Paul's father had applied what little capital he had to opening the business, and Lyle and Virginia agreed to work there for a modest salary and split of the profits. The relation had carried them through some rough times, but everyone, except Paul, understood the business was due for change, to grow into something new or die.

For Paul, the business was old, depressing, and certainly

not in his sites for his future. His morning and late afternoon routines at the shop were as much as he could handle. For him life centered on school and basketbal and not in that order. As soon as he had completed his sweeping, he pulled on his coat and ran the three blocks home to gather up his brand new, white canvas, high-top basketball shoes and his kid brother and head off to school.

The basketball shoes represented a significant milestone for Paul. As a sophomore, he had made the high school's varsity basketball team and Dad had purchased him a pair of Chuck Taylor Converse All-Stars just in time for their first game. It was the first time his father had acknowledged Paul's skill, success, and love for the game. It was also the first game his father had ever attended.

* * *

I had been dozing off for several minutes when Mom had come into the room to give Dad his pain medication. I was not aware of how long she had been in the room, but when I started she apologized for interrupting me.

"Randall, sorry to startle you. It just took me back to better times when I saw you sitting there with your eyes closed. You look so much like your dad. I won't disturb you anymore. I'll just give your dad something for his pain and let you have your time with him, alone. When he starts to groan, I just don't know if he is hurting or just dreaming." Mom, pulled the stopper out of the small bottle she had picked up from the bed stand. She placed a small drop of the opioid into the corner of Dad's mouth and quietly sat beside me, forgetting that she had intended to leave me alone with him. Her reddened eyes belied the memories of better times with her husband of more than 50 years.

"Mom, I am surprised that Dad is holding on to that book.

I tried to lightly take it from him to put it on the bed stand, but he had none of it. In fact, he grabbed onto it pretty tightly," I noted.

Mom just nodded. "You know as he was getting bad, he had asked me to make sure he could hold onto this so as he would not lose it. He said it reminded him of a number of things he still needed to do."

"What does he think, that he is going to take it with him? Do you think he would mind if I took a look at what he has written?" No sooner had I asked than I realized how thoughtless I must sound to Mom. Here her husband, my father, is passing away and I am talking as though he is not lying right next to me, disparaging his privacy and seeking her approval to have access to what? His secrets? His concerns? His fears?

Mom, surprised me as she always did. She gently leaned over to Paul, gave him a kiss, whispered something into his ear and gently removed the book from his hands. She then quietly stood up, placed the book in my lap and said "Don't tell me anything." and left as silently as she had entered.

I was dumbfounded. I had no idea what to do at this moment, feeling as though I now have access to something I should not know, or perhaps access to something my father had longed to say, but had no idea how to. I chose to believe the latter.

Chapter 3

Dad, I am sorry for leaving. August 8, 1943

We need to do things in our lives that we think are right. I think this is one of those times. Forgive me and be proud of me; I am going to be a soldier.

It had been an hour since they had returned from the bus station after sending Paul off. As soon as they had returned home, Dad had disappeared upstairs. Mom and William could hear the sound of sobbing upstairs. She cautioned William that this was something his dad had never prepared for. "It is necessary to leave Dad to some peace and quiet. He'll come down when he is ready."

Both could hear a door open and close, the quiet, deliberate footfalls coming down the steps into the entry. Paul's father gathered his wife and remaining son together in the sitting room. Tears were streaming down his face. It was particularly disconcerting for William in that he had never seen Dad cry before. "Mother and William, I want you both to know how proud I am of Paul for doing what he is doing, but I fear I may never see him again."

* * *

Basic training had been a pretty different experience than anything he had expected. He recalled grinning in spite of being scared as hell as he first stepped off the bus. He had been scared. anxious, apprehensive, and energized as never before. It now struck him; he was on his own. The heat was already suffocating even though it was still only the first week of June. Back home, June was wonderful, warm during the day, with just a hint of cool in the evening coming from being over 6,000 feet above sea level. In Fort Collins, it was daily blue skies only interrupted for a couple hours each late afternoon for rain showers. Here, it was 95 degrees at 6:00 in the evening, and humid . . . the sweat continuously beaded on Paul's forehead, dripping down his face, stinging his eyes. Not too bad, but certainly, not great. He had escaped Fort Collins, trading one "fort" for another. The new fort, Fort Benning, in Georgia and the 1st Infantry Division would change his life. Mom had been dead set against him joining the Army and Dad had not known that he had planned to enlist. He was shocked when Paul announced to the family he had graduated from high school early and would be leaving to join the Army in a week. He had not provided them much notice; it was intentional to give them less opportunity to deter him. The excitement had been real and overwhelming; yes, excitement, but also trepidation, about this new challenge. He could not shake the anxiety about what he left behind: the caring family he had always been able to rely upon and a potential scholarship for a college education, something always out of reach for his father.

All-in-all, basic training had not been as bad as his friends had suggested; it had been worse. Yes, Paul had to endure a complete lack of privacy, marching, shooting, fox hole digging, studying, marching, grenade throwing, defense drills, and yet again more marching. He had little time to even think about home. Although he had thought his being an athlete and exceptional student would serve him well, it never prepped him for the monotony of long hikes or the fear of crawling under barb wire and real machine gun fire. Fun times. After four months, Paul had begun to question the wisdom of his choice. Even so, he was happy to be out of Fort Collins and serving his country. Basic training was complete and Paul was on his way to join the 1st Infantry Division in England.

* * *

After thumbing through Dad's blue journal, I could see he had been pretty inconsistent in documenting his life. He sometimes had entries for several days in a row, only to be followed by gaps that appeared to extend for years. The entries themselves varied in length from only a couple of lines to some entries that extended for several pages in Dad's small, controlled hand writing. The book was almost completely full and included several loose sheets that suggested that he had kept the book with him, occasionally returning to entries to provide updates, almost as afterthoughts.

I would never have expected Dad to be one that would have maintained a journal. He had always been one of few words, but as a kid, I thought this was a result of having little to say to me or my brother. I had not given him credit for the potential of having some level of deeper thinking or emotional intelligence. Actually, I had thought of Dad as always being somewhat one-dimensional, just focused at making money and providing for our family. Keeping a journal was something I had equated to sensitivity and personal awareness, two traits that I would never have assigned to Dad.

Although I had known Dad had served in the Army in WWII, he rarely discussed it, and it did not seem that he had kept any contact with any army buddies. For me, every time Veteran's Day came around I had a degree of sorrow for Dad. For him, the Army and war appeared to be distant memories, pages of life that had turned, never to be referenced again. "Mom, you used to have some old boxes of pictures. Anything in them from when Dad was young?"

No sooner had the words fallen from my mouth than I realized how disruptive my talking out loud might be to Dad. Thankfully, he was lying peacefully, so peacefully that I actually leaned over him turning my head so that my ear was close to his lips just so that I might hear the short breaths validating that he was still with us.

As I stood back up, I felt Mom's left hand on my arm. She gently pulled me out of the room with her right index finger raised to her lips as an admonishment to me to be quiet, but also as if she was leading me to some secret place, confidential only to her, and now me. At the end of the hallway was the doorway leading to the basement, the family storage area. Selfishly, I had always wanted to ferret though the boxes stacked down here to see what long-forgotten items from my childhood still existed here.

"Randall, it has always been a mess down here, and I am sorry to say it has gotten a lot worse since Dad's health has been failing." Behind a number of boxes strewn on the floor were a couple of chrome, wheeled shelving units packed with additional boxes filled with decorations for Christmas, Halloween, Easter, and Thanksgiving. Given the dust gathered on them, it was apparent that Mom had stopped decorating for the seasons several years earlier. As she pulled on a rolling shelving unit, she asked, "Here, can you give me hand pulling this thing out of the way? Back there, against the wall, you see that plastic filing box?"

I pulled the shelf to the middle of the room, making room

among the boxes, pushing them out of the way with my foot. In the farthest quarter of the basement, next to the water heater was a large plastic storage tub with a hinged top. Thank goodness, the tub was strong and had good hand holds, it was heavy and obviously full. "God, Mom, what do you have in here?"

"Who knows? I started years ago, to consolidate this into books that might be good to hand down to you, but I always seem, to get distracted. I'll pull out a picture, stare at it, and before you know it the day's gone. I still need to get it organized so I am glad you asked. Let's take it upstairs to the kitchen. There, you can spread out on the table."

As I lugged the box up the steps, I could not help but wonder how I never knew about this potential treasure trove about my family's past. I placed the box on the floor in the kitchen and quietly walked back into Dad's room to snag the journal I had left on my chair.

* * *

Paul, stepped into what would become his new home and new family for the next several months. It would be a family eventually; however, today, he could feel the indifference upon first entering the barracks, leaving him feeling alone and out of place, five thousand miles and an ocean away from home.

The barracks for Paul's platoon was empty except for four soldiers taking a break from the day's activities. Apparently, downtime was a part of the daily routine, something that was necessary but needed to be managed effectively in order to maintain moral. The only greeting upon entering came from a private who was so pre-occupied with cleaning his rifle that he could not be troubled with actually standing and shaking hands with his new compatriot. He remained seated, head bowed over his rifle. Without interruption, he continued wiping the stock of the M-1 with a rag, raised his eyes to glance at Paul then down to Paul's duffel bag with SIMMONS in block black lettering emblazoned across its side. "Simmons, your bunk's back to the right," gesturing with his thumb and returning to his gun as if Paul had not existed.

The barracks was laid out as a long rectangle with 16 bunks lining each side, enough for 32 soldiers. Between each set of bunks, there was just enough room for two green footlockers, one for each soldier. At the rear, there stood a second door, exiting the barrack to the latrine. Moving down the aisle, first to the right, in a lower bunk lay a soldier with his boots crossed reading a *Look* magazine. Beyond him, also on the right, sat a soldier in the standard drab olive-green T-shirt and boxers slowly polishing his boots. At the far end of the barracks by the latrine door was his bunk with a strip of adhesive tape with the same style, black block letters "SIMMONS" as marked his duffle.

Next to Paul's bunk, sat a large man, silently reading a book. He was still wearing the drab olive-colored pants and black boots of the US Army uniform; he, too, had discarded the standard uniform buttoned shirt in deference for an equally drab olive-colored T-shirt. Even though Paul was tall at 6'2" and athletic, this fellow made Paul feel puny. Standing up and smiling, Paul's neighbor for the next several months stood and extended a hand. "Hi, I'm Orley. I take it you are Simmons?" Orley's, deep but soft voice somehow belied his sheer size. He stood at least two to three inches taller than Paul, but the truly impressive aspect of his size was his physique. He looked as though he could take on the Germans with bare hands. The arms, muscled and defined were twice the size of Paul's. Paul estimated this man probably tipped the scales at 250, and none of it was fat.

In spite of his intimidating size, Orley's smile was disarming. Happy to shake hands, Paul introduced himself. "Paul

Simmons. Is it always this quiet and friendly?" nodding to the individuals and referring to the indifference that permeated the barrack at this time of day.

"Hey, folks need their personal space and time. Not much of it here. They are all good guys, as soon as you get to know them. Paul, pretty soon you'll be just like them, cherishing those few moments to yourself." Since joining the Army, Orley was the only man to refer to Paul by his first name, and he would continue to do so from that time on. Regardless of his rank, it would soon become pretty clear to Paul, Orley was a real leader in the platoon. Orley's use of "Paul" would catch on with the rest of the platoon quickly. Everybody was referred to by last name or nickname: Orley, Hernandez, Baker, "Flash" and such, but the use of "Simmons" was discarded by everyone in the platoon within a couple of weeks. Paul remained just "Paul."

"What's that that you're reading?" asked Paul, more out of a desire just to speak to someone other than genuine interest.

"*A Tale of Two Cities*. You know it's a classic I skimmed through it when I was in school, but I never really appreciated it at the time. The descriptions are amazing; you can close your eyes and imagine what London and Paris must have been like 150 years ago. Thank God, we live today and not then. You know, soon enough you and I are going to see Paris for ourselves." Orley smiled again and added, "Let's hope it's a hell of a lot nicer than the Paris of Dickens and the Revolution."

Paul had never read *A Tale of Two Cities*, but was reluctant to let the conversation die, plus he did not want to come across as being ignorant of the "classic" to his new friend. "So, you like the book? I wasn't expecting there to be much time to read here."

"Time is one thing we have plenty of. Not that we don't keep busy most the time, but we have a lot of time where you have to be creative to avoid boredom. Some play sports, you can always catch on with a game of baseball or basketball. If you want to head over the Brit sector catching on with a soccer or rugby game is always easy. We have movies at night. I prefer reading and smoking. That said, I do have to admit busting some of the British heads in rugby is great. Even after getting themselves all bloodied, they still are happy sharing a couple beers to recount the highlights of the match. Good guys." At that, Orley pulled a pack of cigarettes he had rolled up in the sleeve of his tee-shirt, snapped in expertly against his hand to eject two smokes and handed one to Paul. Paul had never smoked prior to meeting Orley. It was a habit he'd never relinquish from this day forward.

"By the way, my next book will be something called *Berlin Alexanderplatz* by some guy named Doblin. Lieutenant Jameson recommended it. He said it is about the underworld of Berlin in the 20's. Sounds interesting. Given we are not planning to stop our move across Europe until we get to Berlin, I think it sounds like a good choice."

"So, you pick books just because they are about places we're going to?" prompted Paul.

"That's one way to look at it, but no. For example, The Tale of Two Cities is kind of like being about resurrection; new life for Paris. A freeing from the social injustice put upon the people by others in power; the aristocracy, and later the revolutionaries. I think that's why we're here; to free the people from the Nazi's. It's why I left college - to fight fascism."

Chapter 4

I PULLED TWO FLAT, cardboard boxes from the plastic tub lying on the floor and placed them on the table. One was marked "Paul" and the other "William," my Uncle Bill. Even though everyone else referred to him as William, he was always Uncle Bill to me. I removed the lid from my dad's box and tipped its contents onto the kitchen table. The contents were a jumble of school papers, newspaper clippings and black and white photos, the types of photos that we had forgotten long ago, the small glossy ones with the cut curvy edges on baryta paper. It was like stepping back in time. I was surprised that any of the old-school papers had survived the years. Report cards, reports written in Dad's juvenile hand, and even examples of drawings were all here. Dad's high school diploma was also here. He had graduated from Fort Collins High School in June of 1943 just in time to go to war. Flipping through his report cards, it was apparent Dad had been a better student than I had been, and I had been a good student. I could find no grades other than "A." Excellent student and an athlete, pretty impressive.

I planned to return to the box later, but now I wanted to dig into another gem I had noticed and already pulled from the box: the scrap book Mom had started, but never completed.

It was hard to imagine the book not being complete because it was already stuffed well beyond what the binding had been designed for. In the front cover, Mom had written "Paul Simmons and family." The first couple pages included some obligatory pictures of Dad as a baby, Dad as a little boy with Uncle Bill, as a baby, but, unfortunately no pictures of the boys with Grandpa and Grandma Simmons.

After plodding past these first few pages, I was taken aback by large glossy picture of Dad in a way I had never imagined. I had known he had been a basketball player in high school and a good one at that, but this picture showed a young man in absolute confidence jumping over another while shooting the basketball with his right hand, a pretty amazing image given this was a time where the two-handed set shot was the standard. The backside of the picture was marked with the logo of the Denver Post, the main regional paper at the time, with the scrawled message "to Paul Simmons, see you in the pros." On the facing page was a newspaper clipping with the head line "Simmons Takes a Lesson from Sailors' Playbook." The 1943 article was from the local newspaper in Fort Collins, *The Coloradoan*, and was drawing parallels between Paul and All American Kenny Sailors, the creator of the jump shot. The comparison was used to draw attention to the Fort Collins High's big win over Laramie High. Paul, although only a junior at the time, had been one of the premier high school basketball players in Colorado.

On the next page, there were two pictures of Dad in the Army. They were the only two pictures I had ever seen of him in uniform. On the back of the first picture, in cursive was written **Paul at boot camp at Fort Benning Alabama – 1943**. I showed Dad by himself standing ramrod straight. One could almost sense that youthful confidence that comes with supreme ignorance of the world, and complete cluelessness as to his own ignorance. He was invincible.

The second picture included Dad with several others in uniform leaning against a weathered wooden shed. The writing on the reverse side was in a different pen and I can only assume it was Dad's hand writing. The back was only titled Orley, me, and the guys. The picture showed a different look for Dad. The youthful exuberance replaced with the look of comfort and true friendship. Dad, was second from the left in the picture. The soldier to Dad's left, I could only assume, was Orley. He dwarfed Dad and had his right arm wrapped around him as if Dad were his kid brother. In Orley's left hand, a cigarette was clamped between his curled index and middle fingers. A cigarette draped from the corner of Dad's mouth; a look I had become accustomed to over the years. Three other young men looked to be completely indifferent to the photographer and preoccupied in discussion.

The change in Dad's face over the span of less than a year was striking, moving from late adolescence to being a man. Growing up came quickly in uniform.

* * *

Boredom and anticipation, not a good combination. By the time Paul joined the 1st, the Division had already seen extensive duty in the war, having returned from seven months of heavy action in Sicily. It was in Sicily as part of the 7th army that the Division had its first taste of amphibious landings. They had landed in the Gulf of Gela in South -Central Sicily. The weather and seas had been horrendous making the first challenge of the mass landing just keeping one's food down. The initial Axis defenses had been pretty limited. The real fighting started as the infantry moved inland. Now that the 1st was preparing for another amphibious landing, many were expecting to be a repeat of the Sicily experience, albeit on a larger scale.

Private Orley and Private Paul Simmons viewed themselves as a pretty formidable duo. As members of the same platoon, they quickly had developed a friendship forged out of the fire of war, two people that would have likely never met in another time. Orley, a philosophical 20-year-old, had come from the sleepy town of San Diego in southern California. His descriptions of home been seemed as foreign to Paul as the English countryside in which they were now residing. The idea of living someplace where snow didn't exist, where frigid cold weather was any time the thermometer dropped below 50 degrees, and the beaches extended as far as you could see to the north and south. For Paul, coming from the base of the Rocky Mountains, snow would regularly be expected in early October and as late as May. It was not unusual to see snowflakes even in early June. Paul made up his mind to move to southern California as soon as the war was won.

Orley was only a couple of years older than Paul, but exuded an air of maturity and complete confidence borne out of having actually been part of the previous Allied campaign at Gela. Having joined the army two years earlier, he had infinitely more battle experience than Paul and was prepared to share descriptions of his experiences at every opportunity. At first, it had been off-putting to Paul, but he had begun to live vicariously through this sharing and now perceived himself as a battle-hardened soldier, fully prepared for the planned invasion of Normandy, Operation Neptune.

The preparation over the past month had been mind-numbing. In between the war gaming and exercises, it had been a steady diet of study, tactic development, learning and reviewing specific objectives for each and every platoon. Once through the battery of planning, it was back to the beginning to ensure there were no questions, no doubts, no uncertainty at the time of the invasion. Repetition had become a way of life. Everyone had become anxious for the first day of Operation Overlord, the Western Europe offensive and Operation Neptune, in particular.

* * *

June 5, 1944 - I am unable to sleep. Today had been a day of incredible activity, preparing for tomorrow. I should be bone tired, but I cannot even close my eyes. Nobody spoke today. It was if everyone was preoccupied with their own thoughts. I know I was. I could not help wondering if it will hurt when I get shot. What will I say if I meet God tomorrow? Will I be brave? Will I see my family again? Do you think God really forgives us? For everything?

Orley is particularly quiet. Normally he keeps us all light with his banter, but today, even at breaks, he remained mute, his eyes dropped to staring at the ground as a dog that had just been punished. It is disconcerting to see him this way. He has been our emotional leader for the past few months. In the one time we did talk today, he had only taken the time to pass a note on to me with his parents' address while admonishing me to see them when I got back to the States. "Paul make sure you tell them I died bravely.

I think my time is up. I know I will not make it through tomorrow." I gave him my address, too, with Mom and Dad's names.

It is hard to imagine how big and powerful the ocean really is, that is until you are on a boat that is getting tossed about as a toy in bath tub. Today the ocean was intent on reminding us of its strength and complete authority over us mere men. With our Landing Craft Transport, known as an LCT, there was no contest in dealing with the sea; if the ocean wanted to win, it would. The LCT was small, 36 feet long and just over 11 feet wide. It had a shallow draft enabling it to quickly offload equipment and soldiers on the beach, but making it completely unwieldy, when buffeted by waves of any significance. Certainly, the seaworthiness of this ponderous boat was brought into question with the waves pounding us the morning of June 6, 1944. The challenges and risks became more acute after stuffing this small boat with three dozen soldiers with full packs.

The men leaned into the Landing Craft Transport's side walls and to each other just to avoid being thrown to the deck. It was doubly important to stay standing; the mixture of vomit from sea sickness combined with the sea water splashing over the wooden walls had become a slimy wash that no one wanted to sit in. It was bad enough the rancid mix washed over their boots with each rock of the boat. The odor was overpowering; mixed with the salt air and cold humidity, you could almost feel the smell. It permeated the fatigues. In spite of the seriousness of the day, Paul could not help but smile at the thought that flying bullets might be a preferential change in venue.

Paul and Orley were standing next to the steel ramp at the

front of the LCT; they would be the first off from the starboard side of their boat. Orley first, Paul second. Orley's head rocked back and forth, not to the sway of the ship, but as if it was part of some internal clock ticking away the seconds.

Paul could just make out Orley's mantra over the creaks of the boat and the banging of the waves. "Today, please not today. Today, please not today." Paul tipped his head and turned as far to the left as the crowded quarters and his full pack would allow to see if anyone else from his platoon had noticed Orley. No one could notice. Their faces looked blank, zombies with no expression, numbed by the realization of what they were committed to. The reality of D-Day had set in.

Paul nudged Orley. "Orley, stop the chant, man. You're freaking me out."

Orley, turned around as best as he could, tears streaming down his face. "Paul, as soon as that gate falls, I'm taking one. I know it! I can even feel the burn; right here." With that comment, Orley rubbed his hand across the right side of his face, from the nose sideways to his ear. "I'm done. Promise not tell my family I was afraid. Promise!"

"I promise, but today isn't going to be your day and it sure as hell isn't going to be mine, either. Swap places with me so you can't take one when the ramp drops. I'll be first off."

Paul and Orley swapped places. Now that Orley was behind him, Paul had no idea if this change stopped his head bobbing, but at least he would not have to watch it continuously through the remainder of the crossing. He placed his head in helmet against the LCT's wood side wall, closed his eyes, and began to pray, not that he would live through the day, but that he could maintain his faith and not be afraid to die. Then he chickened out and began to pray that he be spared today. Time stood still.

* * *

The pounding of the artillery had become huge and overwhelming. They could feel the concussions shaking the LCT's walls. The vibration shook Paul out of his meditative state. The sounds of the waves pounding the LCT had been replaced by pounding thuds, accentuated by "thwips" and "pops" from bullets cutting the air overhead. Paul could feel the occasional impact on the steel ramp of bullets fired from the bluffs; the very bluffs they would soon be attacking. The impacts were hard, loud, and still hurt like Hades as they transferred their energy to the steel and then into him as he leaned against the inside of this life protecting ramp.

It was just after 7:00 in the morning; the sun had just broken through the clouds. "GO! GO! GO!" The ramped dropped. The platoon only had a few moments to empty the LCT before they would become sitting targets to the gunners from the German 352nd Infantry. The longer they took to disembark the more at risk they were, and more at risk the boat became. The boat had a couple machine guns in the rear, but the defense was meaningless against the onslaught from the bluffs. They were either ramp up and pulled into reverse within three to four minutes, or they were goners.

They were goners. The LCT had beached itself on a sandbar farther out than had been planned. Whereas Paul had expected to jump into a couple feet of water, in the worst case, his feet didn't touch bottom until his nostrils filled with sea water. "Shit . . . cold and I'm drowning" is all Paul could think as the wave rolled by giving him at least a brief moment to catch a breath. The craziness of landing was accentuated by a "THWOP - THWOP - THOWP." Not a loud noise but certainly belying the size of bullets flying above and striking into the LCT. Paul gulped in air just in time to have the huge frame of Orley land on top of him driving Paul back under the surf. Paul's head broke back through the surface having pushed Orley off his back. "Shit, Orley!" Paul yelled as he snagged Orley's back collar and began to pull him toward the beach. Orley's head fell below the water. As Paul, pulled him back up he realized Orley's helmet was lost, not a good thing. Flipping him around to get Orley to snap out of it, he looked at only half a face. The entire right hand side was gone. Really gone. Nothing but space where once had been an eye, ear, cheek. It was amazing that his hairline remained. Paul could not bring himself to let go of Orley, to let him sink quickly in the gray water now stained red. Paul turned to the beach, the bombs, bullets, smoke, and the bluffs that represented both death and his only potential salvation.

* * *

They had been dropped a full 100 yards out in the surf and now were faced with swimming as much as walking these hundred yards, all with full packs and M-1 rifles raised above their heads and the water. Only half the platoon had made it off the LCT. The boat had caught a mortar shell before it could empty. The pilot would never get to extricate himself from the sand bar to retrieve another platoon of soldiers.

The going was slow, but it seemed more so given the surreal surroundings. Men wading, bodies floating, swamped boats, swirling smoke. The noise that had been so loud initially, had become muffled, as if Paul had cotton in his ears. Everything seemed to stand still. Paul had no idea how long it took to get to the beach. He could not even remember dragging Orley's lifeless body behind him. He did feel as though this might be what hell is like: no God and no way out. With each step, the beach appeared to move further off into the distance. Paul was Sisyphus, always pushing towards, but never achieving the objective. Motivation finally came from the bullets plopping in the water, constantly resulting in new and fresh adrenaline rushes, prompting Paul to strength and speed he thought himself incapable to deliver. Twenty yards from the beach, the water had dropped to his waist and Paul's pace quickened. He could see his Lieutenant Jameson to his right making progress to the beach reaching back with his arm to wave what remained of his team on.

Upon reaching the beach, Orley's sheer size and weight, accentuated by full pack made it impossible for Paul to pull him out of the waves. Paul fell to the beach, letting go of Orley's collar. An unknown hand grabbed Paul's pack strap, pulling him back to his feet. "Got 'a move, soldier. Now!" This all the motivation he needed. Up and running, Paul never looked back to his savior, but knowing full well that that hand was the only thing that had kept him from death. Running, running. The beach seemed to extend forever, much longer than expected from the aerial reconnaissance pictures they had been reviewed over and over. They had expected a beach to be no deeper than a hundred yards before they would reach the relative safety of a sand sea wall and the opportunity to regroup before a second assault to the base of the bluffs.

Unfortunately, the LCT had drifted east during the crossing. The team had thought they were landing in the eastern center section of Omaha Beach in an area referred to as Easy Red. The rough seas had pushed them to the far eastern section of Omaha Beach to a section called Fox Green, a section in which the beaches extended for as much as two hundred yards. Two hundred yards without cover, without protection, without hope. Paul could see flash of guns through the smoke surrounding a bunker nestled into the side of the bluff.

As Paul collapsed behind protection of the seawall, he could not help but realize that his success in making it this far was only the result of having so many other targets available to the gunners on the hill. He survived this far because others were dying on that same beach. Paul rolled onto his back, pushing his pack into the sand to stare back at the carnage occurring behind him, taking time to collect himself before climbing up and over the pebble wall separating the beach from the beginning of the bluffs. Scanning to his left as he looked out to the sea, he could see the second wave of landing craft approaching the beaches. Smoke swirls wafted by the breezes stood out as dirty finger smudges on this picture of impending death. Closer to the beach, unlucky LCTs from the initial landing wave lay as dead sentries, providing a vivid warning as to the risks.

Paul scanned the beach to find what had been his best friend. He was lost among the numerous bodies being continuously washed by the lapping waves. The beach had fewer casualties than he expected. Apparently, the gunners on the bluffs found the slow-moving soldiers wading through ocean waves an easier target.

Paul closed his eyes and tried to close out the noise. The pounding of the early morning artillery from the battle ships had long subsided and been replaced by the smaller artillery and snapping of the machine guns from the German bunkers. Paul needed to get himself focused again; the past several minutes had seemed like hours, and he needed to let the adrenaline rush subside.

To either side, Paul saw soldiers just as himself, waiting for someone, anyone, to take control and push them on. For the past six months, this void had been filled by the now lost, big brotherly, Orley, Sergeant Constantine, and Lieutenant Jameson. Paul scanned up and down the embankment for either of the remaining two. Twenty yards to his east, Paul saw the Lieutenant had gathered half a dozen soldiers and was giving orders, pointing to a wash to their left leading up to and providing some modest protected access up the bluff.

The Lieutenant crawled westward toward Paul gathering

soldiers behind him as he approached. "You, you, and you," the last "you" referring to Paul, "we're heading up this wash." He pointed to the right to a slight depression in the bluff wall. "That is where we are going, soldiers. Time to take it out."

The Lieutenant held a grenade in his left hand and his carbine in his right and yelled above the din, "Now!"

At the Lieutenant's bark, the group to the east and four soldiers that included the Lieutenant moved, over the sea wall, across the heavily pebbled ground to the sandy bluffs. Paul could hear the clicking of rounds ricocheting off the pebbles. The sound was discomforting; but not nearly so much as the sound of the thuds signaling rounds had found their mark, the flesh of American soldiers.

The four that made Paul's group had made it to the cover of ground that was below the bunkers effective line of fire. For a few moments, at least, they would be safe . . . at least until another machine gunner to their east or west found them and elected to fire laterally across the bluff, picking them off as easy targets. The four now found themselves scrambling up the slippery sandstone wash extending upwards between the bunker and a machine gunner nest. The slope of the climb required the team to crawl on all fours to avoid sliding backwards. Holding his M-1 rifle tightly in both hands as he traversed upwards, the abrasive ground scraping through uniform and skin, Paul moved quickly, hoping to get behind the German machine gunners before being spotted. Speed was critical.

The onslaught of tracer rounds had sparked a grass fire to the east on the bluff providing a slight cover of smoke, but the cover was temporary and intermittent. As the breeze wafted the smoke, Paul could see the first machine gun battery to his right. The German gunners from the 352nd infantry were completely unaware of their peril from soldiers no more than 10 yards to their right. Paul quickly pulled up his M-1 to fire for the first time to take a human life. Adrenaline pumping, he pulled the trigger twice from a distance close enough to see the dirty sweat lining the German gunner's face, streaming from the corners of his eyes. The excitement, the adrenaline, the fatigue . . . who knows, both rounds missed their mark, pulled high. As the gunner pivoted his machine gun, the dreaded MG 34, to face Paul, Paul was deafened by the snap-snap originating from his Lieutenant's carbine muzzle, no more than 6 inches from his ear. The Lieutenant dropped both the gunner and the assistant gunner.

Onwards and upwards. The group moved with a general leftward arc to their climb, bringing them to the concrete walls of the bunker that was raining death on those on the beach.

Chapter 5

I THUMBED THROUGH A couple of more pages before, putting the photo album aside to read though some additional passages in the journal, getting some insights to the person I had never thought of as being young. As a kid, your only perception of your father is that of just being a father, nothing before, nothing after, never anything but your father, at least until he had withered away to just an old man.

* * *

I never met Matthias, but I have grown to respect him. To Hilke, your husband was good, but not lucky. Please forgive me . . .

It is amazing how our thoughts of what is "normal" can change based on our surroundings. For Paul, this was now normal. He sat in a fox hole, well not so much a fox hole as an enlarged bomb crater, with two of his remaining compatriots from his original platoon. They had been redeployed several days earlier to the front as reinforcements to blunt a push by the German 5th and 6th Panzer Armies along with the German 7th Army. The US Army had been completely surprised by the Blitzkrieg attack through a weakly defended and densely forested area, the Ardennes Mountains. It had been more than six months since embarking on the drive to Paris.

Fatigue had set in. For Paul, it was a good thing; it kept him from thinking about the lack of reinforcements and their dwindling ammunition supply. He had not slept more than a few 30 minute stints over the past four days. His energy had been borrowed only from the common objective of saving friends he had never met, just grunts like him defending Bastogne. To be successful, they had to break through German forces surrounding the town.

Although cold during the day, it became miserable once the sun dropped below the tree lines. Cloud cover was the only saving grace in that it served as a modest blanket over the country-side, perhaps the only thing saving the three soldiers from hypothermia. Even though night had fallen several hours earlier, the hillside had never become truly dark; the snow reflecting the diffuse moonlight eliminated any hope of using the cover of darkness to advance. Trees at the crest provided cover for the German machine gunners, making it imperative to keep one's head down and below snow level to avoid a quick demise.

The three had burrowed under the snow to access tree branches and rocks to line the bottom of their foxhole to provide some reprieve from the perpetual mud. Keeping dry was critical to staying alive to fight tomorrow.

The three soldiers had lost the rest of their platoon earlier in the day, and they had debated their options vigorously before night set in. Tactically, Paul could see they had few options. Moving forward now meant stepping into the direct fire of heavy machine guns. Escape also was not an option in that the ground behind them provided no cover whatsoever. They had elected to stay put until the moon declined in the night sky and then advance up the hill on their bellies under the cover of snow. In the meantime, they would snipe any Germans that ventured beyond the tree line. It was highly likely that they would meet their makers within the next three hours.

The noise of the heavy panzer tanks had stopped shortly after sundown. The three had assumed this only provided a brief respite before they regrouped for their attack on Bastogne in the morning. Hopefully, the three could make the wake-up call more eventful. In any case, they had promised each other that they would not stop until their bullets ran out.

Samuels, Baker and Paul peered out from the edge of their foxhole. They had mounded snow into 10-12 inch walls with a small opening just large enough for which to sight and shoot their M1s. They had hoped the snow would obscure their view from the prying eyes above. They had no idea if it would work, but at this time they had few options. It hearkened Paul back to the days of his childhood snow ball fights and snow forts. So far, the tactic had worked; no fire had been directed their way for the past three hours, while at the same time they had alternated taking watch through the 6" hole in the snow.

Patience never had been one of Paul's strong points and faced with another two to three hours of waiting on the moon was taking its toll. He was finding it difficult to concentrate as he watched through the hole. He thanked goodness when Baker began to talk, providing some relief from the build-up of tension that had obviously gripped all three.

In Baker's soft southern drawl, "Paul, anythin' moving yet?"

Paul, pulled back from his sighting and looked to Baker then to Samuels and then back to Baker. "It is so still. No movement, no noise, not anything. With the reflection off the snow, though, my eyes are starting to play games with me ... you know seeing phantom motions. I close my eyes and open them, the phantoms are gone, and it is just snow."

"You know; I am wondering if the folks shootin' at us feel the same as we do? You know, thinkin' they're right and that they're just defendin' their land. I have a hard time getting' how they can all be so bad."

Samuels straightened up to listen.

Baker continued, "My Grandma is German, right off the boat and she's good and right. She can't understand how this all happened. Her sister is still alive and lives in a town called Muenster. She tried to get out back in '39 but was stopped. Not all of the Germans are bad."

Samuels commented, "It's a disease. The hatred spewed from Hitler since the 30's was bound to take hold. It provided someone besides themselves to blame for their problems . . . too seductive to let it pass. Yeah, not all bad, just seduced."

"Seriously, we are facing death in a couple hours because of the Krauts up that hill" motioning with his thumb towards the tree line behind him, "and you are defending them. Maybe we should put our hands up now and throw ourselves on their mercy." Paul was exasperated. "Samuels, aren't you a Jew. How can you defend any Kraut?"

"Paul, I might be Jewish, but I am also German. My folks immigrated in the 20's. They had nothing at home, nothing to keep them there and they love the good ole USA. I still have family in Germany. Hopefully, they will still be alive when we liberate them." Samuel's countered. "Even though my family and religion may have been forsaken by my Fatherland, I cannot imagine that my family has been forsaken by their friends in that land."

Baker commented, staring into the night, "Damned it all. I hope you're right, but you know the rumors don't look good for your kind. I suspect you might be soundin' a lot more like Paul in a couple of months. That is if we make it through t-night. Paul, anythin' movin' yet"

Paul flipped his head back to his sighting and quietly held up his hand to his buddies signaling to pipe down.

*　*　*

For the Panzer Army, the 47th Panzer Division, the fighting had been too easy. The Americans had been taken by complete surprise. They were now poised to push into Bastogne, providing critical control of roadways and the logistical advantages of such control. Ultimately, defending Bastogne was the Allied force's goal.

Matthias Rieker had been on the move for the past three days. He had once been proud member of the German 5th Army, the linchpin to the drive to Antwerp, putting a dagger into the heart of the Allied push into Germany. The Reich was on the move, and Matthias was now distraught.

Several months ago, Matthias had become all too aware of the lies foisted on the German people by their Fuhrer. Throughout his life, Protestant values had driven home the pure evil of lying. Now lies threatened to kill his nation, but, ironically, now his lies were likely the only thing that had kept him and his family alive. His wife, Hilke, was a "mischling," a mutt, half Jew, half Gentile; a fact they had needed to bury deep, far below prying eyes. Matthias and Hilke had long ago recognized they could not acknowledge the Jewish blood that coursed through Hilke's veins. Pure Arian heritage was a prerequisite to wealth, status, freedom, and life, itself. They had ostracized themselves from Hilke's parents and grandparents in 1938 and had ensured there was no contact ever since. This had actually been Hilke's parents' idea.

As heart breaking the separation, it was likely the only thing that had prevented Hilke and Matthias from being relocated to a labor camp. Hilke's parents and grandparents had not been so lucky and had long since been moved to a labor camp in the south. Last year, Hilke had given up all hope of any reunion with rumors of the labor camps being nothing more than fronts for extermination factories. She had become an alien in her own country, completely alone. Matthias was now forced to fight a war he did not want and did not believe in. Hilke was alone in Dresden waiting for the Russians; fearing her fellow Germans, praying for the Americans.

* * *

The 47th Panzer division had pushed forward for three straight days, crushing all Allied defenses thrown at it. The velocity and veracity of the push had provided Matthias hope he might use the resulting chaos to finally escape his German co-patriots and give himself up to the Americans. He had hoped his rank of "Hauptmann" would provide access to some leniency upon his capture and provide him the opportunity to share what he knew of the German attack plans and the weaknesses of his division, invisible to the Allies, but to him, so apparent. For Matthias the repulse the German offensive was critical for peace. In his mind destruction of the Reich was the only hope for Germany. Matthias had come to the stark realization that if he lived, it likely meant Reich had been victorious and the whole world had lost. If Germany lost in this bid to push back the Allies, he too would likely die. He prayed for forgiveness and for the deliverance of the Allies.

He had long ago acknowledged both the error and the futility of the Reich's quest to control the European continent. "Übel", evil, is how he had come to view Hitler and his ilk. Anything he could do in his role to minimize their success in murder had become his challenge. Today, the American's pinned down below were surprised, exposed, and hopeless. He had a choice, participate and lead the blood bath or, without recourse, become a traitor to the Third Reich. The choice had seemed so easy and straight forward, until he had come to realization it could very likely mean his life would end today.

Prior to today's engagement, Matthias had extoled his platoon to concentrate their fire on a few target areas and conserve ammunition. Although conservation was a real need with their limited ammo supply, he had been ultraconservative in limiting the amount he allocated to the team under the guise of maintaining adequate supply for the push into Bastogne. In reality, he was using the limited allocation of rounds and replacement barrels to reduce his team's rate of fire. Their machine guns were exceptional in tearing apart the enemy both figuratively and literally. His goal, limit his squad's success without making his intentions transparent. Their ability to take lives was limited only by his ability to restrict their rate of fire.

This night would provide him the opportunity he had been awaiting. The fighting during the day was particularly violent and revolting. His German machine gunners had established positions on the top of a rise hidden in heavy tree line. Below them American soldiers had been pinned down, sheltered behind logs and rock walls or hidden in the many craters carved out by the artillery hail from the past several days. The Americans were already dead; they had just not realized it, yet.

For those Americans that had not perished in the day's onslaught, they could only thank the ineffective logistics rapidly thrown together for the offensive. Ironically, in spite of Matthias's overly conservative allocation of ammo to his men, the Germans had, in reality, run short of ammunition for the deadly Maschinengewehr 42, or MG 42. At 1,200 rounds per minute, the gun was a gift from the Devil, himself, but chewed through the ammo at an alarming rate They had needed to pull back in their shower of steel and lead to provide time for additional supply to arrive.

In Matthias's platoon, he had quietly made sure the three infantrymen charged with keeping the machine gun firing by running for additional barrels and ammo never achieved their objective. He calmly dispatched them one by one with his Lugar as soon as they moved out of the gunner's vision. His gunner team was the last to experience Matthias's treason. As they trained their fire, he quietly disposed of them with a three quick bullets the backs of their heads. Even as he committed treason against the Third Reich, he was confident he had redeemed his soul.

This time of year, night came early. With the sunset, the flow of lead from German gunners had quieted, only to be replaced by booming of artillery and the rumble of the Panzers as they turned north to encircle Bastogne. Matthias remained behind, his platoon lying only meters from him, mute and lifeless. Hauptmann Rieker had taken each of their lives in the hope their deaths might save lives tomorrow.

He sat silently, his back against the ice-covered wall that had provided cover from the helpless American souls hundreds of meters down the slope. Beside him lay a pair of semi-functional binoculars with one eyepiece shattered, his Lugar P08 pistol void of any shells, his journal in which he had just completed documenting his admission of treason against the Third Reich, and a smoldering cigarette. In his lap was a half-finished letter to his wife. He struggled under moonlight and through tears to write what would likely be his last words to Hilke; words that she would unlikely ever see. His pencil, a stub no more than 10 centimeters in length, made his writing even less legible that normal.

He hoped Hilke had left Dresden several months ago, to the refuge of Switzerland. They had planned to reunite in Geneva after the war. Matthias had contacted old family friends that had lived in an upstairs apartment on the Rue du Rhone facing Lake Geneva. They had been happy to make room for Hilke if she could only find means to escape Germany. Unfortunately, travel had become extremely difficult over the past year, almost untenable over the three months. If she had not left shortly after they had finalized their plans, he doubted she would ever make it to this new life. In Dresden, there was no doubt that if her heritage was discovered, her homeland would turn on her instantaneously. Matthias feared for her life every day.

Closing his eyes, he could still see Hilke's face as if she was sitting next to him. Closing out the view of bloodstained snow and the stench of gunpowder mixed with rotting flesh, Matthias tried to recall better times, before Germany had invaded Poland and started the downward spiral into oblivion. Hitler's favorite music, Wagner, was well suited for the hell in which they now found themselves.

Matthias jerked his eyes open to a feeling of pure shock and fear; his adrenaline rush moved him to instant awareness of everything around him. He must have dozed off, for how long, he had no idea. If he was to give himself up to the Americans, now was the time. Pulling himself up to a crouch and turning to face downhill, Matthias grabbed his binoculars to take a quick look for movement down the slope.

* * *

It was amazing how six months of kill or be killed had both aged and calmed Paul. Nerves no longer resulted in what he termed as synaptic shorts resulting in premature and inaccurate shots. Now he was the master of his aim . . . as numerous Wiermach soldiers could attest to . . . had they still been living. Paul was also blessed with uncanny vision at night, easily discerning real movement from those phantom movements that would continually distract Baker and Samuels. Baker and Samuels had become keenly aware of Paul's ability to see what they passed over and shoot what they missed.

What Paul now saw was the glint in the moonlight of the sniper's scope. He squeezed the trigger and the glint was gone. There was nothing but silence.

* * *

The moon had fallen below tree line. The snow went from glowing to being a dull, dark gray. Time to move. Paul, Baker, Samuels crawled up and over the edge of their crater in unison. Although the snow was deep enough to keep their burrowing bodies below site lines, the bitter cold had resulted in a hard, cutting surface crust. As they pushed forward the crust cut at any exposed skin, slicing at Paul's face as he crawled. Blood from Paul's forehead oozed down his face to his mouth before freezing. He had no pain from the cuts; he was too chilled to feel. Pain would come later.

The effort was huge. In spite of the cold, Paul was perspiring profusely under his coat. Baker and Samuels labored to his right. They were literally swimming up the slope, though the water in which they swam was nothing more than tiny, sand-sized granules of ice. Baker grabbed Paul's arm and signaled to wait. Although they had progressed no more than fifty yards, he was already spent. He could go no farther. Baker would either freeze to death on the slope, unable to burrow further or die from a bullet by electing to stand and face his enemies directly. He elected to stand. Nothing happened.

Baker took a couple more steps up the hill, still nothing. "Hey you freakin' krauts, come and get me!" Still nothing.

"Boys, we scared them off," Baker chuckled as he reached down to help pull Samuels and then Paul up from the snow. "We win."

The three stood in silence; complete silence except for the sound of them dusting the snow off their bodies.

"Hell, Paul, what happened to you?" Samuels had a look of shock on his face. "Does it hurt?"

Paul's face and coat were smeared with blood. The bleeding had been stemmed by the cold, but the flow had stained his face red; in the dark it looked inky black. The three moved slowly up hill, having no idea of what to expect once they achieved the crest.

* * *

Vacated, quiet, eerily quiet. The three men were the only living beings on the crest. From the American side of the crest, the rise was an uninterrupted white blanket for a hundred yards, except for the three parallel lines marking their ascent up the hill. Beyond a hundred yards, artillery shell craters appeared as black dots across the hillside; freckles on pale white skin. The blood stains of fallen soldiers shown as black brush strokes on a virgin canvas. On the German side of the crest, the signs of huge activity from the earlier day were visible everywhere. The snow had been completely worn away. The clean white blanket of snow replaced by the mud trenches carved by tires and tracks. Spent brass littered the ground, the piles betraying where the murderous gunners had taken up positions.

Paul set off northward along the ridge, in search of the sniper he had taken out during the night. Samuels and Baker trudged after him, each scouring the ground to avoid tripping or slipping in the hazardous, frozen mud. After progressing past two vacated gunner positions, Paul stopped dead; Samuels and Baker quickened their pace to catch up. Face up at Paul's feet, lay the mousey-looking, Hauptmann Rieker, his eyes staring lifelessly skywards. A small, red spot marked the point Paul's shot entered his face just below his right eye. Paul knew the exit point was not so neat. The back of Rieker's head lay in a frozen pool of blood. In one hand, Rieker hand held the broken set of binoculars he had been using to spy down the hill in search of American soldiers . . . to accept his surrender. In the other, a couple sheets of paper were crumpled in a tightly clinched fist.

Paul could not divine what had been Rieker's intensions; however, it was clear he was no sniper. He had no rifle. His only companions were two dead gunners draped over a silent machine gun. Beside the Hauptmann lay what appeared to be a journal and a couple sheets of paper that appeared to be an uncompleted letter.

* * *

I gently unfolded the heavily creased and yellowed sheets of seven-decade-old hand written pages. The first two pages written in German in a faint deliberate pencil, the second two pages in ink, written in English. Flipping to the English pages, it was clear these had been translated for Dad.

> Dearest Hilke:
> I miss you continuously. My heart has become incapable of feeling except for when I think of you. Today my only comfort flows from knowing we are almost done with this terrible war and the devastation it had poured upon our lives. Each night I fear that this night will be my last. Although dying might blot the pain of killing from my memories, I know that in the afterlife I would always regret never again having the caress of your body against

mine, feeling your breath upon my brow, or hearing your voice calling me in from the cold. I need to live to tomorrow.

Your safety is always on my mind. Our Fuhrer is not our friend, not yours, not mine, not our country's. As long as he lives, he represents a threat to all of us. I fear we are too far gone to recover even if saner minds prevailed tomorrow. We have made too many enemies, killed too many friends, left too few options; the world is overwhelmed with a need to punish us . . . and we deserve no mercy.

I hope this letter finds you well in Geneva. I have no idea when I will be able to join you, but trust that even with our separation, I am with you with every breath you take. If I am gone from this earth when this letter comes to you, close your eyes and remember me as we had been when we married. I will visit you in your dreams and protect you from my new afterlife. I now know God will take care of us as we need to be cared for.

If I sound more faithful than you remember, I am. Our Fuhrer has made me a Christian, a real Christian. Until I experienced his terror, his destruction, his evil, I was happy being a Sunday Protestant, quietly adopting the practices and dogma of my parents without understanding why or believing. My faith had been lost, replaced by a Nietzsche-esk personal philosophy based in myself . . . that people are real gods. I could not even acknowledge an all-powerful God could exist. To me, God had become a child's concept that I had outgrown during adolescence.

I WAS WRONG! I think now, Hitler is the personification of evil, beyond any personal capability. He is a product of the Devil; the tool of Satan. I cannot comprehend the existence of pure evil without that of pure good - God. I have come to grips with my failings and now have taken strength in my new faith and belief in good; to do what we all should have done years ago. I no longer fear for myself, but do fear for you.

You will hear that I have done horrible things tonight, but never forget what I have done is ONLY for good. I need to stop our country's murder. I can no longer stand by and participate in the Reich's reign of evil and terror. I have decided to fight for good. Today I took my first, unsteady steps in saving American soldiers lives. I pray for forgiveness in taking German lives. I did not give them a chance to ask their God for forgiveness. Tonight, I will deliver myself into the hands of the Americans and pray for mercy. They owe me nothing, but I will be safe.

When you get this, I will be in a prisoner of war camp. As an officer, I expect to be fine. I hope to help the Americans stop the Reich.

Hilke, I know you understand how I can turn on the Reich to protect Germany; I am just sorry I and others did not act in time to save your parents. Please forgive me.

I have some

At this point the letter abruptly stopped, but included a couple notes in Dad's younger hand.

Translated by John Samuels, December 28, 1944. Letter from Hauptmann Matthias Rieker of Dresden, Germany to his wife Hilke. Hilke died February 13, 1945 in Dresden bombings. I will beg for forgiveness in Heaven.

Chapter 6

A HAND ON MY shoulder gently shook me awake. Looking up I stared into the lively eyes of Uncle Bill. His gentle smile belied the pain he felt for his brother and sister-in-law. "Sam told me you have been here all day, Randall. You want to take a break and head out to grab a quick dinner? I plan to stay the night to give you both some needed rest."

I loved Uncle Bill. He had had a pretty "colorful" past and had driven Dad batty with his lack of reliability more than once, but to me, he was always just Uncle Bill, full of fun and life. It was doubtful that Uncle Bill would be of much use helping out here at the house with Dad. That said, he had been like a big brother to me during some tough times and his company would be welcome.

Mom now had a full-time nurse staying at the house; there was no way she could physically handle Dad by herself. He outweighed her by at least 100 pounds and needed to be turned and cleaned a number of times a day. The nurse stayed in bedroom next door to Dad. Mom had moved to the back bedroom next to the kitchen. I had been relegated to a fourth bedroom that had doubled as an office. I guess for tonight, Uncle Bill would take my room and I'd stay on the sofa in the living room. Although, it would wreak havoc with my back, it gave me an excuse to stay close to Dad, perhaps making up for, in some small way, my lack of visiting over the past decade. My personal life, challenges, and desires had overwhelmed what was really important, family.

It was good the Mom and Dad now lived in a single-story home. At least I would not have to worry about keeping Uncle Bill sober enough to walk up a flight flights of steps after dinner.

"Sure, Uncle Bill. Where you want to go?"

"My call? Excellent. Then its downtown to the Linden Street. There are a couple places I want to show you that I think you'll get a kick out of. By the way, you want to drive? Then I might grab a beer, too. Plus, I think I am getting too damn old to drive at night. My eyes just aren't what they used to be." He chuckled and winked at me at this last comment, suggesting the real issue for not wanting to drive had a lot more to do with the beer he wanted and a lot less with his eyes.

I rolled my eyes and smiled, knowing all too well if dinner ended up with Uncle drinking beer, just as I feared, he would not be much good in helping out that night. Oh well, he was good hearted, if not reliable.

We walked wordlessly to the rental I had parked behind the house. I was disappointed in myself now with my choice in cars. When offered my upgrade at the airport Avis counter, I chose a flashy, fun Ford Mustang without giving a second thought as to the difficulty the low seats might be for my Mom or Uncle... let alone if I actually had to move Dad. Pretty thoughtless, not mean, but thoughtless just the same.

Uncle Bill took a look at the car and chuckled. "Randall, very cool car, but not much of a chance in me getting my butt down onto that seat without your help. Hell, if I do get into it, you're never getting me out. It might have a serious impact on the rent appeal for this beauty in the future... you know fast and sleek and comes with a geriatric map reader in the passenger seat. Let's take my truck instead. You drive." I could see tears welling up in his eyes as he turned to me. "You know I could use a little fun. It's been a pretty shitty couple of months."

The drive to Linden Street was less than a mile and only took a couple of minutes, but it was nice to have the diversion of traffic. I could see that Uncle Bill was taking this harder than I had expected. He wanted to talk, but not at the house . . . and apparently not in the truck, either; he sat perfectly silent until I parked. September nights in Fort Collins were beautiful. The outside mall was packed with college-aged kids and young families. The street was hopping. We had to park almost two blocks away. Before I could even ask Uncle Bill where we were eating, he hopped out. "This way, Randall. You'll like this."

It's funny how returning to a place you loved as a kid could make you forget your troubles, letting you return to an earlier time when you had no cares, when Mom and Dad were there to pick you up if you got into trouble. I felt like kid again. Even Uncle Bill looked younger. Not that his grey hair looked more blond, or that his wrinkles were less visible, or that his paunch less pronounced, but he did seem to have a little bounce return to his step. Yes, he felt it, too.

Uncle Bill passed by one of the trendy bar grills that greeted us at the entrance of the mall, choosing instead to hop into the intimate bistro next door that appeared much too nice for two guys looking to escape reality for just a brief time by grabbing a reasonably priced beer and dinner. At the door, I was surprised when the 30-something year-old host greeted Uncle Bill as "Mister Simmons."

"Hi, Mark. It's been a while. Everything going all right?"

"Pretty good, Mister Simmons." Turning to me, Mark reached out his hand and greeted me "Hello, you must be Randall." I nodded in acknowledgement. "Tim and I have a lot to be thankful for your Dad and Uncle. I have set up a special table for you upstairs, follow-me."

Uncle Bill as "Mister Simmons?" Maybe William, but Mister Simmons? It was a formality I had never attributed to Uncle Bill. Uncle Bill followed Mark up the well-worn oak steps with me trailing behind.

Our table was set up in large, eclectically decorated room, better suited to handling special dinners for the upper crust in town or small group celebrations rather than catering to a dinner for an uncle and his nephew. Save for the large crown molding, the entire ceiling was covered with the ornate tin tiles from an earlier, simpler time. The table had been set up against a wall of huge casement windows facing the street and providing an unimpeded view of the entire length of the outdoor mall's three blocks. Uncle Bill look at me and startled me by saying, "Your Dad did this," pointing out to the street. "You should be proud. I am"

At this Uncle Bill jumped into why we were really here.

* * *

Paul felt happy, sad, confident, scared as hell . . . confused. He was coming home for the first time in three years. The last three years had been spent soldiering during the war and policing afterwards. He had joined the Army an 18-year-old private, was leaving the Army a 21-year-old corporal that was old beyond his years.

He had left home without saying a real goodbye. Leaving as a high school letterman, famous in his little town for a fancy jump shot and was returning a . . . he could not answer this. He was a blank slate. He wanted to believe that he was a work in progress, but he did not believe this to be true. To be a work in progress implied there was a known result he was working towards. He had no such belief. He was no longer a soldier.

High school was a distant memory. College frightened him. He had no job. He had nothing other than the hope his family was there for him.

Air breaks hissed as the bus pulled over to the curb and stopped. The door pushed awkwardly outward and people began to lazily pull themselves from their seats to file off. Paul delayed getting up. It was so disconcerting. He had faced death countless times, had had close friends die in his arms. He had killed, first awkwardly, then with a disconnected professionalism. He had made an intimate act impersonal. He was afraid he has lost his humanity. He had killed bad people for sure. He had saved lives. He had also killed innocent people and that haunted him. He had begun to keep track of things he needed to rectify; things for which he wanted, no needed, forgiveness. They were in his journal. The journal had meaning and importance to him. But now he was just another person stepping off a nondescript bus in "small-town, USA."

As he stepped into the bus doorway, any concerns and reservations melted away. Dad, Mom, William, Lyle, and Virginia were all there. He had not seen them from his seat; they had pushed themselves so close to bus door, they were blocked from view until Paul stepped into the opening. Dad was crying. Paul had never seen Dad cry. Everything was good.

On the drive home, William monopolized the conversation in the car by firing a litany of questions: "What was it like to be soldier?" "How many Germans did you kill?" "What are the girls like in Paris?" "Are you happy to be home?"

Paul ducked the questions with the adeptness of a professional boxer until the last question. For the first question, he described the barracks and how he lived within rules, rules, and more rules. You did what you were ordered to do and hoped you would be a survivor. For the second, he merely mumbled "I don't know." The third gave him relief from the serious issues that he had faced in war. Being able to talk of pretty girls was the only topic that made sense for a 21-year old. Dealing with life and death daily had robbed him of his youth. The last question had left him silent. He was not sure. The lack of the answer was not lost on Dad as he listened to his two sons speaking in the back seat.

* * *

Paul was thankful that his upstairs attic room was still his, and his alone. It represented a sanctuary for him to get his head together and figure out how best to plug back into his family. He politely excused himself upon pulling his duffle from the car trunk, feigned being gassed from the bus trip and desiring to head up to his room for a quick nap. Although he had no need or desire to nap, laying on his bed staring out the window helped him debate with himself as to what was next for his future. He was not the kid that had left this home three years ago, yet his room was exactly the same; as if time had stood still. As only he could know, it had not. Time to move. Paul swung his legs off the edge of the bed, stood up, spied his room, visualizing how it was time to change.

Calling down the steps, "William, come on up here."

"Oh, come on, Paul, I haven't touched anything in your room. Mom wouldn't let me"

"I know. I just wanted to talk to you about something."

Paul could hear Bill bounding up the steps, two at a time. His head appeared to pop out of the floor as he finished climbing the steps. "Paul, what's up? You want to head out and grab something to eat? Maybe we could get meet some of your old friends at the A&W? I have Dad's keys to the truck."

"Not now. I just wanted to know what your plans were . . . now that you are graduated?" asked Paul. "I was thinking we should both go to college."

"Are you kidding? I just started working at the shop. You know we're expanding what we do, Paul. I can make some real money now and you want me to punt this away to stay in college. Heck, what would we study?"

Paul looked perplexed. "Expanding, into what? How? Has Dad finally decided to give Lyle and Virginia the boot and bring in some real go getters? If he has, they sure didn't seem to upset when they came to the bus station today."

"No, Paul, that's not it at all. Besides, you are being way too rough on Lyle and Virginia. They're like family and, heck, it was their idea to expand." William looked out the window. "For someone so smart, you really don't know much about them. Paul, they held the shop together these last two years. Dad, pretty much stayed at home, read the newspapers, and then would just sit in his office."

"Seriously? Shit, why didn't you say something?"

"When? Paul, you just got here and high-tailed it upstairs. I couldn't say anything in the car, but ask Mom. She'll tell you how sad he has been.

"But, that's behind us now. Dad had already gone over to Lyle and Virginia's place. I think he wants to talk to them about you joining the company."

Paul smiled, "So what are we expanding into?"

William jumped into explaining how Lyle had shared that he thought our growth potential with awnings was pretty limited. In fact, the business had actually begun to decline. Plus, if they were going to add two smart, up-n-comin' studs like he and Paul, they had to be more daring with the business plans. Lyle had pulled out a set of green ledger papers that he and Virginia had pulled together to pitch an expanded new business, home general contracting, to Dad. They had not a clue at how to begin, but they thought their connections with suppliers, knowledge of the town, and good name with the people of Fort Collins, made expansion a real possibility. With the returning GIs and the country's renewed economic optimism, it seemed like a perfect time to jump into construction.

Lyle had thought the shop could serve as a store front for the expanded business of "John Simmons & Sons, General Contractors." He had even set up an appointment for Dad with bank manager to see what they needed to do to prepare a formal business plan and to line up the necessary credit to get the business on its feet. The meeting was to be the following afternoon.

From downstairs, Dad called, "Boys, come on down. It is time we talked."

William looked to Paul and whispered, "Don't say a word about what I just said, Paul. Dad wants this to be a surprise for both of us. He'll be pissed that Lyle let me in on the secret."

Paul glanced down the steps and yelled "Coming, Dad. Give us a second."

"William, but I don't know that I want to jump into the business now. My God, I just got home and I think I need to give myself a chance to make it on my own. I think college is first on my list. I have a whole year to catch up on you." Paul smiled and gave William a brotherly punch to the shoulder. "By the way, how goes engineering? Rumor is engineering is the future of the country."

William rolled his eyes. "I guess it's good. Tougher than I expected, though. Calculus is eating my lunch. Paul, you got to consider the business. It's for all of us. I'll bet Dad can figure out a way for us to do both, don't you think. Heck we can both go to A&M here in town. It might take us longer, but we'll be our own bosses; making a name for ourselves."

In William's face, Paul could see the optimism bursting. This had apparently been something that was so important to him, he was having trouble containing his exuberance.

"Okay, we'll try, but school is number one priority, right?"

"Right," William solemnly responded turning his head away to attempt to hide his grin.

The boys headed downstairs, to hear Dad out.

Chapter 7

Winter had come early in 1948. Halloween had not yet arrived and two snowstorms had already dumped a blanket of white on the town. "Guess what kids?" Paul thought to himself as he drove toward the campus to drop William off for class. "This year the trick will be on you; no treats unless you were willing to traipse through crusty snow and brave the freezing nights of a Colorado winter." Paul hated the winters and had longed to leave for somewhere that never saw snow, the San Diego endless summer Orley had described so often. Southern California would eventually be home.

The last three years had flown by for Paul. He had meant to enroll in school, but with the business, things ALWAYS seemed to come up that compelled him to pour himself full-time into the job. It did not bother him; he was still young. Hell at 23, there was always next year.

In reality, it did not even bother him much that William had followed his brotherly advice, deciding to put the business last and put school as his number one priority. Someday, William's education would be a great addition to the business. So, for now, William was in school and Paul had largely taken over the reins from Dad to run the business.

Lyle and Virginia made his transition from kid to adult, from GI to private citizen, and from Dad's son to boss, a heck of a lot easier than it could have been. They were smart and completely selfless when it came to getting credit for a job well done. They were happy with their share of the profits at the end of each month. Paul had begun to develop a completely different understanding of their relation with Dad. Theirs was one of complete appreciation, trust, and reliance borne out the hard times of the Great Depression. Two families had been thrown together by circumstances beyond their control that had synergistically bonded to create a successful life. Dad and his family brought talent and some money, Lyle and Virginia brought intelligence and a desire to work. Together they had developed a bond of loyalty that, today, Paul was ashamed that he had not grasped as a kid.

Paul was still surprised at Lyle and Virginia's apparent humility. It was if they lacked any ego when it came to being recognized for their ideas or contribution... and their contribution was quietly huge. Three years ago, Paul had not an idea as to what the awning business was, let alone how they would expand into general contracting. Yet, they had persevered and learned together. Together, they had completed a handful of home remodel efforts, built half a dozen homes; selling each for a decent profit, and now were bidding on an opportunity larger than all their previous construction efforts put together. The awning business was pretty much a memory at this point.

Virginia ran the office, took care of the books and pretty much made sure Simmons & Sons stayed current with the bank. She paid the bills to the suppliers and contractors making sure the checks were available for Paul's signature each morning. Most importantly, she made sure they remained frugal, not allowing their growth to get ahead of their cash flow. Lyle worked as the foreman for the construction jobs, occasionally still willing to lend a hand if the job fell behind schedule. Paul, completed the bids, met with the bank to review their line of credit and ensured their permitting was current and proper. Dad, pretty much provided a steadying hand and provided Paul "free" consultation. At 23, Paul no longer minded the guidance. In fact, he appreciated, no, cherished it. The discussions always left him feeling more confident about their decisions. William's contribution: well that would come next year when he finished school.

Paul pulled the truck up to the curb and Bill bounded out. "Paul, thanks for the ride. I will be studying late tonight at the library, so don't worry about picking me up after work. I'll either walk home or hitch a quick ride with a pretty girl from school," his countenance flipping from serious to smiling.

Paul grinned, too. "Good thing. I wasn't planning to give you a ride anyway. We have a ton of work to complete the bid on renovating the Armstrong Hotel. It served well as a barracks during the war, but frankly the GI's staying there while they went to school at Colorado A&M beat the hell out of her and now she needs some real tender, loving care. The Armstrong wants the entire ground floor reworked to make room for two large conference areas and large foyer for the lobby. If we win this bid, it might be the only good thing to come out of that war for me."

William looked down and toed some ice from the walk. "Crap, when does the bid need to be in? I am swamped with mid-terms and I have to nail these exams if I am to stay in the engineering program. I am afraid I will not be able to help"

Paul laughed at the comment since it seemed that William never had time to help with bids. "Lyle, Dad, and I have pulled together most of what we need, William, so don't sweat it. You have go and get ahead of the power curve with school. We really need you if we're going to make this step. We are counting on this deal paying the bills for next year."

William, nodded, turned quietly away and began walking to his classes. To get to his classes, William tramped through a thin, icy crust of snow covering the grass of a cottonwood-lined, commons area about the size of football field. Paul waited in the truck until he saw William's figure duck into the blonde brick, three story building that served as home for the school's aspiring engineers. Paul had been in the building several times. It always left him feeling somehow inadequate as he watched the students moving from class to class, proudly lugging their thick books and slide rules as badges of honor.

Paul put the truck in gear and pulled slowly away from the curb. Today he and Lyle would be spending the majority of the day at Dad's house hammering out the final aspects of their bid. He was optimistic, but somehow had just become less happy than any time since returning home.

* * *

Lyle pulled his legs up onto the spare chair in Dad's office. "I think we are back on schedule and budget. We should be pretty well done with the hotel by the first of May. So, what's next?"

It had been a hectic six months since winning the Armstrong bid. Things had turned tough when they had discovered a need to re-plumb the heating and replace the boiler. Although the additional cost was renegotiated into the contract, they had failed to garner acceptance for a delay in the job's completion date commitment. A performance bonus of 5% awaited them if the Armstrong could reopen in time for the spring. May 1st meant the difference between a big profit and barely break even.

It now looked as though profit was in sight, but it had come with some pretty high personal costs. Lyle had been putting in 12 hours Monday through Saturday, keeping the subcontractors on schedule and riding hard on the quality aspects of the job. Paul had taken responsibility for managing the boiler and plumbing upgrade, leaving him no time to beat the pavement to bid on future business. The effort of soliciting future business had fallen solely on the shoulders of Dad.

The strain had taken the most toll on Dad. The financial risk of the Armstrong job had aged him years over the six months of the project. The relief on Dad's face upon hearing the news from Lyle was obvious now that it appeared they were going to turn a profit. Paul even thought he could see the hint of a smile as Dad's cheeks tightened and the slight indention of dimples showed, something that had been missing for too long. It was becoming obvious to Paul their business was going to have to change significantly if they were to continue to grow.

Paul tentatively suggested "This was tough on all of us. Maybe it's time we looked to add another person to the team."

"Paul, I think you are right. I think it is about time I pulled William back into the team to pull his weight," Dad stated.

"Well that's not exactly what I was thinking. Besides, William will be a full-fledged engineer in a year. Let's not make him pull out of school now. He would have saved us a ton on this last job just by being able to certify our construction plans had he already been a full-fledged engineer. I was actually thinking we should pull in a part-time architect to the business."

Dad rolled his eyes. "You have not talked to William much about his grades, have you? He will be lucky to finish in another year and even at that, since he hasn't been the most stellar student, I am not sure we could not pull in a better engineer to the team. I am beginning to question if I made the right call to make him part of the business."

Paul was shocked. Lyle just quietly pulled his feet down from the chair and stood to leave the room.

"Don't leave, Lyle. You know what I am talking about. You

want to tell Paul how helpful his brother has been the few times he has been on the job site," Dad commented sarcastically.

Lyle turned back to Dad, "John, I don't feel comfortable talking about William. He's a good kid. Maybe he's just not cut out to be an engineer."

"Stop it, Lyle. If we would have put his suggestions into the job, we would have had a mess on our hands today. Instead of getting ready to celebrate success, we would have still been stuck in rework and probably would have had some real dangerous situations with the material savings he was proposing. Thank goodness, some the contractors came forward and forced us to seek out a real professional to engineer some of the support beams we needed for the ground floor. Hell, the whole place could have come down on us during demolition."

Lyle looked at the floor then to me. "He's right, of course," then back to Dad "but, he'll learn. He still has another year of school."

"School, yeah sure. If he could keep his eyes in the books and not on the girls I could agree with you. I just do not see him being much help as an engineer. I'll tell you what, I will put off any conversations with William for the time being. Paul, what do you have in mind for the architect . . . and how do you suggest we pay for him?"

Chapter 8

THREE WEEKS LATER, the final inspection of the Armstrong was complete. With the deposit of the final funds from the Armstrong hotel, it was time to introduce Dad to Paul's idea for the next phase of John Simmons & Sons. A project that would change the complexion of their company for good and make a real impact on the town.

For Paul, the prospect of going to school full-time was fading even though Dad was pushing him to enroll in the upcoming term. For Dad, John Simmons & Sons had been moving along just fine and would benefit greatly in the long-term by having Paul earn a degree in civil engineering. Although Paul's Dad had made his mind up that the investment in William's education was not going to prove to be much of an asset, he had decided that Paul's natural leadership abilities and creativity would ensure the second investment would pay premiums. For John Simmons, putting off the idea of expanding the business only made sense. Paul, on the other hand, was committed to the next phase of the business, as much for proving his faith in his brother was well founded, as it was for the good of the family.

The last three years had been a period of transformation for the business. The importance of awnings had diminished to size to where it had moved from being the life-blood of the business, to a becoming a nuisance, to effectively being shut down. Shuttering awnings had liberated needed office space and freed up resources for the growing construction portion of the company. The construction work had proven profitable, but as Paul had come to realize, the difference between business success and bankruptcy was extremely small, continually dependent on the next job in the queue. In Paul's mind, to slow the business at this time would define and limit the business, crippling its growth and relegating its best days to those in the past. In fact, he thought slowing the pace now would prove the end of the business. He owed it to William, Virginia, Lyle, Mom, and Dad to not let it fail. School would wait.

This summer, William would work full-time with the company, under Paul's direct tutelage. Although William had jumped at the opportunity, Paul had become all too familiar with a pattern with William; jump into an idea with exuberance, only to see the interest wain with time or as the job got tough or whenever he saw a pretty girl. Paul was certain that he would need to ride William hard to get steady contribution. He was hopeful that by the end of the summer, he could make a significantly favorable impact on William's commitment to the business, his future, and his life in general. Most important to Paul was to use this summer to create in Dad's mind, a different image of William's contribution and importance to the business. William would either win over his Dad's trust or be relegated to a role of merely being a tolerated participant in the business due to blood rather than ability, relying on nepotism for his livelihood.

In addition, this summer would be a defining time for the business. Paul had laid out plans for the purchase of a 40-acre plot of land south and east of the college campus for a small housing development of up to 110 homes. It was going to be a new concept for Fort Collins and would put them on the map as a primary construction company in the region. It also would test their mettle for the first time as a developer. The project would mean the addition of a full-time architect for home design, the development of a strategic partnership with a local realtor, and a significantly expanded line of credit at the bank. The promise was large, but the challenges were intimidating.

The selection of the architect had been pretty simple. Limited funding really constricted the search to green hires right out of college. Paying for relocation was out of the question, so limiting the search to people already residing in the region was critical. They eventually settled on a newly graduated architect named Arlin Peeples. Arlin, just a kid really, was someone William had met at college this past year. They had gotten to know each other from their late-night study efforts in the campus library. Arlin had been impossible to miss in the library. To keep his mind alert with his studies, he would periodically jump up from his chair only to fall to the floor, rolling over and over on the cool tile, soaking the coolness up to shock himself back awake. William could not help but laugh at the antic and introduce himself. It was only weeks later that William discovered that Arlin was an exceptionally creative student. Unfortunately for Arlin, but fortunately for Simmons & Sons, his prospects upon graduation had not been great unless he wanted to move to Denver. Although the job with John Simmons & Sons did not pay much, it provided him a means to stay in town with his family and gave him a rare opportunity to make an impression on a new residential concept based on limited number of basic home designs for an entire neighborhood. He would be responsible not only for the initial home designs, but he would also establish basic design options for the interiors and exteriors that enabled each home to have its own individual look while still keeping the economies associated with common construction processes and materials. He took it as a challenge and opportunity to make a mark early in his career.

The project also required the addition of a committed and focused realtor. Joseph Klein and Company, had signed on to the team. Joseph Klein and Company came with a number of contingencies. The participation provided the realtor final approvals on the basic home designs, lot plans, basic construction materials, appliances and pricing. In addition, they wanted a sales office and exclusive rights to market and sell the new properties. Their cut was to be 3.5% of the net selling price of the homes. For their take, they had agreed to develop and provide all marketing materials, provide full-time sales staff support, serve as broker, and, through their banking connections, provide the primary conduit for necessary mortgage funding.

With these two new resources, three huge challenges still loomed. First was garnering a commitment of significant funding from the bank, second, closing on the land parcel purchase, and last aligning with the town on extending their utility and road access.

Virginia and Paul hashed out the proposal to the bank with Paul's Dad. Paul had not anticipated the number of variables Virginia had wisely contributed to the business plan. By the time they were ready to go to the bank, they had supplemented the basic financial overview with details on labor, material suppliers, zoning, typographical maps, some basic home elevations to provide a pictorial look at what they were intending to deliver. The work had been much more extensive than Paul had initially expected to deliver, but after the work, he realized how unrealistic his original thoughts had been. He now felt confident that they now had a plan that not only would pay off financially, but would also make a huge contribution to changing the face of the town.

The development of the proposal had taken a full two months; a quick bank acceptance and funding would be critical if they had any hope of breaking ground on the development next spring. No approval and they would have to scrap the dream for the time being since they would not be able to afford to fund the business opportunity. Failure meant finding and landing another big job to carry the business until an alternative funding source could be found.

Virginia had noticeably aged during the last two months. She and Paul fully recognized the risk associated with their plan. Although they were confident in the future business opportunity, if the funding did not come through, the expanded payroll with William and Arlin, meant some serious belt tightening for everyone.

* * *

The dinner table was particularly quiet. Paul and Dad were pushing around the food on their plates, but had barely taken a taste. William had not yet come home. He had planned to stay late in the University library to study for mid-terms. The past summer had been an exceptional time for William; he had demonstrated an ability and willingness to pull his weight by managing a number of small jobs while freeing up Paul to focus on the development of his business plan. It was a time to show an appreciation to his big brother for his trust. From a purely selfish perspective, he had also begun to see how Paul's vision could mean a big pay-off for the family.

Mom sat with hands clasped in front of her, looking exasperatingly from man to man. Mom, finally broke the silence. "Boys, if this is what a growing business is going to do to you, maybe it is not worth it. You know we have lived through some pretty tough times. You cannot let this effect you this much."

Dad looked up from his plate, stared at Paul then to back to his mother, "Virginia is seriously concerned about how much is riding on the meeting at the bank tomorrow. If it doesn't go well, then we are back too square one. I guess we lay off Arlin and William. Hell, it won't be such a big deal with Arlin, he just started. William will probably be thankful. He can get a head start on his studies."

Paul gazed at Dad. "It is going to be good at the bank tomorrow." It has to be, Paul thought to himself. That said, he had already begun to think about fall back options if the meeting did not go so well. First off, he would have to scrap his plans to move into his own home and his dreams of wealth. Well, quod erit, erit. Maybe it would be a good time to try out San Diego to see if was half as beautiful as Orley made it out to be. God, Orley; that seemed like a lifetime ago.

"Virginia is going to meet us at the Walgreen's diner at 9:00 for a cup of coffee to go over the proposal a final time. Dad, we can all three walk together to the bank. Hopefully, we can be done in time to celebrate over lunch. We get the deal, you're buying."

"Just to let you know, Mom and I already have reservations for all of us at the Armstrong Hotel. They have a small room off the dining hall they have set aside for us at 1:00. Your Mother, William, Lyle, Virginia, Arlin, and Joe Klein will be joining us after the meeting. I may have jumped the gun, but Mom and I felt it was important to acknowledge the effort, success or not. God, let it be a success, because I don't want to face everyone if it is not." Paul's father stated.

Dad stood up from the table, took his full plate to the kitchen. As he walked into the kitchen, he said "Hon, the food looks great. I just am not very hungry. I hope you understand."

Mom, grabbed her plate, too. "That's OK. Just make sure you have an appetite tomorrow."

Paul smiled. He now sat alone with his plate and his

thoughts. Not exactly how he expected the night to end, but probably fitting. Silently he began contemplating if it was okay to ask God to help tomorrow. Although he wanted the help, he felt in his heart, it was presumptuous and selfish to ask God for help in getting the loan. Instead he settled finally on a simple, silent prayer: "Help me to do my best. Calm me. Let me do as you will. Let me not let my family down."

Paul, decided it best to finish his dinner. Now that the table was empty except for his plate it provided a great space to spread out and go over the proposal to anticipate any questions that might come up tomorrow. He struggled with why he felt so much anxiety at this time. They had established a strong line of credit with the bank. They were an account in good standing. Their relation with the bank was nothing but positive. And yet, they were embarking on a whole new phase of their business. He was afraid their history with the bank meant absolutely nothing with the exponential request they now had. More importantly, their project actually would change the town. Building off modernization in the post war world, they would provide a new type of single family housing; affordable, efficient, and stylish. It was important.

* * *

"Paul, what the hell are you doing down here." William was gently shaking Paul to wake him.

"Crap, I must have dozed off. What time is it?" Paul whispered.

"It's after 11. You better head off to bed. I'll clean up here," William offered as Paul slowly pulled himself up to stand and stretch.

"I will take you up on the offer. How'd studying go."

"It went great for the first hour or so, but . . ." William gave a quick wink and shrug.

"What do you mean the 'the first hour or so.' Heck, you were supposed to be at the library since before dinner. What gives? You know Dad is pretty bent regarding your grades. You have to get serious. We need you in the business."

"Paul, come on. You are starting to sound like Dad. If you must know, I am now unequivocally in love. I felt as though I had a religious experience when she sat down next to me in the library." Paul's smile was contagious.

"OK, give. What is her name"

"Samantha, and we are going to have lunch together tomorrow"

"Lunch, no way, William. Mom and Dad are springing for lunch at the Armstrong. You have to be there. Didn't they tell you."

"Omgosh, I completely forgot. One o'clock, right? Yeah, I'll be there. Heck, maybe, Samantha could join us." William saw the shock in Paul's eyes and quickly caught himself... "Well, maybe another time." With that William snagged Paul's plate off the table and quietly walked into the kitchen.

Paul, tiptoed up the steps to bed. Sometimes William was clueless. Kind, but clueless.

Chapter 9

"I'll bet you, you never knew your Mom and I actually dated back before your Dad went to Korea" Uncle Bill blurted out. Upon noting my shocked face, he laughed and slapped his hand down on the table. "Hell, Randall, I didn't think I could ever shock you. It wasn't anything, really. Just a couple of dates for fun. Once she met your Dad, Sam dropped me like a lead balloon. Your Mom and Dad were meant for each other from the get-go. You know that idea of love-at-first sight. Well for them it was true."

"Well, why are you telling me this now? Shit, Dad's not dead yet. You're not saying you want to get back with Mom, are you?"

"Randall, that could not be further from my mind. First off, your Mom is a one-man woman and her man is lying in a bed a mile away. After he passes, he will still be her one man, nothin' going to change that and I would never try. I only brought it up to give you some insight to your Dad. Paul first met your Mom when I was stupid enough to bring her to dinner a couple of weeks after we got approval from the bank for our first round of funding for the small housing development I live in, just across College Boulevard from the campus. It had been a dream come true for us. I remember it like yesterday. Everybody was happy and exhilarated. That development was the spring board for everything your Dad did for this town, but even with the funding approval from the bank, our world kind of went into chaos that night.

"Mark, you mind bringing us a bottle of wine. I think that will be better than a couple of beers to go along with dinner . . . plus, a couple steaks, medium rare . . . Randall, you up for a steak?"

I barely got out a "sure" before Uncle Bill jumped right back into his request to Mark "My nephew and I might be here for a while, so anything else you would suggest with the steaks, just go ahead. I'll trust you." I had a suspicion this would be a typical Uncle Bill night; starting out serious and with a point, but quickly degrading once the booze started to flow. Maybe the saving grace would be he was starting with wine and not bourbon.

Bill turned back to me and smiled, "Mark and Tim are great. Your Dad gave them a little starting money to get the restaurant going and they've turned it into one of the best in Colorado. Good guys, queer as a three-dollar bill, but I love these guys and leave it to your Dad to see their potential."

Mark had just returned to the table with a couple of bottles, smiling. "Randall, I know your Uncle pretty well so I figured we'll keep a second bottle up he, just as a reserve." Mark surprised me when he not only poured glasses for Uncle Bill and me, but he poured out a glass for himself. Taking a small sip, "Not bad, I think you will like it but it needs to breathe a little. Steaks will be on the way shortly. Tim and I will join you after the rush from downstairs slows a little." At that, Mark headed off back downstairs.

I was at a loss at this. "So, Uncle, since when did you become such good buds with restaurateurs that you now eat together? I thought this was just going to be you and me. What gives?"

"Soon enough, Randall. They wanted to tell you a little about your Dad themselves. That's all. How's the wine?"

"It's actually pretty good. I'll bet it's expensive. So back to the infamous dinner where you introduced Mom to Dad; what was the chaos?" I figured if I did not get Uncle Bill back on topic before he started in on the wine, the night would be lost.

I was surprised when Uncle Bill actually began to tear up. His eyes became red and his mouth began to clinch. I could tell this was a tough topic. Finally, his eyes dropping to the glass of wine he had cupped his hands around. "That was the night your Dad found out he was going back into the Army. You know, the Korean War." With this Uncle Bill grabbed the bottle and refilled his glass.

"Shit, I was such an ass that night. I accused him of messing up our family's future. Saying that if he hadn't gone to fight in WWII the government would not be tapping him for this war. I actually went so far as to say good riddance and never come back. Randall, I was really bad and I never really had the chance to ask him to forgive me before he headed off to Korea. Anyway, I think he forgave me as soon as foul words spewed from my mouth, but he never forgave himself for the impact to the business and his dreams.

"You know your Dad never had a choice. He wasn't married, he didn't have kids, he wasn't in school, and he was a young army veteran; never had a chance. It was back to a hell hole thousands of miles from home . . . and he only had a couple of weeks to report."

With that an older man in a dapper suit showed up at our table with a couple huge ribeye steaks. "Hi, I am Tim. I really hope you enjoy dinner tonight, Randall."

* * *

Paul's hands were trembling after having read the letter from the Selective Service System at dinner. He had received an order to report for an "Armed Forces Physical Examination" at the Greyhound Bus Depot on Monday, April 17th, 1950, less than a week from this evening. "Mom, Dad, William, this doesn't have to change anything. We should still move on the development."

Dad stared at Paul. "Paul, there is no way in hell we can pull this off without you . . . and William no more comments from you. We will just wait until this mess in Korea is over. I will sit down with Virginia and you tomorrow and we will just have to figure out a way to put this on the back burner until you come home. No if's or but's."

William was stewing. It was unclear if he was more upset about Paul going back into the army, the delay of potential wealth through the development, or being humiliated by being ignored in front of his new girl, Samantha. Dad had not even bothered to acknowledge him as he talked about what they were going to do now that Paul was back in the army. Heck, hadn't he proven himself this past summer to be capable? Couldn't he be a solution to keep the development on track? What did Virginia and Paul have that he didn't? Then the answers struck him like a ton of bricks; talent, smarts, commitment, and Dad's trust. Hell, they had everything the company needed. William, sat quietly, realizing now how he had let down the family. Even worse, Samantha had not taken her eyes of Paul for more than a few moments ever since sitting down at the table. It was obvious; tonight, William had lost his illusions of self-respect and self-worth plus he had lost his girl.

* * *

Uncle Bill, pushed his plate back from the edge of the table. He had pretty much demolished the huge steak. I had to admit the steak was probably one of the best I'd ever had. It looked like the only real difference between Bill's appetite and my appetite was the commitment to wine. I was on my second glass and Bill had just drained what was left of the second bottle into his glass.

Mark had just returned from the main restaurant downstairs. "Sorry, Tim and I have not been able to break away to join you for dinner. It has been hectic downstairs." Looking at the two emptied plates, "Wow, it looks as though you REALLY liked the dinner. Tim will be so happy. By chance have you left some room for a desert? This morning I made a cheesecake just for you two. Plus, I have a great port I've wanted to break into."

"I have to say, that was one of the best steaks I can remember. Uncle Bill, you up for Mark's cheesecake."

"I do not know where I would put it, Randall. Besides, I think I kind of overindulged on the wine; it was superb. I didn't bring my reading glasses and I did not recognize the label."

Mark smiled and winked, "I thought you might like it. It's actually a Petite Sirah out of an up-and-coming winery in Temecula, California. Randall isn't that close to your home?" Without even waiting for my answer Mark jumped right in to describing how the spicy, plummy taste seemed to go so well with red meats. He obviously knew his food and drink.

Although I had no doubt Uncle Bill loved the wine, he pretty much loved any wine that poured, in this case, maybe too much. His eyes divulged that none of Mark's description was sinking in; perhaps if Mark had come up a couple glasses earlier?

"Mark, I hate to say this, but I think my uncle and I are going to have to pass on the cheesecake. I hope Tim and you are not too disappointed, but from Uncle Bill's eyes, I think it might be time for us to head home. Plus, I suspect my Mom will be sending out a search party for us shortly. Maybe we should just pay the check and we can swing by again over the next couple of days."

To this Mark laughed and said "There's no check from us, Randall. Never is and never will be. We owe more to your Dad and Mister Simmons that we could ever pay back with meals." With that he stepped to Uncle Bill's side and grasped one arm. "Randall if you catch your uncle's other arm; I think it best if we help him down the steps. They can be pretty tricky. And I am going to hold you to your offer to swing by again. Tim and I always enjoy sharing stories about your Dad."

Chapter 10

Even with the ride home being short, Uncle Bill had fallen sound asleep and was sawing logs by the time I pulled in behind the house on Armstrong Street. I had briefly thought of driving him to his house, but leaving him without his truck didn't seem right and it was too far for me to walk home. So Uncle Bill would be staying with Mom and me tonight. Thank goodness, Mom had decided to hire the live-in nurse.

Uncle Bill, groggy and muddled, woke up just enough to allow me to walk him into our home. It was all I could do just getting him up the entry steps to the front door; it would be next to impossible to walk him through the house to my bedroom; at least without waking the entire house. Bill got the couch tonight.

It had been a fun and relaxing night, and I was not ready to turn in. Except for the tic-toc-tic-toc of the grandfather clock in the living room, Uncle Bill's snoring, and the dry, short breaths coming from Dad's mouth, the house was eerily quiet. I sat down with a cup of late-night coffee at the kitchen table to open the box Mom and I had pulled up from the basement earlier in the day. I had barely started to rummage through it earlier in the day, and I now wanted to see if Mom had saved anything from the time before she married Paul. Before digging into the box, I grabbed Dad's blue book off the table and began to flip through some of the pages I had yet to read.

Johnny Jackson, you deserved better. I guess you know what it meant to be a real man. Sorry I never returned the favor . . .

    I remember a Johnny Jackson from Dad's business when I had been a kid. I kind of doubted this was the same guy. Johnny had been a quiet, big black guy that came to our family back when I had been a child. He had worked for Dad for several years until he had passed away quietly during my junior year of high school. Some of my friends thought he was kind of creepy because he would talk to himself while he was working. I figured he just had a lot to say, but didn't have many folks he felt comfortable talking with. Initially, I never knew why Dad had invited him into our family, but that was just Dad. I read on.

* * *

'I hate this country' was all Paul could think as he hopped out of the jeep in January of 1951. It was humid and cold, maybe not bitter, but cold in any case. Pusan was dirty, congested, surrounded by desolate low mountains; generally miserable, but at least it was far from the front.

    Pusan was a port city in the far southeasterly part of South Korea. It had been the center of heavy fighting several months earlier as the Chinese and NKPA, North Korean People's Army, had been converging on the city in a push to drive the United Nation defenses into the ocean. Thankfully, they failed and the United States 8th Army had responded by surprising the NKPR with a counter attack led by an amphibious landing at Inchon, close to Seoul. The tides had certainly turned. Now if President Truman would just get out of MacArthur's way and let him win, maybe Paul could return home sooner than later.

Paul never did understand Truman. He had been instrumental in making the hard decision during WW II, perhaps the hardest decision, to win the war and save lives. Now this same man's complacency and a new war had uprooted him out of his life in Colorado only to be set down in a country, 6,000 miles away; a country where millions of civilians had been killed and were continuing to be killed, and yet his president apparently had no interest in winning the war. What a waste. He hoped he was not destined to be thrown on the waste pile as had been so many US soldiers before him in the interest of what? a stalemate with the two-bit dictator, Kim Il-Sung, or some improbable hope of keeping China complacent?

Paul's previous army service along his successful experience in business and construction had landed him in what he had thought would be a reasonably safe role as a Sergeant with the US 8th Army Corp of Engineers based out of Pusan. His duty largely revolved around road bed grading to ensure the routes north out of Pusan remained adequately smooth for truck traffic while keeping them raised above the flooded rice fields that dominated this portion of the country. This was all going to change quickly with his redeployment north. It looked as though the rest of his time in Korea was destined to be spent too close to the front for his comfort, only several miles south of the 38th parallel separating North and South Korea.

To date, the work was long, tedious, and safe. It sure as hell beat what he remembered of being shot at during the Battle of the Bulge. Now WWII seemed a lifetime ago. Paul's days now were consumed keeping the grading equipment in adequate repair to keep the supply logistics running unimpeded to the north. It was pretty much the same each and every day. Even though he had only been in Korea for three months, he had settled into the monotony of continuous road repair.

In one respect, he was thankful to be in a role where nobody was shooting at him, but this current job exposed him to a different danger, one more insidious in nature. His routine now concluded each day with a visit to a bar in town, one typically patronized by other NCOs from the engineers and supply corps. Night meant drinking cheap bourbon with his fellow sergeants from his platoon. Sergeants Simmons, Grey, Henry, Knight, and Halsey pretty much closed the bar each night. A Sergeant Jackson, the only negro sergeant in the platoon was not included in their small clique and yet also ended the day in the same bar, drinking with a small group of negro NCO's from a different platoon. They had taken up residence at the far end of the simple room. Paul Simmons guessed segregation would be with people for a while whether the US Army wanted it or not.

For Paul, evenings began with the same embarrassment; Grey would begin by making some pejorative loud comment regarding their black compatriots in the bar. Henry, Halsey, and Knight would nervously and quietly chuckle. Grey, gaining fortitude from his white buddies would then follow-up his first disparaging comment with equally despicable comments targeted specifically at his negro counterparts. Paul had determined early on that Grey was a jerk and chastised himself for being too much a coward to put Grey in his place. Tonight, would be no different. If he had any real grit, he would stand up and put his fist into Grey's mouth and then head right over the Jackson's group to make new friends. Maybe tomorrow. Tonight, he would continue being an apparent bigot via complacency. Okay, he was guilty, but it was a feeling that a couple glasses of bourbon would numb.

Having been drafted against his will into the service for this war, isolated from actual battle, hearing more horrific stories every day, it was easy to become disaffected. He found himself seeking release through unconsciously developing self-destructive habits. He now opened his eyes in the morning looking forward to the night of drunkenness that would follow the day's work. His responsibilities to his platoon and country had become secondary. He had also developed an affinity to finishing the night off liaising with local women with whom he had nothing in common other than being lonely. This was hardly the Paul that had haled from Fort Collins. It was also not a person Paul could be proud of.

In spite of his decline into debauchery, his time in Korea was not all a bad thing. He had to come to acknowledge and enjoy a diversity of life that he could never have experienced back home. First off, his company was integrated. In Fort Collins, he could not recall ever having seen a negro, let alone eaten with one, elbow to elbow. Secondly, the Korean culture was SO different than anything he had ever experienced: the food, the language, the religion, the art; there was nothing that was comparable back home. Lastly, the people, well, they looked and acted so differently. And the women, they seemed to genuinely love the GI. Something good could come from this. Well, one could hope.

Tomorrow, this would change, as his company was to pull out in the morning, moving north to a camp bordering the southern portion of a Chinese stronghold, an area referred to as the "Iron Triangle" about 60 miles north of Seoul. Even with the additional danger. the majority of the sergeants in the company were looking forward to the change. Paul was not.

* * *

This was so different from anything Paul had experienced in the previous war. The fighting, although furious, was so diffuse, with fighting centered around small outposts. The 8th had troops stationed on top and around naked, harsh mountains formally assigned hill numbers, but known more commonly by the troops by names such as "Bald Mountain," "Pork Chop Hill," and such. Paul had been raised at the foot of the Rockies in Colorado, majestic, picturesque mountains covered with cooling blue-green pines, rippling rivers and streams, and abundant wildlife. And the smell, almost perfume-like. No such thing here. These mountains were dead, rough, gray/brown completely devoid of vegetation and animal life, except for the 100 or so soldiers clinging to each of them.

This was an odd war. Troops from the good ole USA, France, and Australia sitting atop one hill peering over a dead valley at their enemy, the PRC troops, or the more fanatical NKPA, sitting on the next hilltop 500 meters away. Both sides staring at each other, daring each other to attack. For the US, the effort had largely turned into a battle of attrition with each side lobbing deadly mortar rounds at their enemy. The US took pride in being more efficient in the killing.

The engineering corps was charged with making sure these US outposts did not become isolated. Their first objective was to keep the service road from the Main Line of Resistance (MLR) open. It was maintained daily. Mortars and landmines made the job significantly more dangerous than Paul had expected. Every morning, small craters needed filling and repair. The land mines were another problem entirely. Even though the bulldozer's blade and sheer mass pretty much protected the driver from any blast, the damage to the dozer meant road repairs were delayed constantly, putting at risk the resupply to outposts. A delay of a half day in getting food and ammunition to the soldiers could be the difference in life and death. Delays were not acceptable.

A solution to the land-mines came out of a bleary-eyed and rare discussion between Paul and the black Sergeant Jackson. The booze that night had been particularly bad, but Paul and Jackson had no desire to turn in early. Although they rarely socialized together, tonight circumstances left them alone in the makeshift NCO tent. It had proven to be an excellent opportunity to get to know each other a little and to tackle a common problem: land mines.

"Sergeant Simmons, you OK with me sittin' here?" Without waiting for an answer, Jackson dropped heavily into the empty bar stool next to Paul. Jackson had obviously been drinking as heavily and every bit as long as Paul had this evening. His eyes were red-rimmed and he was having trouble talking.

Paul was too drunk to be surprised by Jackson's uninvited visit. "Heck, yes, Sergeant Jackson. Sit your ass down and have a whiskey wif me." Amazing as it was, introductions complete, they were now, apparently, friends for life.

Jackson was older than Paul by a full half decade, and had dealt with the discrimination of the old South his entire life. Even though he was bright, creative, and unusually articulate, when sober, Jackson had welcomed being drafted by the army selective service. For him the draft provided liberation from poverty and discrimination. For Paul, the same draft represented shackles. Perspective was everything.

Without any preamble, Jackson looked directly into Paul's eyes, "So, Simmons, what are we gonna do about those land-mines?"

"What do you mean, Jackson?"

"Well, not to be insensitive to those smarty college boys, but they don't seem to know shit about the land mines we are getting blown up by every day. I think it's about time we take the problem into our own hands, and I think I have a way to knock out those mines without killing ourselves. I was thinking if we could figure out a way to whip the ground with chains or something, you know, ahead of the dozers we could set those puppies off without ruining our tractors. You got any ideas?"

Paul's eyes started to light up "Hell, yes."

With that Paul and Jackson pestered the bartender for a pencil and some paper, and before dawn, Jackson and Simmons had penciled out a rotating bar laced with replaceable chains. The motion would be driven from the bulldozer drive train with a simple gear box. As the tractor engine RPM increased, so would the flailing action of the chains. As the chains flailed, slapping the ground, the land mines would be blown up at least six feet in front of the dozer, not under one of the dozer's treads. Okay, the driver would have to replace the chain, but that was a heck of lot easier than fixing a track or a transmission. Neither Paul nor Jackson knew how to make the gear box or a clutch system to turn the flail on and off, but they figured there were a number of "college boy" engineers in camp that might be able to fabricate something.

Within a week, a crude, but effective, gear box and flail rotor had been pulled together in the equipment shed and Paul had convinced a couple mechanics to rig up two dozers with the new flail, one for Paul's squad and one for Jackson's. The two sergeants had become famous within the small confines of the company.

Unfortunately, creativity and success did little to ingratiate the colored Jackson with Sergeants Grey, Henry, Knight, and Halsey. It shocked Paul that fame with the flail innovation had fueled the strong racist beliefs in his compatriots. Even in the army, skin color overwhelmed the respect and admiration that should have been granted. By the end of the following week, Paul had returned to evening drinking with his white Sergeants and Jackson had once again relegated himself to the corner of the tent.

* * *

Grey winked toward the trio of Henry, Halsey, and Knight, then turned to Paul. "So, Simmons, what's that uppity nigger like?" nodding his head towards Jackson. Grey was an old-school, Mississippi Democrat that had either never gotten the message of the 13th through 15th Amendments or was just a downright despicable person. Paul suspected Grey had never even read the Constitution, let alone understand it, and yes, he was truly an ass.

All Paul could respond with was a "Huh?" and a look of shock.

Grey continued, "Shit, Simmons, you know what I mean. He was all proud of that chain flail thing. Big fucking deal. Any of us would have come up with the same thing if we could have had the mechanics work with us. Hell, we all know they pulled together the link to tractor drive just because Jackson is black as night just like them. Those negroes all stick together."

Having regained his composure, Paul said, "Grey, you are so full of it. Jackson's a stand-up guy. You'd like him. Let's call him over to have a drink with us."

The other three sergeants at the bar stayed silent trying to avoid being pulled into an uncomfortable discussion, at least until they had poured a couple more glasses of liquid fortification into their gullet.

"Jackson, what the hell, join us." Paul yelled. Then under breath turning back to the sergeants at the bar, "Grey, now shut up and don't be a jerk." Although he only addressed Grey, by name, it was clear he was admonishing them all to keep their racist comments to themselves.

Sergeant Jackson looked up uncomfortably at Paul and his

buddies before slowly gathering up his beer and the letter he had been writing. He folded the letter and stuffed it and his pencil into his breast pocket and moved over to Paul's table. Paul had to push his and Grey's chairs to the side to make room for another chair. Grey stared at Jackson. Henry, Knight, and Halsey just stared at their beers, apparently, they had become mute.

"So, Paul, how'd your flail do today? Ours ran fine, but didn't get any mines. At least the privates have stopped pissing their pants out of fear of blowing themselves up every time they have to run the tractor." At this Jackson started to laugh. "Guys, it's a joke! You can smile man!"

"You'll have to let up on them a while, Jackson. You know, we are drinking with some good ole' boys that have never had the pleasure of the company of someone with such a perfect tan like yours."

Grey finally cracked a smile. "Paul, I guess you are right. Welcome aboard, Jackson, to the infamous drunk boat. We move on to whiskey at ten." At this Grey, Henry, Knight, and Halsey all stood up and extended their hands to shake. Jackson thought he was now one of the team, perhaps a not a full member of the first team, but member in any case. He was mistaken. It is sad how mean and disingenuous folks can really be.

The following morning Paul's squad had drawn the unenviable duty of maintaining a section of the service road closest to two particularly nasty and dangerous US Outposts: Hills 266 and 255. In addition, they would also begin work on deepening and reinforcing the almost 400 yards of communication trench critical for accessing the top of the hills. Paul had suspected the 2nd Infantry units occupying these hills were destined for glory as part of the US frontline against the Chinese.

For the engineers, the duty was not only back-breaking, it was extremely dangerous. Landmines and mortar fire from

Soviet manufactured guns were prevalent, and the danger had been exasperated by confusion introduced by a steady flow of refugees from the north. In general, these were fine people just fleeing the oppression and murder at the hands of Kim Il-Sung, but intermingled with the safety-seeking civilians were a small number of NKPA soldiers who had traded in their cotton padded white telltale pants and coats for typical simple black peasant garb in hope of infiltrating the US lines. The US troops now had to check and recheck the passing refugees to make sure one was not armed and intent on murder. The NKPA infiltrators could be armed with any number or weapons, but most likely it would be an outdated Hanyang 88 bolt-action rifle or the Soviet built the PPSh41 submachine gun, an incredibly efficient killing machine. The submachine gun, or "burp gun," had become the North Koreans' weapon of choice in that even in the hands of an inexperienced warrior, it was deadly at close ranges. Unsuspecting GIs died daily at the hands of these supposedly harmless refugees. Truly innocent refugees ended up being shot even more often by nervous soldiers trying to defend themselves. Paul had no idea how many US troops and innocent civilians had already died as a result of the North Korean subterfuge.

In this region, most of the civilian refugees were escaping the area around Kaesong and were intent on moving on as quickly south as possible crossing over the Han River to a region controlled by United Nations forces. A handful of refugees had stopped their exodus once they reached the US Camp Castle, effectively turning the camp into an asylum of safety. Camp Castle was also the home to Paul's unit. For these refugees, Paul had begun to develop a unique appreciation and respect. Anyone that could deal with the heartbreak these people had experienced in the north and yet share what little they had with the GI was amazing. It was here that Paul had met Seo-Young.

Chapter 11

Today was pretty much as every day inside the Iron Triangle this time of year. It was bitter cold and the view was crowded with bald, craggy hills that held no real value to mankind other than they were a proxy for how well or bad the war was going for your particular side. A meaningless hill being in US or Chinese control somehow gave politicians a sign they were winning or losing the war. Here the dead, worthless land resembled the sepia tone photos from the 20's and 30's, devoid of all color save a monochromatic shading of browns. Unfortunately, human blood spilled in maintaining ownership of these meaningless hills was just as meaningless to the leaders thousands of miles away. Today, it was a stalemate between forces, and all was quiet.

Private Harris was charged with running the dozer this morning. He loved this duty and proved to be extremely proficient with the operation of this 15-ton stodgy behemoth, the Caterpillar D7. This tractor, albeit slow, was a reliable, stable, and a reasonably maneuverable beast, at least in the hands of Harris. He had just completed pushing tons of broken rock and stone to form a defense wall for the initial length of the critical communications trench serving Hill 266. What he accomplished in less than an hour saved the rest of the squad weeks of work, time that they did not have. That said, getting the dozer up the hill had been precarious at best. Twice Harris had been targeted by mortar rounds, the second coming as he was pre-occupied with saving the tractor and himself when the rock floor failed and crumbled along the entire length of his left tract, leaving the dozer lurching precariously to the port. For a just a brief moment, Harris considered jumping from the tractor before it would slide further and roll on its side. Gathering his courage, Harris collected himself to ride out the slide; jumping was not a guarantee of safety. It would likely just put him on the same crumbling surface as the tractor, to get crushed between rock and steel.

Thankfully, the left tract finally grabbed solid rock righting the tractor before he needed to abandon the ride. When asked how he kept his composure during the slide when the mortar shell hit, all he could say was "What mortar?" The whole episode took no more than 10 seconds, but it had been a very long 10 seconds.

The squad had moved back an additional thousand yards from the trenchers that were exposed to mortar fire to the comparative safety of the service road to break for a quick lunch. Paul had ordered Harris to evaluate the dozer's left tract to see if repair would be required before restarting the work on Hill 266. They could not afford to strand their dozer in range of the mortar fire.

Food came via a two-wheeled, oxen-pulled cart driven by an old man and his daughter. The young woman was striking. As soon as the ox stopped she hopped from the cart and began to hand out little grass-woven baskets to the soldiers. The baskets were filled with an assortment of short-grained white rice, kimchi, and grilled pork ribs, called galbi. It was a great break from the military k rations they had become accustomed to. It was obvious, this pair had taken it upon themselves to treat the soldiers as heroes and, hopefully, their country's saviors. Upon closer look, Paul could now see the woman was younger than he originally thought. She was really only a young girl. One young enough to only be concerned with school, family, and fun; not the daily dose of death she saw here. She moved away from the cart and sat quietly by be herself next to Private Harris as he worked on the bull dozer while the rest of the soldiers ate their meal.

Ignoring the father, Paul stood up and quietly moved toward girl. "Thank you for the food. It is really delicious. So, what is your name?"

The girl raised her eyes to look at Paul, but kept her head tilted downwards and made no verbal response. Paul assumed she was bashful, afraid, or more likely both and certainly understood little English. Oh well, he had tried. As Paul began to turn away, the girl reached out her hand and quietly grabbed his pant leg. Startled by the contact Paul responded "What the . . ."

The young woman's eyes darted to her father then back to Paul and she turned her head slowly, almost imperceptibly from side to side. Paul took a quick glance over to the old man and realized instantly his error.

The old man he had mistaken as the father was no such thing. Having seen the girl grab the soldiers leg he knew he was discovered. Jumping quickly to the cart. He reached inside to pull the deadly "burp" gun from where it had been hiding below the food-filled, harmless lunch baskets. He turned towards the girl and Paul pulling the trigger at the same time, spitting an arc of lead toward the American.

Paul jumped in front of the girl while pulling his military issue Colt 45 from his hip holster. Adrenaline was no longer an enemy for Paul as it had been when he first became a soldier. Now he had now mastered his nerves, and the adrenaline merely made him acute, faster and accurate. Paul put four quick rounds into the old man's chest dropping him almost instantly, but not before carnage had been inflicted. With the first snapping from the machine gun, all the squad members dropped their lunches and had either grabbed for weapons or jumped for cover. All members but Harris. He had had his back to the team working on the track as the old man had opened up with the sub-machine gun, had taken one of the first bullets to the right side of his neck, and was now bleeding profusely. He had sat down against the track and would bleed out quickly. There was nothing that could be done to save him.

The young girl had moved to Harris's side and was holding her hands against the wound trying to squelch the bleeding. Harris looked at her, smiled, and was gone. The bleeding slowed to a trickle. Seo-Young cried. "I so sorry! I so sorry! He was going to kill my Auntee. I so sorry."

After radioing for a medic, Paul and the team had settled to hear Seo-Young's story. She had no idea who the old man had been other than he had stopped her just before she was to enter Camp Castle today to sell her lunches. She had been bringing lunches each day for the past three weeks to earn what little money she could for her Aunt and her Aunt's family.

Seo-Young's father had been an instructor at the centuries-old Koryo Songgyungwan University before the war when the NKPA had crossed over the 38th parallel to impose their will on the south. Her family had gone into hiding until, upon giving up hope of rescue, they had decided to run. Two months ago, their journey stopped. Her family was destroyed just as they were to cross over the Han river to safety.

Her mother had been beaten until she fell unconscious onto her face. The North Korean Officer that had captured them, pulled her up to her knees by the hair just to fire his pistol into the back of her head. Her father was forced to watch. He then was beaten, pulled to his feet, had his hands tied behind his back and began the long march back to the north; no doubt, a march that would end at one of the many labor death camps that defined the North Korean dictator Kim Il-Sung.

By sheer luck, Seo-Young would owe her life to a bowel-movement. She had moved off the road to hide behind some bushes to relieve herself when she heard the sound of her mother's scream. Staying low to the ground, Seo-Young saw and heard everything. She continued to lay hidden long after the North Koreans had left, frozen in fear. After night fall, she had recovered from her fear and shock to rise and return to the road. She held her mother's lifeless hand until the sky to the east began to show grey with the earliest morning light. She then slid into the water to cross to the south. She had made it to her Auntee three weeks ago, and had finally started falling into a good routine, until today.

* * *

I pulled a yellow, lined sheet of tablet paper from Dad's blue book. This one looked to be written in the hand of an older "Paul," lacking the free flow of Dad's earlier years. In spite of the relative newness to the book, the paper had obviously been folded and unfolded a number of times. I handled it gently as to not tear the folds.

So young, but too old.
Wise, but not so much as to intimidate.
I think your soul is better than mine;
I need to work on mine for a little longer
Maybe our souls are but a work in progress
Moving on from this Earth as soon as complete.
  . . . unless borne good as yours.

I think yours was always good and complete;
A marked contrast to the one borrowing my body,
Portending to probity and mercy;
All the while looking not to be truly discovered.
But, alas your years were too short.
Perhaps the soul always knew when its life here was to be done
Racing to finish long before mine.
Yes, I misled, ignored and lied to you,

* * *

Jackson and Paul sat quietly together, both staring at their drinks; a beer for Jackson, a watered-down whiskey in front of Paul. "I fell asleep at the switch today, Jackson. I royally fucked up. No way I should have missed that the chink was not a refugee. He was way too quiet."

"Bullshit, Paul. You didn't do anything wrong. Funny how you white guys are willin' to take blame when there is no blame to be had, but when there is, most of you just point the finger at someone else. Thank God you are not like the rest. Shit, if Grey was here, he'd be blamin' me saying my bein' colored attracted the..."

Jackson, stopped mid-sentence as he saw a little girl walking over to their table. "Hey, Paul, don't look now, but I think you have a new kid." Smiling he continued, "and you didn't even have the fun dinking her mom."

"Shut it, Jackson. Man, her Mom's dead; killed a couple of months ago, up north." The girl had been shadowing Paul ever since Harris's murder this afternoon. He had thought he would get a couple hours of peace from her by ducking into the bar.

He had been annoyed when Seo-Young had not given up and gone home to her Auntee. Instead, she had taken up vigil by the door, sitting in the dust with her back propped against a tent post.

Seo-Young pulled up a chair and hopped up on her knees bringing her head to the same level as Jackson and Paul. "So are you going to buy me a drink Mister Army Man. And you still owe me for lunch today."

Paul was shocked that a girl no more than 12 years old could act as though the actions of today had never happened. She had really developed a tough skin, or she put on one hell of an act.

"Little girl, you're way too young to be in here. Why aren't you at home safe with your Auntee?" Then shooing her away with his hand the same way one might with a bothersome fly, Paul continued, "Go on, git out 'a here."

"No way, Mister Army Man. I can't go home without my money. No money, Auntee cannot make food tomorrow. We go hungry. And I am not too young to be here. I think of age as being about how many years you have left. Maybe I am a lot older than you, Mister Army Man. My life might end tomorrow, but you will likely live long and have lots of "Seo-Youngs" as your children. So please do not tell me to leave."

Paul was taken back, not only by the little girl's moxie, but by the sheer sadness of realizing she was right. He probably would live years longer than her and it hurt to be confronted with the truth. "Seo-Young, you have a lot of years left," he lied. "Heck, this damned war should be over soon and you can go home."

"I have no home, Mister Army Man. You want to take me with you when you leave?"

"Oh, sure, kid, I'd love to, but you know tough it is for us GI's to adopt one of you?" Paul was skating on thin ice now. He had no idea what was involved with adopting a child in Korea or if it was even possible. The only thing he knew for sure was that he had no intent on bringing Seo-Young back to the States, but he was too chicken to say so.

"I go to the Captain and ask if I can go with you?"

"Jackson, come on, help me out here." Paul looked to his friend and noticed that his tough friend's eyes were brimming with tears.

"Look, Seo-Young, my name is Sergeant Jackson, but you can call me Johnnie. How much does the Mister Army Man owe you for the lunch?"

"Three American dollars is what my Auntee needs. And she will make you good lunch for tomorrow."

Jackson leaned to his side while admonishing Paul. Pulling out a small leather pouch with a fold-over flap held closed with snap, he said "Paul I think I can cover the lunch, but you have to pick of the tab for our drinks." Without waiting for Paul's agreement, he dumped his money out onto the table; a couple dollar bills and some assorted change. After counting out the change to make up the third dollar, Jackson pushed the money across the table to the little girl and waited for her to confirm the count.

Seo-Young grabbed up the money and deftly deposited it into a small pocket in the front of her peasant pants. "Tomorrow you like lunch and, Mister Army Man, you can check to see how you can take me home to USA?"

"Yeah, sure. Tomorrow, but don't hold me to it. It might take a while to figure out how I can adopt you."? With that Seo-Young smiled, spun around and walked out.

"Paul, you really goin' to adopt her?"

"Heck, no, Jackson, but she'll never know."

"But, that's so wrong man. You got 'a tell her. You know, you got 'a be honest. We are honest men. When we lie it kills us. She's had enough heart-ache. It's not fair to get her hopes up and then dash them again."

Paul stared at his hands. Without looking at Jackson he said, "I guess you are right, but not tomorrow, okay? Heck, she might actually grow on me and . . . who knows."

* * *

Paul was greeted by his captain as he exited his barracks. The meeting was a first in a number of ways. First off, prior to this morning, Paul could not recall ever seeing the Captain prior to breakfast. Secondly, the captain was rarely unaccompanied by one of his lieutenants when dealing with the noncoms. Lastly, the captain had checked his bravado for this morning's request; and yes, it was a request; not an order.

"Good morning, Sergeant."

"Good morning, Sir"

"Sergeant, in a couple of days after a brief memorial service, we will be returning Harris's body stateside. You probably did not know this, but his Dad was my Sergeant back when I went through basic and now I feel compelled to write a letter about his son's passing. I do not have the slightest idea what to say. You have any suggestions or words of wisdom?"

"Sir, Harris, was a good soldier. I am sure that you must have a standard memo to inform the family?"

"Of course, and that is the point, I think I need to do better. His Daddy deserves it. He was a fine man and one that I still respect to this day."

"Sir, not to be presumptuous, but, if you provide me the liberty, I would be honored to draft the letter to his family."

"Thank you, Paul. Do you mind if I call you Paul?" Paul, shook his head. "I will ask the Lieutenant to assign a different Sergeant to your squad for today. You think you could have a draft to me just after lunch?"

Paul returned to his barracks without breakfast. He had never written a letter to inform a family that their son had now become another one of the thousands of casualties of American casualties of the war. He felt he needed to provide honor to Harris while not endorsing what he considered to be a meaningless war. The war may be wasteful, but Harris was not a waste. He had been a fine talented, and God-fearing man that was just in the wrong place at the wrong time.

Paul was disappointed in himself in that the most difficult part of starting the letter was not concern over communicating a wrenching message to a son's father and mother, but recollecting Harris's first name, Jerry. Paul had consciously avoided getting close to his team. Harris had been a brave soul, one that shared his faith and beliefs openly, one that he could count on to sacrifice himself for his fellow soldier. Paul made a personal commitment to get to know his squad members on a personal basis, beginning tomorrow. He knew this may not be smart from a military perspective. Yes, it was harder to order a friend to potential death in battle, as if it was easy to send anyone to their death, but to keep his humanity, it was necessary. Forgetting Jerry's name was just a sign he was slipping away from the person he had been. He pulled out a lined, yellow pad of paper and a pencil.

March 21, 1951

Dear Mr. and Mrs. Harris:

I write to inform you of the tragic death of your son, Jerome, who was lost to us this past Wednesday in the field of battle in Korea. His death represents a deep loss for all of us and I can only hope you can take some comfort in knowing he died protecting a peace-loving people and in the service of his country.

Jerome was an example to all of us; a devoted individual that subordinated his safety for that of his fellow man. As we mourn his passing, we will also celebrate his life. Let Jerome's passing not throw us into grief, but embolden our faith in God. Take comfort in knowing that Jerry's faith in God ensures life is not lost.

I pray his devotion to duty has more quickly brought us closer to a day of peace in this country, a day in which evil perishes and we can live in respect and harmony together.

Sincerely yours,

Paul, folded the sheet in half three times over, stuffed it into his breast pocket, and headed to his Captain's quarters.

* * *

Tomorrow, Paul would be returning home. His 21 months of required duty was up. It had been a time much different than that of WWII. In this war, Paul had spent his entire time relegated to two encampments: his first several months had been spent grading roads just north of Pusan, while the past year had largely been spent maintaining logistics routes in and out of Camp Castle. He had settled into a routine that pretty much looked the same every day. Morning would start with calisthenics for the squads; the exercise was an effective means to shake out the cobwebs from the previous night. Breakfast was spent with his fellow sergeants, including Jackson. Somewhere along the way, Grey had apparently gotten over his racist ways and had welcomed Jackson as part of the gang.

The sergeants melted away to complete their assigned daily duty roster.

Seo-Young had become a mascot for Paul's squad, accompanying them on almost all of their assignments except for the most dangerous; those involving the service road leading to hills 255 and 266, or even more dangerous, rebuilding and reinforcing the rifle trenches that encircled the hills. Not only was this last responsibility dangerous, being well within range of enemy light artillery and rifle fire, but backbreaking as well. The rifle trenches required almost continuous rebuilding and reinforcement with sandbags and timbers; all needed to be carried manually up the almost 400-meter trail, rising several hundred feet.

On most days, Seo-Young would only leave the squad to refill their canteens or to bring them their lunch. For lunch, she would normally bring along her Auntee to serve the soldiers. They had uncomfortably become a family, using lunch to learn about each other, their families, their lives, their beliefs, and their hopes. By late afternoon, Seo-Young would return to her home with Auntee, and Paul and the rest of the sergeants returned to camp for debriefing.

Evening was the same every day. Dinner at the mess hall and then Paul, Jackson, Grey, Henry, Knight, and Halsey would meander over to the noncom "club" for drinks consisting of warm beer or watered down, poor quality liquor. From an outsider perspective, tonight started out looking the same, but in reality, it was a night of celebration. Jackson had surprised everyone by pulling a couple bottles of George Dickel No. 12 Tennessee Whisky from behind the bar. Where it came from or how Jackson got it, who knew?

"Gentlemen, I have saved this for when I was to go home, but I think it best to celebrate the first of us getting out of this hell-hole." He plopped the first of the two bottles in the center of the table along with six small glasses, five riding on finger tips of his right hand with the sixth sitting over the cap of the bottle. Pulling the sixth glass off the bottle, Jackson proceeded to peel away the foil and pull the first bottle's cork stopper. Placing it in front of Paul, he smiled and said, "Okay, Sergeant Simmons, please honor us with the first pour."

Once drinks were in hand, Jackson pulled up his glass "I hear, George Dickel will tickle anything. We are all tickled to death to wish you the best in your escape . . ."

" . . . and we all hate him for it!" piped in Grey, smiling as he eagerly put the glass to his lips.

It did not take long for the six hard men to finish off the first and make a significant dent in the second bottle of Dickel. Soon speech was slurred and the men had degraded to poor jokes and slapping each other on the back as congratulations for their witticisms.

Grey pulled himself from the stool. "I have to piss like a race horse. I'll be right back." He drifted toward the door, lightly bouncing off the next table, a couple stools, and finally the door jamb that had been plugged into the tent opening.

Paul noticed Halsey and Knight smiling broadly as Grey exited. "What's up with you two? You look as though you have stolen the cookies and gotten away with the crime."

At that second Grey yelled, "Get down, grenade!" and a grenade careened off the bar and settled next to their table. Paul lit off his stool and dove over the bar with Henry hitting the ground with the bartender, just hoping that somehow the cheap wooden bar would provide some protection. Knight and Halsey leapt to the door and dove to the ground rolling out of sight. Everything was quiet.

After several seconds, which seemed like minutes, Grey popped through the door smiling and laughing with Knight and Halsey. "Got you fucks. It's a joke!"

Paul, Henry, and the bartender slowly pulled themselves up from behind the bar. "What the hell, Grey. You are more of an ass than I thought." Looking over the bar, "Where's Jackson?"

They all heard him, breathing loud and whispering "God help me, God help me . . . ." Jackson lay on the floor, face down, with his arms bent to bring his clutched fists to just below his cheeks. His eyes were closed. It was obvious he had not heard Grey's admission of the sick joke and he was not hearing anything now.

Paul and Henry walked out from behind the bar. Paul knelt down beside Jackson.

While Paul tended to Jackson, Henry alternatively proceeded directly to Grey, knocking him to the ground with a right and then kicking him in the side with his size 10 infantry boot. He then dropped to the floor with his back against the bar. Knight and Halsey had obviously known of the joke, but now saw there was no humor in what Grey had perpetrated. Grey was a sick fuck.

Paul gently rolled Jackson over by the shoulder. "Jackson. Jackson. Johnny, it's okay. It was a joke, man. You're okay." Paul looked to where Jackson had been laying and saw that he had proven that he was the only man among them. The hand grenade, just a small, shiny green pineapple-looking, oblong steel ball, still lay on the ground where Jackson had fallen. Instead of jumping to safety, Jackson had jumped on the grenade to ensure the safety of his friends.

In that split second, something had slipped in Jackson's mind and he was now caught in a loop; not realizing the emergency was over, not realizing it was a joke, not realizing he was not going to die now. He was still stuck in a world where a grenade pushed into his gut was going to take his life and he could not break out.

*　*　*

The night's antics would delay Paul's return home by a day. After hearing of the story of the hand grenade hoax, the captain had met with Camp Castle's commander to discuss what disciplinary actions, if any, would be taken. Even though Paul, Jackson, and Henry had been cleared of any wrong doing, the commander was debating what to do with Halsey, Knight, and Grey. For the Captain, his career was likely over. For the three sergeants, there was no doubt. For them, the only remaining question was if and how long they would spend in the brig.

For Jackson, the issue was more concerning. His mind had not recovered and had spent the balance of the night and all of today in the infirmary sitting in a chair, rocking rhythmically forward and backward almost as if he was listening to a moving piece of music. Paul believed Jackson was still caught in his prayer for salvation. The Commander was sure of only one thing: what Jackson needed was not likely to be found in Camp Castle in the middle of war. His staff was now working through the mechanics and bureaucracy to have Jackson return stateside as soon as possible. Tomorrow, Jackson would begin his journey home with Paul, but his return would be interrupted by a stay in Osaka, Japan at the army's 279th General Hospital. They would have to figure out the best disposition for Jackson's care.

As Paul hopped into the jeep to leave camp, he scanned the hillside one last time. He saw Seo-Young standing alone by the mess hall, looking at Paul with tear-filled eyes. Paul had never followed up on the question of adoption, choosing instead to ignore and defer. He never intended to hurt Seo-Young, but how could he possibly take her home. He turned his eyes to road ahead of the jeep as it lurched to motion.

Seo-Young was killed the following year by the NKPA, a full two weeks after the armistice was signed with North Korea. Apparently, Kim Il-Sung was not concerned for the 12-year-old either.

Chapter 12

My coffee had grown cold; probably for the best. The caffeine would just ensure I would not be sleeping tonight. I pushed back in my chair and pulled my hands up behind my head to stretch. I had been sitting here entirely too long. There was a slight stirring noise coming from beyond the living room, Dad's last bedroom.

I flipped off the lights in the kitchen and felt my way through the dining room and living room in the dark, not wanting to wake Uncle Bill. A feeble light had been left on in Dad's room, and I could see the nurse's back as he hovered over Dad. I thought I remembered Mom introducing him as Jenkins. "Hi, Nurse Jenkins," I whispered, not wanting to shock him. Dad's nurse broke two of my mental models for the profession. First, he was a guy and I had been conditioned to think of the field as primarily staffed by females. Secondly, the guy looked to be more at home as a bar bouncer than a nurse. Mom was adamant she wanted to hire a male nurse believing a man could more easily handle Dad's size to care for him. At 230 pounds, Dad represented a pretty significant mass to maneuver.

"Oh, hi, Randall. Hey just call me Bob." Bob pulled his

stethoscope from his ears and draped it around his neck. As he moved to the other side of the bed, he said, "I hope I didn't wake you, but it is time to do a little clean up and give your Dad a little pain medication to allow him to sleep. If you want, you can help me change his diaper. We need to keep him clean to make sure we do not complicate his condition"

"'Complicate his condition'! Fuck! He is dying!" is all I could think. Instead, I said "Sure." Cleaning my Dad of his excrement was not what I had planned for tonight. I had half wished I had just stayed in the kitchen to allow the very competent Nurse Jenkins do his job.

I think Bob saw the anxiety in my face. He said, "Look, let me give him a drop of the morphine sulfate before we try to roll him on his side. He gets pretty uncomfortable when he is moved. You know you really don't need to help, but . . . I think you might not mind it as much as you think."

"No really, I'm okay," Hell, what else could I say? I did not want to come across as the selfish, prudish, and shallow person I really was.

Dad then surprised us both. Quietly, "Randall, how long have you been there? I have so much to tell you." For the first time today his eyes had cleared. It is tough to describe the look, but they were alive now, kind of like the difference in water between stagnant pond and that of a fresh stream. Yes, they were both water, but the stream was clean, fresh, and inviting; whereas the pond looked drab and dead in comparison. Dad's eyes had just become the stream.

Bob, looked to me and then pantomimed, "This can wait; you talk with your Dad. I can come back later," and he quietly slipped out of the room.

"Dad, I just got here. What can I get for you?" My eyes were starting to puddle. God knows why. You see I never cry, but just seeing Dad was kind of overwhelming me.

"Just a sip of water, OK? My mouth is so dry it is hard to talk."

I turned to the night stand and poured him a little water. I was unsure how to do this. I had no idea if he would have problems swallowing. As I put the glass to his lips and tilted, his right arm moved up to the cup and pushed my hand to greedily tilt it faster.

"A little more, son, please," and I refilled the glass and put it to his lips to allow him to quench his thirst. After finishing the second cup, he smiled and then said, "Now at least I might be able to piss."

"Dad, are you hurting? Do you need some of your medicine?"

"Not yet, Johnny just told me to back off it if I could. He said it was fogging my mind and making me slur. Hell, he hasn't been able to put two words together for years, and now he is lecturing me about speech."

"Dad? What are you talking about? Who is Johnny?" I asked, fearing the answer.

"Johnny tells me you've been looking at my book. You've been learning a little about your good ole' Dad. At least that's what Johnny said."

How could Dad know I had been looking at his book and who the hell was Johnny? The only Johnny I had known passed away years ago and would rarely talk.

"That's what I want to talk with you about, Randall. I was just talking with some of my friends. I haven't seen them for so long." Dad started to cry. Then his eyes started to glaze over again.

* * *

After being away for almost two years, Paul was expecting to feel out of place and outdated. He had no idea how to plug back into the family, and he had begun to doubt he still held value for the business. He was wrong. It seemed as though time had stood still while he was gone. He would fit back in as easily as a hand in a well-worn glove. Sure, there had been some change; William had finally graduated and now was a full-fledged engineer and Dad and Mom were looking older, but in general things had not changed much.

The company had yet to break ground on the housing development project, but thankfully, it had not been put on ice completely. Paul had fretted during his deployment that any delay would require aggressive cost cutting in the business, laying off Arlin and likely scuttling the business relation they had put together with Joseph Klein and Company. Either of these actions would likely have put a death nail in the project. It would be devastating to the business.

Even more of concern to Paul was the fate of his brother. Between his Dad, Virginia, and Lyle, William really did not have a champion. Hell, it would be hard for even Paul to come up with a business reason for keeping William over either Arlin of Joe Klein.

Dad had been unwilling to discuss the business in his letters to Paul and Paul had taken this as a bad omen . . . a very bad omen. He had convinced himself the business was struggling and he expected the worst. The 50's were going to be a boom time for Fort Collins and Simmons & Sons could ill afford to miss out on the opportunity. Paul was convinced that during this decade, the town would double in population as the war veterans returned to the states and moved west in search of the American Dream.

Fortunately, most of his worries had been unfounded. Dad, Virginia, and Lyle had seen the same potential for the business and their pending housing development. They were committed to doing whatever possible to keep the company, the WHOLE company, together until they could start generating some cash flow. Once again, Virginia, and Lyle had surprised him at their selflessness and loyalty to his Dad and the family. Virginia had actually taken a night job and sacrificed her salary from the company until they could get their financial footing re-established. Lyle took over all project management until William could join, full-time. In addition to Virginia and Lyle's contribution, Arlin had elected to take a pay cut and had moved into Paul's old room, at Dad's insistence, to make ends meet. Even William was showing signs of maturity and commitment to the business. His weekends were no longer filled with coeds; instead they were consumed with manual work. He now served as a laborer under Lyle's tutelage, learning how to actually be a builder along with being an engineer. Dad and Mom eked by on their savings.

Joe Klein had been a huge asset to the team during Paul's absence. He and Virginia had begun to tag-team their efforts with the City Council to negotiate the almost endless set of infrastructure requirements required for the development. At first the challenges seemed insurmountable as the two sides debated timing, costs, and the sizing of the investments. The issues under discussion included road access, schools, signal lights, additional police and fire department staffing and hookups for electrical, natural gas, water, and sewer. The only area related to infrastructure that did not seem problematic was telephone service. AT&T was just happy to have an excuse to expand their service and revenue base and had agreed to fund the installation of phone lines at no additional cost to the development. They had alternated between negotiating the increased size of governmental services that would need to be created, led by Joe, while Virginia argued the cost assumptions supporting these services. One thing had become clear: the town was going to get Simmons & Sons to fund as much of the infrastructure as possible up front.

After two full years of negotiation, it now appeared the two sides had achieved some breakthroughs and had progressed to the point that breaking ground was imminent. The majority of investments would be funded via an increase in property taxes for those living in the development. Simmons & Sons had agreed to fund the installation of two traffic lights; one each on the main roads bordering the north and west sides of the development. In addition, they had agreed to restructure the development layout to provide for a separate access road to minimize congestion on Fort Collins's main north/south road, College Boulevard. This represented a major concession on behalf of Simmons & Sons in that it meant they would need to reallocate a chunk of land to the street rather than homes. Ultimately, William and Arlin revised the development site layout plan to accommodate the additional street, resulting in the loss 8 of the original 110 home lots. The development would ultimately be 102 homes.

Paul came home to a family waiting to welcome him back once again and a business ready to make it's biggest move yet. He could not be happier, that was until he walked into the kitchen for his first dinner after returning home. He was shocked by the hustle and bustle; he had expected to have a quiet evening with Mom and Dad, but instead the house was the home to an extended "family" reunion. Arlin, Virginia, and Dad were engrossed in a set of blue prints spread out on the kitchen table. William and Lyle were setting the table in the dining room. Joe Klein had donned an apron over his white shirt and tie and was fretting over something cooking on the stove. His son, Joe, Jr., was washing pans in the sink. Paul's Mom's back was to him as she and another young woman were slicing bread and tearing a salad. Paul's heart felt as though it had skipped a beat and all of a sudden, he was anxious. The woman, Samantha, was the woman his brother had been dating when Paul left for Korea. She was also the only woman Paul had ever fallen in love with, head over heels in love with her.

Paul pulled William into the living room. "William, I didn't know you were still dating that girl. Samantha, right?"

"Not even sly, Paul. We haven't dated in years. She fell for you the first time she saw you at that dinner when you announced your free, all expense-paid vacation to Korea and you damn well knew it.

"Not that I mind, you know. The world would not want me to waste these good looks on just one woman. I mean I have to stay free, even it is just for the benefit of our fairer sex." Paul smiled, "She's been asking Mom about you since the day you left. She eats dinner with us a couple times a week, and I suspect Mom invited her. You upset?"

"Heck, no! Can you reintroduce us? You know, so I don't come across as presumptuous; you know, expecting something?"

"Big brother, why not? You steal her from me and now you are asking me to be complicit in the theft?" He shrugged his shoulders and raised his hands then smiled and said "Follow me. She has been waiting to see you for two years and now she's pretending she didn't notice you came in. I guess if I don't provide a little push, you love birds might never talk. That would be real awkward"

"Sam, could you come on in here? You've got to see your bashful knight in shining armor" he yelled and then laughed.

Paul was mortified. He debated punching William, running, or? And then Sam walked through the door and he knew exactly what to do. He gave her a hug and kiss, shocking even himself. He would forever be grateful to William.

* * *

Marriage looked good on Paul and Sam. It had been a whirlwind from first date to wedding in a matter of eight weeks. For Paul and Sam even the abbreviated engagement had been too long. They could not imagine ever being apart.

The wedding was small; only including Paul's and Sam's direct families. For Sam, this meant her Mother and Father had driven up from Denver the previous day and had stayed in a small motor inn just south of down-town. In Paul's case the "direct" family included the entire Simmons & Sons team. Sam had actually suggested inviting the extended Simmons "family." She had become part of this family over the past two years and could not imagine getting married without them and their support.

After the wedding, Mom had pulled together an informal feast at the house for the two families. Dinner had been moved into the backyard to make room for everyone. William and Arlin had pulled the dining room and kitchen tables outside and were now across town putting the finishing touches on a small apartment that would be home for Paul and Sam. Both families had pitched in to furnish and pay the first month's rent. The place was small, but they were sure it would feel like heaven for the newlyweds. Paul had been stuck in a barracks for two years only to return home finding he was now sharing his room with Arlin. Sam had shared her room at the campus with a roommate for years. They now had room for themselves.

The newlyweds pulled up to the house in a lightly used Ford sedan Paul had purchased when he first got home. He had figured it was about time he owned a car. Driving around town in the old company truck or borrowing Dad and Mom's car just wasn't right for a 27-year old part owner of the towns largest real estate developer to be, that is. Pulling in right in front of them came William and Arlin in the company truck. He yanked open the rear doors revealing a large steel tub filled with ice and cold Budweiser beers. William had already started celebrating. He had barely let the truck stop before popping open his door and hopping out. He was holding up a beer as if in toast to the bride and groom, but Paul assumed he had been drinking while driving and was merely trying to keep the beer foam from spilling on his new suit. Arlin also had a beer in hand as he got out of the passenger side, but had obviously not finished as many as William.

"Congrats, guys. They have one heck of a spread for you out back. Let's go have some fun!" yelled William as he headed through the grass lawn towards the front door

Arlin, deferring to the walkway merely smiled and waved. "Paul, Sam, I am so glad you let me come to the wedding. You guys are going to be so surprised at what your families did for you." At that he popped in through the front door, right behind William.

Paul looked to Sam. "You know they just left the beer. You think they forgot?" He smiled, "Okay, Sam, you grab that handle and I get this one. See what you missed by not staying with William?"

At this Paul stopped, "Hey what do you say? We could leave the tub and just take a few to our new apartment and bag the party. I am pretty excited to see what they have done with it. Given that William and Arlin have been there all day drinking, we might want to check to make sure they didn't burn it down."

"Let's go, big boy, we won't stay long. I am sure our families will want to wish us the best. They'll be the ones shooing us off to our new home soon enough. Grab your side, that is unless you don't think you are strong enough to carry it. I mean I do see how you have let yourself go since getting out of the army." Sam laughed as she put her hand into the tub, scooping up some water and flicking it at Paul.

With that they picked up the tub of beer and walked together into the house. It was a game that would be played out for years. Playing with each other, contemplating something crazy, then doing the right thing, always with a smile.

* * *

I pulled myself up from the chair, thankful that I got to see Dad come out of his fog, even for just a brief moment. I was beginning to forget how vibrant a man he had been. I needed some context to jar my memory. This had been just what I needed. I only wish Mom and Uncle Bill could have been with me.

Bob was quietly waiting just outside the bedroom door, leaning against the hallway wall. "Randall, I'm glad you got to talk with your Dad. He comes awake every now and again, but I can never tell when it is going to happen. You mind if I go in to finish up? You go to bed. I'll take care of him."

To that, I just nodded. "Thanks, Bob, but I think I am going to head into the kitchen and finish up with some things." With that I padded off through the living room with Uncle Bill's snoring, through the dining room and back into the kitchen. I dumped out the stale coffee and started a fresh pot brewing. I suspected it would be a long night, but I felt as though I did not have enough time to finish everything I needed to do, to learn what I needed to know.

As the coffee started to drip, I walked to the kitchen table and pulled open the box I had intended to dig into earlier. I noticed a well-worn, brown, accordion style folder with "1952 to" written in blue ink. Somewhere along the way the file had become filled and dumped into the box without ever noting the final date pertaining to the contents. The folder was old enough not to have the elastic ties we see today; instead it was cinched shut with a heavy brown ribbon tied in a bow.

I returned to the coffee maker, poured a cup of fresh, hot coffee and sat down at the table to explore the folder's contents. I kicked my feet up onto a chair so I could use my lap as a table to facilitate my research. I pulled opened the folder, emptied the contents on my lap and returned the folder to the table, planning to refill it as I progressed through the stack of papers.

The first item I turned over was a familiar picture. It was a black and white picture of Mom and Dad on their wedding day. They were so young and vibrant. Sometimes I could still see traces of that look in Mom, but Dad's face had aged significantly since that day, almost to a point I would not recognize them as the same person. The newlywed's smiles were exuberant, but natural. They were smiles I had become accustomed to over the years as commonplace. So, common that when they disappeared for some brief times, it was unsettling and frightening. For those tough times when the smiles were absent, it was as if my parents had become absent.

Unlike contemporary weddings that have become huge, expensive events driven by the need to impress, this picture showed two individuals with no concerns other than to celebrate their love for one another. I know that neither my grandparents nor my Mom and Dad had much money at that time, but from the look in their faces, I could tell it did not matter. Dad was wearing a suit and Mom looked to be wearing a basic light-colored, short-sleeved, button-up dress. I suspect this dress had not actually been a "wedding" dress as much as just nice dress Mom had already owned. Such were the times in the early fifty's.

The next picture I turned over was one that I had never seen before. It was also from Mom and Dad's wedding day, but this one included a number of other people. I flipped the picture over to see the names of those that had been at the wedding.

On the far right of the picture stood Virginia and Lyle. I had developed a huge affinity to these two even though they had passed away when I was a kid. It was a treat to see them. As a young boy, I didn't know much about them other than they were "family" and for Dad, it was as if they were his uncle and aunt. There was Grandma, smiling just like always. She also had died when I was a kid. I could not remember seeing many pictures of her in our house. Next to Grandma was Uncle Bill. He looked already two sheets to the wind. In the picture, it looked as if he had dark rings around his eyes. From experience, I knew these to be the red rimmed eyes that accompanied his drinking. His smile was so big, he looked to be a fool, but from my talk with him earlier this evening, I knew that smile to be confessing to his true admiration of and his happiness for his brother. Next to Uncle Bill was Arlin Peeples. Arlin now lived in San Diego, not far from my wife and I. He occasionally pops in for dinner.

On the other side of the bride and groom were a couple middle-aged folks I did not recognize. From the back I, could see they were my Mom's parents. Sheila and Richards Corrs. They were the two grandparents I never met. I had always felt as though I was missing part of a family, knowing these people were part of my blood line, but never having had the chance to meet them. Next to the Corrs was Joe Klein. He was another person I had never met, but I had heard so much about him from my family, I suspect he was a pretty impressive individual. His son had stayed involved with the business and was an equally impressive person. He still is.

Grandpa wasn't in the picture. He must have been holding the camera.

There was a folded note paper clipped to the picture. All it said was . . .

Mom and Dad, Thank you. I guess we are here to stay.

Love, Paul

in Dad's handwriting. It looked as if he had finally recognized Fort Collins as his home for good.

Chapter 13

THE 40 ACRES of the development had now been scraped by graders; shaving bushes, weeds, and small trees as if whiskers swept away by a razor blade. The grading process had been repeated a number of times to lower the street and raise the house pads. It would be critical to complete the first three homes before the snow of winter hit. The goal was to have these first three homes finished and furnished as models by September 1.

The first model would also double as The Joe Klein and Company office, exclusive realtors for the Simmons & Sons development. The office would be set up in the garage to ensure the house remained as true to function as possible. The garage office served a second purpose for the development. Connected garages were new and in this case the garage actually had room for two cars, an extreme luxury in 1953. It made the houses stand out from any of their competition and really had not added much in the way of construction cost. The hope was that selling this as an option, the second stall in the garage would substantially augment profits.

A large trench had been cut down the middle of the street. This would provide for laying the first stretch of utilities. A second set of trenches had been cut into the ground spanning off at a 90-degree angle providing sewer, water and natural gas to the individual housing pads that would soon be the new homes for families. Paul straddled the trench that would ultimately lead to their first model home. While staring at the vacant lot, visualizing the house, "So you really think this can be completed in a few months?" he said to no one in particular.

Lyle and Arlin nodded to William. "You keep the money flowing, I keep on schedule," replied William.

In private, Paul had had extreme doubts about William's ability to keep the project moving consistent with their plans. In public, he had been Williams biggest proponent; he prayed he would be up to the challenge. William had grown up a lot since Paul had left for Korea; this would be his first real challenge to manage a big project. Lyle had agreed to split time between the remodeling business and the new home construction to provide William with general contracting and management experience. Paul and Arlin would handle the streets and utilities to keep the city on track.

The sewer, gas, and water pipes were to be delivered later this afternoon with the total section to be completed by the end of the following week. At that time, the trenches could be filled allowing them to begin the process of setting curbs, sidewalks and paving. Laying the driveways would be delayed until house framing was completed for the models.

As of now everything was quiet on the site except for the four men making a final inspection to ensure there were no surprises that could delay the utilities. Piled at the rear of the model home lots were sections of wood that had been sized off site to construct the forms for pouring the concrete foundation. Their newest purchase, a Hough loader/backhoe that had been used to dig the trenches, was now waiting to take a crack at digging the basements for the home foundations.

Although expensive, the Hough was already paying dividends. In one scoop, it did more than a man could do in 10 to 15 minutes and it was a heck of a lot safer since men no longer needed to be in the trenches until they needed to join the pipes. For the basements, Paul and William figured that unless they ran into some big rocks the Hough would be able to cut out each basement in a matter of days. If the Hough worked as well as planned, Paul and Virginia had budgeted the purchase of a second tractor next spring to double their home building capacity if demand dictated.

The only real challenge they were facing was that of the typical Fort Collins spring and summer weather. Late afternoons were marked by some pretty horrendous thundershowers, or hail, or both, pretty much dictating a work stoppage from three to six pm. On rare occasions, they could expect to see a twister funnel reaching to earth. Thank goodness, it was even rarer to have the twister turn into a full-blown tornado.

As such, they had negotiated with the contractors and equipment operators a workday that started at 6:30 in the morning and ended my 3:00. If rain came early preventing additional work, they would still be paid for the entire day but released early. Unfortunately, this did not apply to the primary track of utilities. The Fort Collins Council had demanded the pipe be laid by city workers and, therefore, their hours prevailed. Essentially their work day would start at 9:00 but would still effectively stop around three, unless they were lucky enough to be spared the rain.

They had hoped to construct 25 homes in their first twelve months, selling 22 and keeping three as models. In following 12 months their plans called for an additional 35 homes to be built and sold, with the remaining 42 home to constructed and sold the following year, along with the final sale of the model homes. As part of the process, Paul would pull in

Virginia to formally begin their efforts to size and target their next development over the next several months. Paul had planned to complete most of this effort on his own, recognizing Virginia would be mostly consumed just keeping the office and finances running in support of the committed development.

Although he had not discussed a change in the business with Lyle or his Dad, Paul had actually hoped that once their first year was complete, revenues from the new home sales would allow Simmons & Sons to cease their remodeling efforts and focus strictly on new construction, liberating Lyle to focus on the next development with Arlin and Joe. Joe had already effectively turned over the reins for selling the development to his son and was ready for the next challenge. Now that the process had kicked off, Paul's plans would center on the success of this plot of dirt for the next few years.

* * *

Paul and William had had little time to talk over the past two weeks. Their respective roles had pretty much kept them at opposite ends of town: Paul in the old office, downtown with Virginia, Arlin, and Dad while William was at the building site except for the brief times he popped into the office to pick up work orders and contractor plans for the day. Paul had asked William to join him and Sam this evening for dinner. He felt they had a lot to talk about. In particular, he wanted to let William know how proud he was of how he was managing the housing development construction projects. The development was moving ahead without interruption under a maturity Paul had not realized William possessed. It had given Paul pause to consider making a move he had been contemplating for years and now seemed like the right time. He had enrolled in the business administration program at the newly renamed

Colorado State University. With William's engineering and his business education, they would be a great one-two punch for the family business for their next phase of growth. School would still take a backseat to the business, but Paul was confident that if he could cut his time back with Simmons & Sons to a few days a week, he could complete school almost as a full-time student.

William had been excited at the dinner offer. He relished the fact that it was free and that Sam was a pretty darn good cook; he greedily accepted. The timing was great in that it would also let him share some pretty big news with Paul and Sam, a secret he was busting to tell them about.

Paul had picked up William at Dad's home shortly after six and they had ridden in silence together to his apartment, neither having prescience as to the other's news.

Upon opening the front door, Paul called, "Sam, were here and I have some real exciting news to tell you guys over dinner."

Beyond the small sitting area, they could see Sam sitting at the kitchen with her back toward the front door. She never moved. No "Hi," no acknowledgment, whatsoever. Something was seriously wrong. Sam stayed still, sitting at the kitchen table facing the window over the sink as Paul entered the Kitchen. William silently trailed behind.

"Hey, hon, you okay? Something the matter?" Paul whispered as he knelt beside her to bring his face close to hers.

Sam turned to face the two brothers, tears streaming from her eyes; the telephone set was sitting in her lap.

"Paul, I think I should go and let you two talk. Let's touch base tomorrow for breakfast at the Northern café before heading to the building site." With that William turned to slip back out of the apartment the same way he had come in.

"Stop, William, you may as well hear this now." Sam's voice stopped William mid-stride. "You're going to be the uncle.

Paul, you are going to be a Daddy." At this she smiled at Paul, stood and threw her arms around him. Burrowing her face into his neck she whispered, "You happy?"

To this Paul began to cry. She had never seen Paul cry. William stared in disbelief; he too, had never seen Paul cry. "Hell, yes I'm happy. Happy more than I can say. I'm going to be a Dad!"

"Then I'm happy, too." Then to William, "Now, William, don't go blabbing this to Mom and Dad. I want to surprise them."

"Well, we should go out to celebrate rather than eat in. Sam, I hope that's okay?"

"It's going to have to be okay, because I actually forgot to get any dinner started. I've been just sitting here imaging what our baby is going to look like and how our lives are going to change. I kind of scared myself."

With this William said, "Then let's head out. How about we eat at Nino's? . . . and Paul, I'll pay . . . I'm going to be an uncle"

The final comment as is atypical in that William had become almost miserly since the project had broken ground; he rarely offered to pay for anything. In fact, he had expected he would get stuck with the breakfast tab tomorrow morning. Paul could only assume William had been caught up in the euphoria of becoming an uncle, a nice change.

* * *

Dinner at Nino's was a treat that the three had rarely had. The restaurant was an authentic Italian haven with pastas, fish, and veal dishes that truly excited the pallets of the typical Fort Collins resident whose only exposure to "authentic" Italian was Chef Boy-Ar-Dee from a can. This was not just a treat, but an experience. The table cloths were crisp and white, their waiter in contrast dressed in a black suit. Flowers adorned the table.

The waiter placed a large leather folder on the table at each of their settings. The folder held a menu encompassing massive selection of dishes and antipasti.

The waiter then discretely handed a smaller menu to William for the wine selection. Even though William knew little about wines, he took obvious pleasure in the selection process, reading the brief overview of each wine before settling on the house red, more as a result of price rather than any true taste preference.

To embrace the evening and the event, the three ordered a plate of cheeses and olives along with a wonderful selection of cured prosciutto and a salami called tartufo. They had never had prosciutto before; it was delicious. To be daring, they also ordered a dish to share of antipasto di octopus. It was left largely untouched by Paul and Sam. They found the chewy texture, fishy taste off-putting. Even though William was equally repulsed by the texture, he gamely choked down what Sam and Paul had left, not wanting to waste such an expensive plate of food no matter the taste. He was thankful when the waiter materialized at his side to refill his wine glass.

Holding his glass out over the table and high above his head, William spurted out loudly, "To the future parents."

Sam looked sheepishly around as she picked up glass "Shhhh, William, we want to surprise Mom and Dad. Someone might hear and spoil the news."

To that, Paul raised his glass, too and yelled, "To the expectant mom and my future baby" If someone in Nino's that night knew the Simmons family, the secret was now history. They all laughed.

"So, William, you said you had some news, something you've been busting a gut to share all night. What gives?"

"So maybe not as exciting as being pregnant, but huge in my life. I am moving out of Mom and Dad's house."

"What? Really? Where are you going?

"Well, rumor has it there are some real nice homes being built on the south end of town. Hell, I even might know the guys that are building them." At that he stopped to let it sink in to Paul and Sam. "I am buying a house on Yale Court, just about halfway down the street, on the right. It should be completed by the end of next month."

"Now I know why you have been such a tight wad the last few months. Saving, saving, saving. Good for you and congratulations, too."

"So, you want some ideas on colors, William?" Sam asked.

"Too late. Arlin already pulled together a color pallet that looks great... and is all man. Hell, Sam, if you picked the colors the house would look great, but women would think I was ready to settle down and get married! Can't have that, can we? Okay, big brother, that is my news, what's your big news?"

To that, Paul, merely said, "Geez, I can't remember, but whatever it was, it cannot compare to you guys." Paul made a mental note to drop by the campus on the way to breakfast with William tomorrow morning to withdraw from the fall session.

Chapter 14

Business had been good to Simmons & Sons in 1953, very good and they planned on 1954 being every bit as exceptional. They had the three model homes available to prospective customers by mid-August in 1953, and the interest had been better than expected. Joe Klein had successfully opened his sales office in the first model home's finished garage, essentially providing him a second location for his realty business, rent free.

By the end of the calendar year, Simmons & Sons had completed and sold their first five homes and had an additional five in the queue at various levels of completion. The plan was for William to build to a forecast using a pre-defined model layout to ensure the neighborhood would maintain some diversity in houses. Prospective customers would order their preferred model on a first-come, first-served basis, picking from the allotted plots allocated to their model of choice. Once their desired model was sold out, it would not be available until the next phase of construction.

Arlin had suggested they define phases by street, selling out the majority of one phase, or street, before beginning the next. Based on this process, each phase would constitute between 30 and 35 homes. One of their largest concerns centered on the risk of having one model being substantially less popular than the remaining models, stranding unsold, unfinished models from a prior phase.

The concern had been unfounded. Demand had exceeded their expectations. Instead the risk now centered around their underestimate of the popularity of the two-stall garage option. So far, they had been successful in selling the step up from the standard single stall garage to the optional two stall version to roughly a third of the customers; however, Joe Klein had stressed they could have easily moved this ratio to two thirds of the homebuyers if the inventory and been planned. The profit potential was huge. For houses ranging in standard price from $19,900 to $21,950, the additional option price of $1,495 was extremely profitable, especially when considering they had estimated the incremental cost at less than $700 per home. Paul and William had decided to double the allocation of two stall garage homes for the rest the first phase. They would reevaluate the allocation before starting the next two phases of construction.

By the end of 1953, Simmons & Sons had expended almost a quarter of a million dollars, but had exited the year at a positive cash generation pace that would begin paying back a substantial portion of their bank loans. At year-end, they had conserved enough cash to complete three of the five homes currently under construction while breaking ground for an additional three units. In total, they still owed the bank $150,000, spread over three separate loans. Virginia's business projections showed that they should be able to reduce this amount by almost half in 1954; 1955 would be gravy and position them well for their next development.

Now the company could finally begin paying themselves a real salary. Arlin remained their lowest salaried employee at $4,500 per year, but at a time when the national average for household income was only $4,100, he was thrilled and thankful to the Simmons family. For Virginia and Lyle, they had elected to forego a share of the profits for a more attractive salary. The two of them were pulling in more than $11,000; an income that would now let them put aside some significant savings for their retirement.

* * *

I flipped through the next several sheets of paper in my lap to get to a folder titled merely, "The Mattsons." I had never heard the name come up in discussions so I opened the folder and dug in. The first sheet was a carbon-copy typewritten sheet with notations in the margins in Dad's telltale hand.

Mr. and Mrs. Richard Mattson
1231 N Harvard
Fort Collins, Colorado 90523

September 12, 1953

Dear Mr. and Mrs. Richard Mattson:
    It is unfortunate to hear that as a result of the recent layoff at Johnson Hydraulics, Richard has lost his position. We at Simmons & Sons certainly hope you are successful in your efforts to find a suitable new position. We will certainly be on the lookout for positions on your behalf.
    That said, we will not be in a position to return you the $3,500.00 you provided as the down payment on 1514 Yale Court. The contract in force provides no contingencies and specifically states you have already established funding to fulfill on your obligations to complete the real estate transaction. As such, the down payment was specifically defined in the contract terms

as 'non-refundable, contingent upon the satisfactory performance of Simmons & Sons in compliance with contractual terms.

Please note your removal of the normal and customary financing contingency was instrumental in my company's acceptance of your offer reflecting a full 5% discount in the purchase price. As such the purchase price was reduced from our standard $21,950.00 to $20,850.00. In good faith, we have completed the home to your specified trim selection, flooring, and color pallet. I trust you will fulfill on your obligations in support of the scheduled closing date of September 24, 1954.

If this continues to present an issue or if you intend not to fulfill on your obligations, please notify us through return mail as soon as possible so that we might refer this to our attorney for resolution.

Regards,
Latimer Simmons, Simmons & Sons

Latimer was Grandad and a name I had rarely heard over the years. He had died early in my life and I really had only fleeting recollections of him. As a kid, Latimer had been an outdated name for an outdated man. I preferred Grandad.

In the margins, Dad had made notes that had included the cost implications to potentially repaint the exterior of the home and replace the kitchen countertops, presumably to address the preferences of an alternative buyer if the sale ultimately fell through. In addition, Dad's notes stated that it was likely we were going to have to resell this property and layoffs at Johnson Hydraulics might result in some required belt-tightening and reduced demand for their existing home inventory. Growing up, I can recall Dad stating Johnson Hydraulics was one of the top three employers in town. That had been a long time ago.

* * *

"Paul, we just cannot afford it now. I am likely going to have to leave town just to get a job. Right now, jobs are tough to find. I've heard rumors of a company out of California may be starting up in Loveland, but that would be such a long drive and even that is still a pipe dream if that comes through. We just can't afford to go through with the new house. You have to get your Dad to give us a break," Richard pleaded. Mrs. Mattson just sat quietly next to her husband.

Paul had rehearsed this confrontation a number of times over the past couple of days. He and his Dad had agreed that they would not, could not refund the entirety of the Mattson's down payment. A contract was a contract and, hell Richard had driven a tough bargain. They had ultimately settled on a price well below what the rest of the homes were selling for. The reason for the lowered price? Well, Paul had to agree he had come to respect Richard and his moxie through the negotiation process, and Richard's final offer to remove the financing condition cinching the deal. Plus, after a month of the Mattson's touring the models and pestering Klein's agents, he had been happy just to get their "John Hancock's" on a piece of paper. Joe would still need to hash it out with his agents to determine an equitable way to split the commission; the Mattson's had developed separate relations with the two agents and Joe Klein's son.

The rehearsal had not helped Paul to feel comfortable going into the conversation. The plan was to stick to the "no refund" 100% and when the discussion began to escalate, he would offer to look at a compromise deal based on the actual cost, labor and materials, for Simmons & Sons to repaint the house and make flooring and countertop changes inside. Of course, he would have to "convince" his Dad to accept the compromise.

Although the likelihood that having the sale fall through actually resulting in changes being required was highly unlikely, Paul and his Dad had agreed they might as well ensure these were funded, just in case. In reality, they would make out much better if the deal fell through. Not only would they end up keeping all, or at least the lion's share, of the down payment, they would also likely resell the house for an additional eleven hundred bucks. For all intents, the deal falling through meant they would get substantially more profit from the home than they had already budgeted for.

Paul's negotiation discomfort was not founded in a concern that he could not prevail. Hell, they had a contract and they were fully within their legal rights not to provide a dime back. They had completed the house, the Mattsons had completed their walk through, the certificate of occupancy was all there was left to complete the Simmons & Sons obligation and it was in process and was to be delivered the following day. No, the issue Paul wrestled with was that it just did not feel right. He was being dishonest and he knew it. A good Christian should be concerned for their brother and sister more than for their pocket book.

In his own mind, Paul had needed to justify his actions based on the potential that the market might nose dive, making the sale of their existing inventory tough. The layoff at Johnson Hydraulics was just an omen of tough times ahead. In reality, he could not even fool himself; everything in town looked to be on the upbeat. The town had even revised their council structure to accommodate the future anticipated growth. There were already rumors circulating in the Chamber of Commerce regarding two major corporations, one from New York and one from California, looking to establish major greenfield manufacturing in town or just outside the city limits. If true, Simmons & Sons would have no issues selling out their last phase of their current development and the proposed larger development even farther to the south. Certainly, he felt if he ever needed to try out his justification for not returning 100% of the down payment with Sam, he knew it would never fly. Let's face it, he had just gotten greedy.

"Richard, Mary, you know I would like to refund the down payment," he lied, "but times are tough and I see no way to do it, especially since we have already installed the living room carpeting, and the linoleum. All the color choices have been yours. I have no doubt they look wonderful, but it is highly unlikely someone else would choose them. We would have to replace the flooring and repaint. We might need to replace countertops and it would all just delay selling the house longer . . . and that is expensive." Paul stopped to let the Mattsons take in the argument. Although he expected them to come back with some retort discounting everything he had said, he now realized Richard's layoff had taken all the salt out of him. He had no fight left.

Richard and Mary Mattson looked to each other, Mary's cheeks lined from tears. They quietly rose from their chairs and shuffled out the office door. Why should winning make Paul feel so shitty.

Paul would never see Richard Mattson again.

* * *

I, woke with a start. Across the table sat Uncle Bill with a newspaper in hand. Next to Uncle Bill sat Bob, the nurse, wolfing down a plate of scrambled eggs and bacon. Mom was at the stove frying up some more bacon and a couple eggs that would soon be flipped over easy.

"So how long did you stay awake last night, Bright Eyes?" asked Uncle Bill.

"God knows. I don't recall what time it was. I just started digging into a folder" I nodded toward the folder now lying horizontally across the corner of the plastic storage tub, "and I don't recall much after that. That's until now. Oh, my God, my neck is so stiff."

Mom flipped the eggs and turned with an empty plate in hand. "I'm surprised you didn't fall over in the night. I found you splayed back with your feet up on Bob's chair. Your chin was resting on your chest. Randall, you looked so uncomfortable. By the way, eggs over easy or over hard?"

"Just like they are, Mom, will be fine." Mom slid the eggs from the pan to the plate like an experienced short order cook and handed the plate to me.

"Bacon and toast are almost ready" she said.

"Sam if you have an extra slice of toast and some bacon, that would great." Said Uncle Bill with his eyes just barely peeping over the top of the business section.

"Mom, this folder about the Mattson's? You know anything about them?"

"Randall, that was a long time ago and so out of character for your Dad. Don't hold it against him. I don't think your Dad ever got over the guilt of Richard killing himself. It was so terrible. One day everything was great, and the Mattsons were planning to move into the house next door to your Uncle Bill. The next day Richard is laid off, the following day he shoots himself with a pistol. So sad."

Mom sat down at the table after pouring herself a cup of coffee. "You know that was just before we had Cal. Quite frankly if it had not been for your brother being so young, I probably would have divorced your Dad right then and there." Then she smiled, "I wasn't too happy with Grandad either.

"I could not believe that they would not give the Mattson's money back. We would have made do just fine, but they got way too caught up in being the big guys in town. They got a big shot of ego that overwhelmed their humility and humanity. I guess if there was one thing good that came from the Mattson's loss was Dad's heart. I cannot recall him losing his way like that again."

"Wow, I didn't know. Sorry to dredge up that old memory." Then I continued, "You have any idea whatever happened to Mrs. Mattson?"

"Actually, I don't. You know your Dad would look for her occasionally over the years to say he was sorry, but I think he just finally gave up." With that, Mom hopped up and scurried back to the stove. "I hope you men like your bacon crispy. I let it get over done."

Picking up Dad's Blue book and flipping through to pages I had yet to read; in pencil . . .

Mrs. Mattson, I am so sorry about Richard. I know you cannot forgive me today, but maybe someday you will find a way in your heart to see me in a different light, better light than I deserve. I don't know how to make it up to you.

Then in blue ball point ink, another entry . . .

I guess Mary is better today; so am I. Paid in full, $10,000. January 3, 1963

"You know, Mom, I think he found Mary Mattson just after I was born."

Mom turned and looked to me, eyes questioning.

Chapter 15

CAL WAS BORN on the 3rd day of November, 1953. It had not been quite the surprising event Paul had expected. Sam had actually started experiencing labor early in the evening right after dinner. They had debated staying at home, since her water had not yet broken. Being the level-headed parents-to-be they envisioned themselves as, they elected to calmly load themselves into their Ford, drive the two miles of snow crusted streets to the hospital, and check Sam in for the night.

Initially, the nurse that had greeted them at the door was inclined to send the straight back home until Sam doubled over with the pain of a contraction, one of her strongest, yet. At that, the nurse retreated to the hall behind the admissions counter, snagged a wheelchair and returned. Once she had Sam comfortably positioned in the chair, she began to push Sam into the hallway, turning her head to Paul as she walked, "You will have some paper work to fill out at the admissions desk. I will be right back after I get your wife . . . she is your wife, right? . . . to the maternity ward."

At the ripe old age of 28 and having lived in Fort Collins the majority of his life, this was the first time Paul could remember being in the Larimer County Hospital. It was so bright and smelled antiseptic. He wondered how the doctors and nurses worked here. There was no color, no fresh smells, just the footfall noise of soft-soled shoes slapping against the monochrome gray, cold linoleum, square tile floors. It struck Paul as odd and ironic that a place that had been made specifically to provide care to humans would be so lacking in human qualities. He could not wait to get his wife and child back home and out of here. He was starting to wish he and Sam had just decided to spend the night at home in their apartment.

At the desk, Paul filled out the standard papers required to admit his wife. He had also brought his check book in case he would be required to pay the hospital up front for their services. The administrative nurse laughed at him when he pulled out his check book. "Honey, don't worry about it now. I suspect we all know where we can get ahold of Paul Simmons if you don't pay your bill. You know my family just moved into one of your new homes. I never thought we'd be able to afford a place like that. It's just beautiful and kids just love each having their own rooms. Now after we get done here, you can go up to the second floor, maternity. Your wife will be taken care of wonderfully and you can try to make yourself comfortable in the waiting room."

"Thanks, and I am certainly glad you like your home. You know we are planning on a couple more phases plus we are going to open another development just to the south if you know anyone interested."

At that, Paul heard William bust through the hospital double doors; his Mom and Dad trailing behind. "So, did we miss it, Is it a boy or a girl? Come on . . ."

"Time out, William. There is no baby yet, we just got Sam checked in. I suspect it is going to be a long night, so, really, you guys don't need to wait with me. But thanks anyway."

"Well, son, maybe we will stay for just a bit. I suspect they will shoo' us out of the waiting room by 8:00 in any case." Dad said, looking to the nurse as if waiting for confirmation.

"Mr. Simmons, your Dad is right. Everyone, but you will need to leave in 30 minutes or so. Perhaps one of your family members might like to pack you some snacks for the evening. It might be hours before your wife delivers."

Mom smiled "I beat you to it," she said as she pulled up a brown paper sack by the handles. "This is for you, Paul. I packed a couple apples, a muffin and a Thermos filled with some iced tea. Let's head upstairs for at least a little while."

"You know where you're going, Mom? William asked.

"Where do you think you two were born? Now march to the elevator."

* * *

"Mister Simmons? Mister Simmons?"

Paul stirred and opened his eyes to what he took as Sam's doctor. He was dressed in a light green set of scrubs consisting of a short-sleeved shirt and drawstring pants. He still had on his scrub hat, giving the impression he had a light green bouffant.

"Yes, I'm Mister Simmons. Is Sam okay?"

To this, the doctor merely smiled and said, "Samantha came through it wonderfully and you now have a handsome baby boy. If you will follow me, I think we will break a couple rules and bring you into the delivery room."

The hallway was eerily quiet, as they padded to the room marked "Delivery Room #1".

"It has been a particularly quiet night, so not much activity. It is usually a lot busier than this, so normally I don't bring fathers back here. You are in for a treat." With that he swept open the door to expose a nurse dressed in the identical scrub setup as the doctor. She had just placed a newborn at the breast of the new mother, his wife, Sam.

Sam looked to Paul, then back the baby. "Cal, you want to say hi to your Dad?" She paused, "I guess not. You are more interested in the boob. You are Daddy's boy."

Paul was shocked at her comment given that two strangers were in the room with them, but then again, he figured prudence went out the door once his wife spread her legs to enable the doctor and nurse to bring this new child into the world.

Paul laughed.

* * *

Paul, Virginia, and Arlin were now in the final stretch of pulling together proposals for the next development. Proposals, plural, was important to note. After their first effort, they realized they needed focused proposals that anticipated the needs of the respective stakeholders. As such, they now had proposals structured for the zoning commission, their bank, and the utilities commission. The last had been the primary stumbling block in the first development, so this time they had put some extra effort into developing a set of targeted funding proposals based on the city's own projections of tax revenue growth. Developments like the one Simmons & Sons were proposing were integral to these projections. The team had pulled together what Virginia referred to as 10-year pro-forma of the tax revenue impact, showing that their project would be exceptionally valuable to the city of Fort Collins's coffers.

Paul had assumed the business plan they had pulled together for the bank would sail through approval with minimal concerns. They had reduced their current loan balances ahead of schedule and had elected to limit their request to that of a line of credit of up to $75,000. They had mistakenly understood what would concern the bank.

Their first warning that the financing might come with some unforeseen challenges came when Paul took a call from James

Horton, the bank's Vice President of Business Accounts asking Paul to make sure that he brought his Dad to their meeting to review the Simmons & Sons business plan and the request for the line of credit. James and Paul's Dad had known each other for years, but rarely did the two have cause to get together. They had run in very different circles from their early days as kids. Paul had met with James many times over the past couple years; their initial meeting back when they garnered his approval for their first round of bank funding. He inferred from James's call and his insistence on expanding their meeting as a vote of no confidence in Paul. He fumed.

"You will not believe what that SOB, James Horton, just did."

"What's that?" asked Virginia.

"He just pretty much demanded I bring Dad along to the meeting this afternoon to discuss our business plan. Not that I wouldn't love to have him there, but the idea that we are not capable of addressing his questions really ticks me off. Heck, Dad is pretty much part-time now and it's my company, too."

Arlin sat quietly bouncing his eyes between Paul and Virginia, then asked, "Did he say why he wanted your Dad at the meeting? I mean, maybe something else is going on."

To that, Virginia agreed, "Arlin, you might be right. We've had a great relation with the bank, and we've certainly proved we can manage the business. I cannot believe Horton would have any doubts in our ability to deliver on what we say."

"Okay, okay. Maybe you're right. Maybe something else is going on . . . you know, like wanting to know from Dad what the bank should get us for Christmas presents. I do not buy it, but I'll give Dad a call anyway to tell him we'll pick him up at the house a little before one this afternoon. It will make sense to run through the plan assumptions with him once again since he will now be in the meeting.

* * *

The appointment with James Horton was scheduled for 3:00 pm. Paul, Lattimore, Virginia, and Arlin approached the receptionist 15 minutes to the hour and asked to see Mister Horton for their three o'clock meeting.

"You know I don't see that he has any meetings this afternoon, but let me bring him on down to meet you. Who can I say is calling?"

"We are from Simmons & Sons. We have had this appointment for some time, but just this morning we changed the attendees. Maybe there has been some confusion," Dad responded.

"No problem. Please take a seat and make yourself comfortable. I will be right back."

Several minutes later, Paul noticed the receptionist approaching from the steps, followed by a man, about his own age; someone he had never met. Eagerly approaching, the man held out his hand to greet the four, moving from right to left, Virginia, Paul, Arlin, and lastly Paul's Dad, thereby avoiding making a potentially embarrassing mistake by guessing who might be the most important member of this management team. "You probably expected my Dad, Jim. I am Landon Horton, but please, just call me Lanny. I always hated the name Landon . . . so hoity-toity.

"Dad's waiting for us in the conference room upstairs." With that, Lanny turned and started out in the same direction from which he had just come, obviously expecting Simmons & Sons to follow.

The conference room was amazing; walnut paneling, intricately carved crown molding outlining a glossy-smooth plaster ceiling, all surrounding a huge conference table that looked too big to fit through the double-hung, eight panel doors. Pouring a cup of coffee from a stainless-steel percolator was the senior Horton.

"Folks come on in. We have some coffee and some donuts over here. I thought it was about time to get us all together to have a frank talk." Jim placed his cup on a plate with a couple donuts and several cookies and a napkin. He passed on the silverware. He was apparently comfortable eating with fingers. "Seriously, guys, grab some food. If you don't dig in, I'll be tempted to eat seconds. I have no self-control when it comes to donuts." His last comment was not necessary. It was apparent. Jim had to push the scale somewhere north of 250 even though he looked to be no more than five and a half feet tall. He certainly did not miss too many meals and the sedentary life of the banker did not help.

"Lattimore, why don't you sit next to me? It has been a long-time since we've a had a need to talk. Your boy, Paul, and Virginia have been absolutely superior business people. I bet they have you just enjoying life now. You pretty much retired?"

"Hell no, Jim, although I do have to admit I do not feel compelled to head into the office very often anymore." Paul's Dad placed a cup of coffee, sitting appropriately on a saucer, down by Jim and plopped down. "I suspect if I showed up every day, I'd just be getting in the way. Probably screw things up. These guys," nodding across the room to Paul, Virginia, and Arlin, "have been great. So why have you pulled me into this discussion?"

"Soon enough, Lattimore, soon enough." Addressing the rest of the group, "Let's get started, if you are ready?"

To that they found seats at the table, all to one end surrounding the two elders. Jim started, "By now I think you have met Lanny. He just got back from studying banking and accounting at Wharton. I think you will find he will bring a lot to our relation that I just have not been capable of providing."

Looking at Lanny, "Smart, capable, educated, energetic; I was thinking of assigning him to manage your account on behalf of the bank." Lanny blushed at the complement. Jim continued, "but I don't think that might be the best thing for you. Instead, I want you to hire him on as your Controller." At that he stopped and waited for a reply.

Paul did not know what to say or how to respond. Looking at the faces around the table, including Lanny, it was obvious they were as equally dumbfounded. "Mister Horton,"

"Hell, Paul, we've been doing business together now for years and you are on your way to becoming one of my most important customers; please call me Jim."

"Uh, sure. So, Jim, why do you think we need a Controller and what makes you think we can afford to add another senior member to our team?" Arlin, Virginia, and Lattimore sat quietly, letting Paul take the lead.

"Look, Paul, let me be frank," and then turning to Virginia, "Virginia, you have made huge contributions to Simmons & Sons. Your business plan proposals are so good I don't even need to look at them. I know you guys have done your homework. You have developed a skill set that I think Lanny, over there, would be envious of, even given his platinum quality education." Then turning to Paul's Dad, "Lattimore, you have always impressed me with your business instinct, sharp as a knife, and with a heart. Damn impressive. But you two have to be pushing sixty. Am I right?"

To that Paul interrupted "So what's that got to do with our business, Jim?

"Nothing other than you are getting big enough you really need to think of your next step. You have no transition plans for your senior staff. You have outgrown the 'mom and pop shop' if you don't mind me saying. To be clear, I have NO issues with your team or your talents, or your business plan, or anything . . . other than you have reached a size that you only have two choices: get bigger or get smaller. It is inevitable, every company has growing pains or dying pains all the time. Unfortunately, most companies do not realize they have spiraled into dying pains until it is too late. I want to help you with your growing pains."

"So, what are you suggesting?" Paul asked.

Jim sat out pads of papers and pens so that the Simmons & Sons team might take notes, then jumped directly into sharing his thoughts. In general, Jim was afraid that Simmons & Sons had no true succession plans in the case that they lost one of their team. Compounding that concern was the fact that outside of Paul, William, and Arlin the other five integral members of the team, Virginia, Lyle, Joe Klein, himself and Lattimore, all were in excess of 57 years of age, Joe being the oldest at 65. This is in a world where the life expectancy for a person born in the USA around the turn of the century was less than fifty years. They were living on borrowed time. Jim had stressed that he did not expect any of them to keel over in the near term, but it was only prudent to begin planning for some transitions.

There was another reason, Jim was pushing for changes within Simmons & Sons. Their structure was too risky in his opinion. He suggested it was time to move away from the proprietorship and move into a corporate structure, if for no other reason than to limit their liabilities. In the next couple of years, he also fully expected US Treasury recommendations on new corporate structures to prevail with Congress, thereby creating something called a Sub-Chapter S corporation. It would only be a matter of time before this was signed into law, and the current business structure for Simmons & Sons would be outdated. The benefits to Simmons & Sons should be significant: limit their liability to lawsuits and make transitioning the business to heirs easier. However, the law also meant they needed a real accountant to manage the books, fill out tax returns, and manage the ownership shares. Quite frankly, Jim did not see that Simmons & Sons had the requisite skills in house to handle the job, and they were getting big enough to justify the investment.

By the end of the discussion, Jim had convinced them of the need to change their structure. Even if the Subchapter S did not become law, Paul was convinced that incorporating was prudent, if for no other reason than to limit their liability. With building homes, it was only a matter of time before they became embroiled in a lawsuit. There were just too many dollars at stake.

That day, they agreed to a new, two-company structure. The first would be PW Simmons, Inc. and the second would also maintain the Simmons name, but now would just be Simmons Company. PW Simmons would be chartered with new housing and industrial developments. Simmons would be 100% owned by PW Simmons and would focus on renovation and redevelopment. Administration and accounting for both companies would all be handled through PW Simmons. An appropriate cost would be allocated to Simmons for the infrastructure support.

Lanny would join PW Simmons as the new company's corporate controller and treasurer. Virginia would operate as their chief financial officer and drive long-term planning. Over time, Jim stressed that they would need to bring in successors for Lyle and Lattimore to focus on Simmons Co., or else they were putting a very profitable business at risk. Although it wasn't the major contributor to growth for the combined company, the Simmons Company would still be contributing more than 20% of the total profits if managed effectively.

Lastly, the proprietorship essentially provided that Paul, William, and Lattimore all shared equally in Simmons & Sons.

Jim thought this relation might need to be discussed going forward.

On this last point, Paul was glad that Jim had kept his comments brief and non-specific. He presumed that this was Jim's veiled attempt to suggest William should not have an equal part of the company. True, Jim's experience with William's contribution was likely colored by his lack of reliability early on with Simmons & Sons, but he had really buckled down and showed his value over the past two years. He certainly had earned his part in the company. Paul feared Jim was being unfair and jaded with his opinion of William.

After hinting that the control and ownership of the company be altered in the future structure, Jim had stopped.

Paul looked to his Dad. His Dad nodded back to Paul. Paul then looked to Virginia. She nodded in agreement.

Paul responded to Jim's proposal, "Okay, you had us convinced several donuts ago." He smiled and finished, "Jim, this all makes a lot of sense, but now we're going to have to redo our business plans to reflect all these changes. When can we meet again to discuss our funding for the next project?"

"Paul, I am prepared to offer you a line of credit up to $200,000 today in addition to your outstanding loans, so don't sweat it. I'll have the completed documents to you before you leave today. I would not suggest my son leave the bank to join your company if I did not have the utmost faith in your business savvy and planning. You tell me this will work, and I'll get the papers up here."

Paul looked to Lanny, "So Lanny, when do you want to start? Oh, and by the way, how much did your Dad suggest we pay you?"

Chapter 16

THE MENTION OF the Mattsons was sufficient to get Uncle Bill to set aside his newspaper. "Uncle Bill, are we planning on heading back to that restaurant anytime soon? I was looking forward to our talk with Mark and Tim," I prompted Uncle Bill.

"I think that would be good. Let's sit with your Dad a while and then head over for a long lunch"

We both got up and walked through the living room and into Dad's room. We were both pleasantly surprised to see Dad awake and apparently lucid. "So, I haven't died yet. Shoot, that means I have to put up with this gut pain another day. You know I dreamt I died last night and then I was okay."

I did not know exactly what to say to Dad. "Dad, does it hurt a lot?"

"Only when I am breathing, peeing, eating, you know pretty much all the time."

Continuing, I said, "Do you remember talking about Johnny last night?"

"Johnny? You mean, Johnny Jackson? My friend, he died so long ago." Dad started to weep. "You remember Johnny, don't you William?" Dad was looking not at William, but at nurse Bob. "We fixed that fence at your house yesterday." Dad had slipped back in time, into delusion. Oh, but for a brief moment he was here with me.

Mom walked in on us and said. "Boys, why not go get some air. William, I suspect you could certainly use some given how much you must have liked that wine last night. Maybe you can get Tim or Mark to open up a little early for you two. They called earlier this morning to make sure you two got home okay and to invite you back to talk a little. If there is one thing Mark and Tim like more than cooking, it's talking."

"I'm up for it if you are, Uncle Bill."

* * *

William, I have always thought I knew you, but you constantly surprise me. I thought I was the good man of the two of us . . . and you surprised me again. Forgive me.

Paul,

January 3, 1963

Lanny had joined the Simmons & Sons team shortly after his father had hosted what he would come to refer to as the "Come-to-Jesus" meeting to begin forging a path to the future for the business. The move had been rewarding, both developmentally and financially for Lanny. Although his position at the bank certainly provided a nice, consistent, and safe pay, it would have been years before he could aspire to the wealth his father enjoyed. The Simmons family business had had a very good run over the past five years, and he had been lucky enough to participate in the success.

Simmons & Sons had taken his father's advice to heart and

had moved aggressively to put in place a corporate structure creating PW Simmons, Inc. and had added the subsidiary, Simmons Company. The restructuring of the Simmons & Sons had also provided another opportunity for the team and to ensure some business continuity.

As part of the corporate structure, James Horton tentatively suggested the corporate structure might be a good time to expand the ownership to include the significant members of the management team., thereby creating some real incentive to stay with the firm. Although Paul had initially been cool to the topic, he had come to see the wisdom in the move. He was confident in the team they had assembled, and it seemed to make sense that they participate in both risks and rewards in the future.

PW Simmons essentially doubled their closely held stock and redistributed the additional stock in equal parts to Lyle, Virginia, Arlin, Lanny, Joe Jr., Paul, and William. The additional allocation to Paul and William guaranteed the Simmons would maintain ultimate control of the company.

For Lanny, he had moved from a basic bank manager to the Controller and a part owner of the town's most successful real estate developer in a few short years. It had been a very good run.

With the addition of Lanny and his new position, it was obvious PW Simmons had outgrown the old awning shop space. Although the shop held high sentimental value, the space's location on the main street in the town proved to be of even a larger financial value. Its sale had largely funded the business relocation to a newly renovated office space a block west of College Boulevard. The new facilities were a tremendous boon to the team. Although the office required the climbing of stairs to a second floor, the office provided an abundance of square footage, enough to accommodate a staff of up to 20 people, a conference area for clients, and enough room for the business's growing bank of files and plans. The facility also came with the luxury of natural light, beaming in through huge, west-facing windows that spanned the entire width of the office. Gone were the dreary days of laboring in the old awning shop.

Simmons Company occupied a small, walled-off section at the rear of the office, next to the conference area. When not in use, the space doubled as a quiet spot for PW Simmons client discussions and negotiations. Although Simmons Company had largely been managed by Lyle and Lattimore initially, Paul had become more hands on over the past year as Lattimore bowed out of the day-to-day operations. Paul had engaged to outline a path forward to expand Simmons Company's footprint and its impact on the town; truly embracing its original charter of redevelopment. As such, he had also relegated much of the day-to-day business management of PW Simmons to Virginia and Lanny. William still handled all the construction operations for the company.

Lanny walked into the walled off section of the office that had now become Paul's domain with a ledger book tucked under his arm. His face did not provide even a glimmer of the happiness that it normally exhibited. He had not bothered knocking upon entering and now, uninvited, he closed the door and plopped himself down next Paul's desk.

"Paul, I think we have a serious issue to talk about," started Lanny.

No greetings, no jokes, no small talk before jumping into business was unlikeCed's attention. "What's the matter Lanny? You lose your pencil or something?" Paul joked in the normal banter only he and Lanny normally engaged in. In private, Paul would kid Lanny about being a pencil pusher, Lanny would respond by referring to Paul as a B-school drop-out, even though Paul had yet to attend his first day of college. The banter was always good to elicit a smile, but not today.

"No, seriously, Paul, we have a real problem. It involves your brother and I am not sure what to do."

"With William? What happened?"

Lanny placed the ledger on Paul's desk and flipped to a section he marked with a paper clip. He began to go through a series of cash transactions that had been initiated by William during the past year. The description merely referenced MM Enterprises—installment. Normally, Lanny had never questioned transactions that had been initiated by Paul, William, or Lattimore, but in this case, Lanny had been reviewing the previous year's expenses in order to complete the tax returns for the PW Simmons and discovered this particular vendor. Over the period of a year, William had initiated payments of $3,500 to the company, an amount that justified making sure that future payments were completed via check to provide an audit trail. Upon recommending the change to William and offering to add MM to their vendor listing, Lanny had been rebuffed with a "never mind, I don't think I'll be doing business with them in the future, anyway."

"Paul, I asked Arlin and Virginia if they knew anything about an MM Enterprises. They never heard of them." Lanny was looking to Paul as if in hope that, miraculously, Paul would know of the company and the whole thing would be dismissed as a non-issue.

Unfortunately, it was not to happen. "Lanny, did you ask Dad or Lyle? Maybe they know something about it," Paul asked.

"Not yet. I didn't want to this to get out of hand if it was really nothing. Arlin and Virginia do not have any idea as to why I asked; and they certainly have no idea as to the dollar amount involved. So, what do you think we should do?"

Paul was silent, although his mind was going a mile a minute and not on good thoughts, he calmly suggested "Why don't you sit on this for a couple of days? I suspect US Government is not going to fold up if it takes us another week to file our tax returns, right?"

"But what then?" asked Lanny

"Look Lanny and I invited William over for dinner tonight. I don't want to talk about it in front of Sam. It just would not be right. Let me talk with him tomorrow morning."

* * *

William showed up to Paul and Sam's house promptly at seven. Paul and Sam had moved from their apartment two years earlier to a comfortable new home from their second housing development and their first as PW Simmons. The new house was only a short walk from William's home, so he had left his car with the excuse of providing him the opportunity to get some fresh air. In reality, Paul figured it just gave William the freedom to drink a couple additional beers over dinner without any worry of driving home inebriated. Being prepared, Paul had picked up an additional 6-pack of Budweiser on the way home.

"So how goes life for my favorite family?" William yelled as he both knocked and walked in through the front door without waiting for an answer.

"Come on back to the kitchen, William. We are just getting Cal cleaned up."

Smiling, William asked as he walked into the kitchen "Why, what happened to Cal?"

"Uncle Bill!" called little Cal with a tomato-orange stained mouth.

Sam cut in "Cal loves Chef Boy-Ar-Dee spaghetti so much he decided to wear it on his shirt. William. Go ahead a grab a beer while I get him wiped off."

Paul smiled and opened the refrigerator to grab a couple of beers; one for William and one for himself. Paul plopped the two beer bottles down onto the table and popped the caps. "You want to sit in here or in the living room while Sam takes care of your favorite nephew?" Then to Sam, "You mind, honey?"

"No, go ahead. I know you two boys probably want to talk shop or something. I will be right in with Cal once I get him into his PJs."

"Excellent, we can flip on the television. I heard that Cassius Clay's first pro fight is tonight; against some guy named Hunsaker. The paper said Hunsaker is a cop during the day. Clay is going to mop up the floor with him. You want to watch?" William asked.

"Sure."

For the rest of the fight and through most of a reserved dinner, Paul remained quiet. It was a very un-Paul and William evening.

"Why don't you two have a couple fresh beers and head into the living room? I'll be right in after cleaning away the dishes." Sam grabbed a couple beers along with a bottle opener and handed them to William. "William, find something good on television, would you? Paul, can you help me here in the kitchen?"

William headed into the living room, turned the channel and began to fidget with the rabbit-ear antennae.

"What do you need, Sam?"

"What do you mean, asking me that. Hell, Paul, you didn't say but a few words over dinner. What is up with you? You are being positively rude to your brother."

"I guess you're right, but I cannot talk about it now. You want to give me and William some time alone? I'll tell you later what is going on, okay?"

"Okay, but be nice."

Paul turned and walked into the living room and flipped off the television. "William, you and I need to talk."

What had started out as an awkward evening now moved rapidly from clumsy to impossible. Paul laid out the concerns both he and Lanny had regarding MM Enterprises. He went so far as to accuse William of stealing from the firm when William refused to discuss what the expenses were for.

"William, if you are in trouble, Sam and I can help, but you have to tell me what's going on. Hell, this is a lot of money at stake. What did you do?"

"Paul, I really don't want to talk about it; especially with you and don't bring Sam into this, please. I don't want anyone to know about this. Please?" William's eyes belied the helplessness he felt now that the situation had surfaced. "If you want, I will quit the company now. You can take the money out of my share of the profits; there is plenty there that is mine. I wasn't stealing. You have to believe me. Just don't tell anyone." Tears began to run down Williams checks and his voice was beginning to choke.

"William, keep your voice down. I just don't know what to think right now. You say you were not stealing, but, my God, it is thirty-five hundred bucks. That's a lot of money. Lanny and I need to talk about this tomorrow morning. I think you should swing by the office tomorrow. We'll figure this out then, but you have to give me a reason to believe you." Paul fell silent and William slowly got out of his chair and let himself out of the house alone.

"Okay, what was that all about, Paul?" Sam was leaning against the doorjamb leading into the kitchen. "I wasn't listening, but I caught parts of it. Is William stealing from the company?"

"Really, I don't know why he would. We are doing great

and he doesn't have a lot of expenses. I cannot imagine what he would need the money for; unless he has gotten tied into gambling or drugs. I just don't know." Paul hesitated. "Hell, I do know. William, well he drinks so much. Maybe it is drugs or gambling. It is not so unbelievable. Hopefully, I'll know more tomorrow. Let's not talk about it anymore tonight, okay?"

"Okay"

"And don't say anything to Mom or Dad. They would have an aneurism with this."

* * *

Uncle Bill and I were seated at the same table we had occupied just several hours earlier. The daylight had transformed the downstairs restaurant from the upscale, high-end dining experience from the previous evening to a trendy gastro-pub for lunch. Ted apologized for not having a breakfast menu for the two, but offered to whip up something from the kitchen. Uncle Bill politely declined, and asked if he and I could just use the time before lunch to share some stories about my Dad. Understanding, Ted left us with a fresh pot of coffee and then deftly retreated back downstairs. He had to get the kitchen prepped for their lunch crowd.

"Uncle Bill, I'm kind of embarrassed to ask, but whatever happened to you with the company back before I was born? Mom always told me you left the company for a while to do your own thing."

Uncle Bill coughed, "Wow, leave it to Randall to ask the tough question," turning his head as if talking to a third person even though no one else was in the room. "I didn't really leave to do my own thing. I kind of didn't have a choice, but, you know, it was OK. It gave me a time to get to know a lot of new folks. You know folks like Johnny Walker, Jack Daniels, Adolph Coors, and occasionally I had the opportunity to eat with Paul Masson and Mateus. I don't remember much from that time, but we got over it.

* * *

"I don't know what he was thinking and I don't know why he needed the money. Perhaps it's best that I never know." Paul was sitting next to Lanny. Even though it was Sunday morning, they had agreed it was critical to go over the discussion that Paul and William had the previous evening.

"Lanny, is there anything we have to do besides getting the money back? I mean I really do not want to make this any worse than it already is."

"Well, we really should discuss this with the rest of the shareholders, but I guess if we can somehow get the money back from William, I'll be quiet. Besides, I really don't have any proof he did something illegal. We cannot trust him though. You agree? And I think we should ask him to leave his current role heading up our operations?"

"I guess I agree. I will need to make up some excuse as to why William is not going to be a part of our team in the future, but I'm not going to ask him to give up his ownership position. He'll need the income from the business to live on. I sure as hell cannot recommend him to any other companies."

"What about the thirty-five hundred dollars?"

Paul shot back, "I'll take care of that by the end of the week. Don't mention it to anyone. Nobody needs to know Virginia and I paid it back, okay?"

Lanny pushed his chair back from the desk. "I think it has to be okay. Anything else would be bad for William and, even more important, it would be bad for the business. Nobody is going to want to buy a house from a company that has an embezzlement problem. Hell, I won't even talk about this with my father."

"Lanny, I do need to talk with Lyle to see if he can handle the operations at the development. I can give him a call this afternoon and ask him to drop into the office before heading over to the renovation project we have going on Mulberry Street. If you talk with him, don't say anything to him about William. I haven't come up with an excuse yet for William leaving the team."

William was waiting outside the door of the darkened office when Lanny left.

"Paul, can I come in?"

"Sure, close the door." After William closed the door, Paul jumped right in without waiting for any explanation from William. "William, you probably know we cannot have you working here now or in the future. I need to come up with an excuse as to why you are going to be leaving the business."

"Are you going to bring charges against me, brother?" William emphasized brother as if insinuating that Paul was out of line with his dismissal. "You know, I am an owner here, too, and I have just as much say in how this business runs as you do, so please have some respect. By the way, I have come here to resign. You don't need to ask me to leave. I trust you are not going to try to force me to give up my ownership share. I'll give the company the thirty-five hundred out of my share of the profits when we distribute the profits at the end of this quarter. You okay with that?"

"Don't worry about the money. I will have the $3,500 by the end of this week and Lanny will take care of the rest; and no, we will not be asking you to sell out your portion of the company. Nobody outside of you, me, Lanny, and Sam know about this." William cringed at Sam's name. "Look William, Sam overheard us talking last night. Sorry."

"So, are you going to do my job for me? We should spend some time going over the schedules and contractors," William offered.

"I will track down Lyle and have him swing by the office tomorrow to figure out an attack plan to fill in for you until we can find some type of replacement. We might need to pull back on a couple renovation projects though." Paul paused. "If you are okay with meeting with us to discuss the transition it will make it lot easier; especially if we can come up with a reason for the emergency change in our operations management."

"Fuck that, Paul. I don't want to be here in front of the entire staff. Tell the lot of them that I just got caught up in something, don't say what; and that I need some time to work through it. You will have a replacement before you know it and no one will be the wiser. I'll bring by my schedules and plans that I left at the site by the end of today. The contractor listings and progress reports are on my desk out there in the office. I don't want to be here when Lyle gets here. I just don't think I could keep from crying." William looked to floor, turned to the door and walked out.

Paul could see through the doorway that William did not acknowledge Lanny as he walked through the office; he just stared straight ahead and exited. Quietly he overheard Lanny, "what a mess . . ."

Paul whispered, "Shut the fuck up, Lanny."

William started to cry as he walked down the steps for what he thought to be the last time. Not a good day in the office.

Chapter 17

BY THE END of October, nights in Fort Collins could be cold, frigid enough to drive even the toughest person indoors to huddle in an oversized sweater in front of the fireplace. Tonight was no different, but William sat outside on a wrought iron chair, legs crossed and propped up on the table, looking up at a moon and stars that pierced through the blackened sky. Stan Getz's jazz album masterpiece *Moonlight in Vermont* filtered out through the open patio door, the rich, warm, breathy strains of the sax calming his mind. An empty glass occupied his right hand; a half-filled bottle of Jack Daniels, his left. What Getz could not calm, Jack Daniels numbed. He had wrapped himself in a blanket; that and the whiskey were his only protection from the cold. He closed his eyes letting the smooth sax slowly flow over and through his body like honey.

Life had crashed down on him yesterday, crushing his hope and faith in life and family. The weekend had been something to look forward to, a rest from the work week, a time to recharge his batteries, so to speak. Now all he had was time; time to think and reflect on what he had done to deserve this.

The phone began to ring; it had rung several times since he

had been home. He let it ring; he imagined the caller was Paul trying to get ahold of him to talk, as if talking would somehow relieve Paul of his own guilt. "Fuck him!" There was no way that William was going to make this any easier emotionally for his brother. Sure, he would do what he could to transition his job; he still needed the company to be successful, it was his only income, but he did not want to be the only miserable Simmons in town. "Fuck him, fuck him, fuck him."

William refilled his glass. He was not much of a whiskey drinker and really did not want another, but he could think of nothing better to do with his time. He looked up to the sky taking in the unfiltered starlight. Given how cold it was, he had no doubt he had this sky view all to himself; he was getting to enjoy this privately, not having to share it with anybody else in town and certainly, not Paul. Normally on a Sunday night he would go over his schedules and any plan changes then go to bed early. He would be at the construction site by sun up waiting for his crews to make sure he did not waste time or daylight; the days were already getting short in anticipation of winter. There would be no need to go to bed early tonight.

Getz's sax had flipped from the meandering, almost drunk title song on the record to the frenetic *Jaguar* track. It was a disturbing contrast, much like what William had experienced in the last couple days. One moment, everything is working as it should be; he was a success, he was respected, he was making a real difference to the company and to his community. The next, well he was now contemplating moving to another town just to escape the humiliation. He brought the drink to his lips and sipped. No big gulps, just sipping, he wanted to stay in this mood. It did not make sense, but he wanted to stay in this sorrowful mood a while. Drinking too fast would just knock him out and, hell, he'd probably freeze to death. The worst thing, he did not feel guilty about the money, nor would he. Maybe someday Paul would understand why.

He would feel like hell in the morning. Banging head, dry mouth, tired, and lethargic. It is how he would feel most of the time from now on.

* * *

Paul had moved aggressively to replace William as the Operations Manager for their housing development. They already had a number of homes effectively sold, only waiting for construction to be completed to consummate the sale. He wanted to button up the majority of these by Christmas. Being able to log the additional revenue would be a boon for their profit distribution. This was shaping up to be a record year for the company. Secretly, he was even more motivated so that the profits would be sufficient to carry his brother financially through the foreseeable future. Even though he could not understand William's transgression, he did not want him to suffer. Hell, he was family.

Initially, Paul had thought getting a qualified replacement to take over for William was going to be tough. Surprisingly, one of their earliest competitors in town, a hard-core general contractor with years of direct construction experience by the name of Leonard Sky, was more than happy to run from his own business to join PW Simmons. Sky's firm, LSC, Leonard Sky Contracting, had been competing first against Simmons & Sons, and now PW Simmons; it had been losing ground for years. In Sky's mind, joining now was no admission of defeat; that had happened a long time ago. The job offer was a gift of preservation for him and his family. Little did he know how much of a boon it was for PW Simmons. The addition of Sky also came with access to some pretty talented carpenters, as well.

LSC would continue to exist under the direct guidance of Sky's eldest son, but would not compete against PW Simmons in the market space of housing developments as long as Leonard Sky remained under their employ. Instead, LSC would focus strictly on custom home design and construction. Without having to pay for Leonard while getting some relief from overhead burden of the LSC carpenters, Leonard hoped his son could eke out a livelihood in a more synergistic, if not smaller, co-existence with PW Simmons in the Fort Collins region. In any case, this would stave off bankruptcy for a while, at least.

Leonard Sky now sat in the PW Simmons office across the conference table from Paul and Lanny. They were hashing out the specifics of Sky's offer. Sky was happy to accept a modest salary with a small profit sharing provision. Any portion of a profit was likely going to be a lot more lucrative than what he had expected prior to the job offer.

"So, Paul, what the hell is that brother of yours going to be doing with himself now? I know you guys are doing pretty good, but he can't really be thinking of retirement and just living off the company profits, is he? Not that I care, but he's way too young. I hope he's not planning on just taking a little vacation and then having you guys cut me out to make room for him again?"

Paul responded almost too quickly, "Sky, you do not have to worry about William coming back. I think he has set his sights on a different opportunity that has little to do with construction and housing developments. If you are really concerned, we can draft something up to protect you."

At that Lanny piped in, "We cannot guarantee Leonard Sky employment, Paul, but we can do something to make him more comfortable. Perhaps a guaranteed severance payout in the case of us needing to cut our ties without there being cause for a dismissal. I was thinking something like a six-month salary payout, plus you would still get your pro-rata profit sharing. You okay with this?" Paul nodded in agreement.

Sky squinted a little, trying to make it look as though he was still contemplating whether or not to accept the offer. He suspected Lanny and Paul had no idea that he was thrilled with the offer and would have accepted it even without the severance offer. He really had few choices.

In the future Sky, would be surprised to know that Paul and Lanny were fully aware of LSC's business difficulties. Although they had guessed Sky would be happy to accept pretty much any offer they threw on the table, previous to this discussion Lanny and Paul had agreed they would not take advantage of the situation. They could not afford another "William" situation, and they needed Sky committed for the long-term, even though he would never get an equity stake in the company. The meeting was shaping up pretty much as they expected.

Sky reached out his right hand toward Paul to shake. "I think we have a deal. When you want me to start? And Lanny, when do you want me to talk with the carpenters regarding what we discussed about coming on to your payroll?"

"Deal, it is. Lanny, I think you can wrap up the carpenter question with Sky without me. I need to head over to the development to spell Lyle. Sky, if you can start Monday, maybe you can fill out some paperwork today, before leaving?"

Sky smiled, "Hell yes. I'll meet you anywhere you please, Monday morning."

Lanny had not really comprehended how badly things must have been at LSC until he saw Leonard's eyes welling with tears of joy. Lanny could not help thinking, a talented guy like Sky should never have been so hopeless. He was actually happy that William's transgression had led them to save this old, crusty codger.

* * *

I was born on Thanksgiving Day 1962.

Uncle Bill fished out his worn wallet and began to flip through pictures that had apparently been secreted away for years. "Randall, this is one of my favorite pictures." It was an old black and white, 3x5 inch print that had been folded in half to fit in his wallet. Your dad gave me this just after you were born."

He handed me the picture. It was of my Mom holding a baby wrapped in a receiving blanket, lying in her hospital bed. Surrounding the bed was the whole team from PW Simmons: Arlin, Joe, then Dad, half sitting on the bed with Mom. On the other side of the bed was Lyle, Virginia, Granddad and Grandma Simmons. I had seen this picture before and until now had assumed Uncle Bill had taken the picture. "You were not there, were you, Uncle Bill."

"I wanted to be, but I don't think I would have been welcomed into the hospital. I mean, you were born at night, so I was probably in a conversation with a dear bottle of something, no doubt drunk, sitting alone in my living room. Besides, even if I had been sober, no one in that picture would have been glad to see me, let alone be photographed with me" he said as he pointed dismissively at the folks in the picture.

"You know you were a gift to your Dad and Mom, but probably even a bigger gift for me."

* * *

Paul pulled into William's driveway with his brand new Ford. William's car, a shiny light green Buick LeSabre convertible, sat in the open garage. Paul did not get William; his car was always immaculate and cared for, but yet he apparently did not give crap about his house, a house that he, himself, had built.

What had once been a nice green lawn, now was nothing more than weeds and dirt. Paul had to admit to one thing, it sure as hell made it easy to find William's house; just turn on to his street and drive until you see a shitty yard and house that badly needed some fresh paint.

William's home had become antithetical to this quaint, well-kept neighborhood and the neighbors were demanding a change. Phone messages had started to pile up on Paul's office desk prodding him to do something about his brother and his house. It had been several months since Paul had driven this street. He had actually avoided it out of a desire not to run across William by accident. He dreaded having to stop and make some small talk belying his true feelings for his brother. He had never gotten over the $3,500 and likely never would. When he did run into William, he was always shocked by William's attitude; no humility, no regret. It was almost as if he were waiting for Paul to apologize for something. Only God knew what.

Today, however, Paul was not counting on some chance meeting. He was here for a couple of reasons. The first purpose: to tell William he had become an uncle once again; this time to a brand-new baby boy, Randall. Maybe he could talk him into coming by the house to see the family. In spite of the hard feelings from the apparent embezzlement, he still loved his brother and wanted him to know his nephews.

The second reason for the visit was not going to be so pleasant; he was here to demand Paul to clean up the house. Or what? Well, he hoped it did not get that far. Theoretically he really could not do much other than to appeal to William's pride and decency to fix up the place. His neighbors certainly had nothing to do with his dismissal from PW Simmons so there was no reason to punish them. He was hoping to get a commitment for some action. If his appeal failed, he was prepared to pay for a yard service to get the lawn and fencing back in shape and keep it nice.

Sitting in his car, he gave a quick assessment of the property: green grass had pretty much degraded to weedy brown tufts, a couple broken risers where sprinkler heads had once been, punctuated by an old garden hose with a rotary sprinkler spitting a steady stream of water onto some weeds and a long dead tree, creating nothing more than a growing pool of mud that ran up the entire side of concrete walkway leading to William's front door. The wood facia board under the eaves of the roof were in bad need of some scraping and new paint. He would not be surprised if some of the wood would need to be replaced. Thank goodness most of the house was brick. The brick still looked as good as the day William moved in.

Paul opened his car door and stepped out onto the driveway, took a deep breath and marched up the walk to the front door. He stopped briefly to push a weathered, half empty card-board carton filled with some garden tools off the front walk so that he could pass without having to step into the mud. He kidded himself that he wanted to avoid the mud so as not to not to tread dirt into the house, but that was a lie. He really did not give a shit about the William's floor; he just didn't want to mess up his new leather loafers.

Paul knocked at the front door and waited. Not getting any response, he opened the screen door and tried the door knob to see if it was unlocked. The knob turned. Pushing in on the door, Paul quietly called out "William? You here?" Paul caught himself. What a stupid question; if William wasn't here, how could he expect him to answer? Paul called again, "William, are you okay?" Not knowing why, but Paul felt like a criminal, breaking and entering into someone's private domain; but in this case the only thing he would be stealing was little bit of William's time. By the look of the yard, it looked like time was something William had plenty of. "William, you here?" He called more loudly this time.

"Well, I'll be if it isn't my favorite brother. Coming to slum a bit?" William had been watching from an armchair in the living room. The television was on, but no sound emanated from it. In his lap, William, was holding a large, loose leaf binder. He slapped the binder closed and dropped it on the floor next to his seat. Surprisingly, William hopped out of his chair and gave Paul a big hug. "Welcome to casa de William." At this he turned and left the room for the kitchen.

Paul had noticed the prevailing whiskey odor on William. There was no way to tell the smell was from some early day imbibing or just a holdover from the previous night. For William, evening and day ran together and liquor was just the grease to slide from moon to sun. He pretty much smelled like booze all the time. Paul guessed the odor poured from his pores.

Surprisingly, the living room was spotless. He had expected to see the outside decadence to be matched by an equally decrepit interior. "Orderly" and "clean" were the last two adjectives he would have thought of upon seeing the yard, but orderly and clean is exactly what he was seeing. It was as if two different people occupied this house: a lazy slob and a fastidious neatnik. Paul just shook his head, having difficulty processing the apparent dichotomy that was his brother.

From out in the kitchen, "You want a little something to drink; just something to tie you over until lunch?" Without waiting for an answer, the voice continued, "I sure as hell could use something. You know just to clear up those mind cobwebs." William returned to the living room, in one hand a glass filled with an amber liquid. In the other, a glass filled with ice.

Paul sat down on the sofa and placed a stack of phone messages he had been accumulating for the past several weeks on the low coffee table. "So, is the whiskey or the ice for me?" he asked.

"Neither. You didn't ask for anything. You want something?"

"No, not really. William let me jump into it so I can get back to the office to work." Paul proceeded to pull the top note of the pile and read it to William. Likewise, he moved on to the 2nd and 3rd and so on until he had read more than a dozen of the notes.

"William, I am getting these calls every day and a lot of them are repeat calls to complain about how your house looks."

William pushed the stack of notes onto the floor and smiled. "I was wondering how long it would take for you to get up the nerve to come see me and have a little chat. I think it is about time to get some things off our respective chests. You know why my house is always clean inside, but looks like shit outside?" without waiting for Paul to respond, he continued to plow on. "It's because I have a great housekeeper, but she's not so good at yard work. She doesn't complain a bit and I'm sure she is not included in that bunch of telephone messages even though she lives right next door. I think you even might know her. She's Mary Mattson. You remember that name?" William stopped to let the name sink in.

"Mattson? Sure, I remember the Mattsons. Mary's husband lost his job and they backed out on buying a house from us. You telling me Mary and Richard finally ended up buying a house in your neighborhood?"

"Well, not Mary and Richard. Just Mary. You see Richard killed himself back in '53. Sucked down a small hunk of lead from a pistol he had kept from his time in WWII. Apparently, it didn't sit well with the back of his head. I guess he thought he could at least get some money for Mary from his little life insurance policy. Pity, it had a suicide rider that meant the insurance company didn't need to pay up. They didn't owe him a dime. You know how it goes; a contract is a contract. Shit, Paul, he blew himself away for nothing leaving Mary without two pennies to rub together. By the way, that's where the thirty-five hundred bucks went, if you still want to know. I didn't keep a dime. I gave it to her as a return of the down payment from our company; you know that down-payment that you and that fucking father of mine refused to refund. God, Paul, you were pricks. I was so ashamed when I found out Richard killed himself. I've been giving her a couple hundred bucks each month for the housekeeping, just to help her get by."

Paul was dumb struck.

William continued, "I never thought I was stealing. It was money I felt the company took from the Mattsons so the company ought to give it back. It was only right."

Paul regained his composure. "I never knew. Why didn't you ever say something?"

"Paul, I couldn't. I knew if Lanny heard what you and Dad did, he probably would have left the company. Hell, you probably would have lost the entire team. I could not do that to you. It would have killed the company. But hell, Paul, it was only thirty-five hundred bucks. How could you and Dad have been so mean spirited, thoughtless, and greedy?" Paul was shocked to see that William was beginning to weep.

"Wow, I kind of just swept this away from my memories. I never wanted to think about what I did. Damn, Sam would have been so disappointed in me."

"I know, Paul. So, it was better that I got fucked instead of you and Dad, but I need to move on now. I have an opportunity I want to take advantage of, but I cannot do it with the rumor of embezzlement hanging over my head . . . and I want you in this."

"I'll do anything. What do you want me to do? We have to be able to move on. Right?" Paul looked at the coffee table as he spoke. He could not bring himself to look at William. He was filled with regrets on so many levels. He had done the absolute wrong thing regarding the down payment. Now it was time to face up to it. He and his Dad had kept what they were doing secret from everyone: his friends and his family because they had known all along it was wrong. He had not even bothered to follow-up with the Mattsons as any decent human being would have to see how they were fairing. He had treated them as nothing more than a payday. He accused William of stealing while he was the real thief. He had never given William a chance to explain his position. All of this had resulted in ruining the lives of the Mattsons and William, and, in effect, forever damaging his own life and that of his family. Now, he would spend a lifetime trying to make up for the shame he had heaped upon William. But he could never make up for what he did to Mary and Richard.

"I need you to come clean with the family; you know, about what you did."

Paul realized that when William referred to 'the family' he meant Arlin, Lyle, Virginia, Joe Junior and Senior, both Lanny and Jim Horton, in addition to Sam. Sam would be the most difficult and, for him, the only one that really counted. She was the person that trusted, supported, and loved him without question, and he had violated her. He raised his eyes to meet William's gaze. "You are right. I will. I will talk with Dad today on my way home to tell him what you did and what I need to do to earn back my man stripes. Thank you, William."

Paul, stood up and walked to the door. He let himself out without turning to say goodbye. Once he sat in his car, he realized he had not even told William about his new nephew, but that would be okay. There would now be plenty of opportunities for William to get to know Randall and become reacquainted with Cal. Although scared, anxious, and nervous, he felt better than he had in years.

Chapter 18

William was sitting at Paul and Sam's kitchen table. "Paul and Sam, I want you to buy me out of PW Simmons. You don't need me in the company. In fact, I would just be a sore reminder of a topic we need to put behind us now. I really have nothing to offer to the company." At least that is what William intended to say.

They had just enjoyed a fun evening together as a family, Paul, Sam, their two kids and their Uncle Bill. William preferred the 'Uncle Bill' to 'Uncle William.' He liked Uncle Bill because it did not sound so formal and it helped him start anew with his role as uncle to Cal and Randall. It had been a wonderful evening, something they had not enjoyed in almost three years. William had not stepped a foot into this house since that cold day in 1960 when they watched Cassius Clay win his pro boxing debut. It had been long ago. Everything now had been forgiven, if not forgotten . . . yet.

After putting the kids down for bed, Sam had returned to the kitchen only to find the table cleared of dishes and replaced with stacks of papers and car brochures. A large ledger book had been placed at the table's center, and Paul was standing by the table leaning on it with both hands while William was pointing to numbers in the ledger book while speaking animatedly about some topic that had been the secret he had wanted to share with his brother and sister-in-law.

Sam stood on the other side of the table, across from the two men and asked what was so interesting. William flipped the ledger around to face Sam; only too happy to include Sam in his plans.

William had been enamored with cars since his youth, and during the time he had been on his forced "sabbatical" from PW Simmons, the infatuation had morphed in to a full-fledged addiction. He had developed contacts with a number of auto dealerships to begin his journey understanding their business. He had been a quick student, and he was now fully convinced of the financial opportunities that could come from operating a dealership in their own Fort Collins.

There were already three dealerships in town. Getting one of the Big Three automotive manufacturers to agree to a fourth was probably not likely; however, purchasing one of the existing three looked to be a promising option.

In particular, William had developed a relation with the owner of one of the local dealers when he purchased his Buick. He had maintained his friendship with the owner, and now that dealer wanted to sell out and retire. The dealership currently sold both Chevy and Buick. William was confident that with the right money and negotiation, he could also get GMC to add a Cadillac franchise to the mix. This should be a great business opportunity in a growing market and would allow him to exit the construction business completely.

William was convinced of a huge upside for the automotive business in the region. His argument was well thought out and many faceted. It was absolutely true that a number of new companies had either put a new footprint in town or were planning to over the next several years. All of these would bring jobs, a lot of high-paying jobs, along with them. With the jobs came money to buy new cars and cars were required to drive to where the jobs existed; largely on the outskirts of town. It was symbiotic, a virtuous relation. The country was infatuated with cars, and PW Simmons had already benefited from the trend. The majority of the homes they built now included a two-stall garage even though most of the families only owned one car. William wanted to profit from filling that second stall. Paul and Sam absolutely concurred with his assessment of the market and the potential.

To fulfill his dream, he would either need Paul to buy in with him or buy out his share of PW Simmons. William had anticipated Paul was already consumed with leading PW Simmons and the Simmons Company along with being a father to two kids; the youngest just a baby. He would not likely want, or be able, to tackle another set of responsibilities on top of his almost overwhelming work-load. No, William was positive Paul would say no to becoming part owner in a dealership, at least at this time.

Although William had genuinely hoped Paul would join him the car dealership, he was a pragmatist and had, instead, pulled together the alternative proposal to sell his portion of PW Simmons to Paul and Sam. With the help of Lanny, he had established a fair value for his portion of the company and was confident that with the proceeds from the sale and some help from the bank, he could satisfy the conditions for the dealership transfer. He had been surprised at the value Lanny had calculated for PW Simmons. He was potentially wealthier than he had anticipated. As things stood. he would be able to provide a great value to Paul without jeopardizing his chances of becoming Fort Collins newest car dealership owner.

Paul and Sam listened to William run through the numbers. Sam could tell from Paul's questions and the excitement in his eyes that he was dying to throw in with William to buy the dealership. All the same, she knew that his commitment to his family and PW Simmons would prevent him from getting too excited.

William had the same sense and as he moved through the business opportunity, his excitement gave way to sorrow. Sorrow in knowing his big brother would by all means do the right thing and not even ask to participate as a partner in the dealership. He would pass on the opportunity, not because it was not interesting and exciting, but because of his sense of responsibility.

It was exactly what William had expected, yet he had not been prepared for the look on Paul's face. William had seen this look long ago, when as a kid, his brother had passed on getting his letterman jacket, knowing that the family could not really afford the purchase. Even though their Mom and Dad had scrimped and saved to buy him the jacket, he had asked, no forced, Mom and Dad to return it to the store. Paul had wanted that jacket so badly. The look on Paul's face was the same this evening as they stood around the kitchen table.

William stopped. "I take it back. I don't want you to buy me out. Forget it, I have another idea."

Completely winging it, William put aside his plans and jumped into outlining a plan that would include Paul and Sam in selling cars. "Guys, look, Virginia's talents are being wasted in PW Simmons now that Lanny had joined the team. She has a business mind that is exceptional and you both know it. Let's set it up as another subsidiary of PW Simmons. I'll run the dealership and bring Virginia over as the business manager. She'll run the financing and the day-to-day operations. I handle the marketing, sales and maintenance. Lanny can leverage his role over the accounting department that already exists at the dealership.

Although it was pretty clear that William was flying blind on his recommendations, it really did ring true on a number of counts. First off, Virginia had given up a lot of her responsibilities with the addition of Lanny and it was a waste. Even though she was approaching 60, she showed no signs of slowing down or desiring a smaller role in the company. She would fill a huge role in what William was outlining and would need to be a quick study in the position, but there was no doubt she could do it. Finance was a huge driver in defining whether a car dealer would succeed or fail, and Virginia would make sure it succeeded.

Likewise, Lyle was not ready for retirement. He was and likely would continue to run Simmons Company just fine without intervention from Paul. That part of the business was not growing, but it continued to churn out profits month after month.

The largest part of the business would remain, at least for the time being, the house development portion of PW Simmons. Paul realized that between Arlin, Sky, and Lanny, they had it covered well. His role would really migrate to being the CEO of the entire company. Sure, they would need to hire some new blood to provide for some degree of a succession plan for the business, but that was just a good business practice; whether they purchased the dealership or not.

Really only two issues remained. The first was convincing the rest of the PW Simmons stock holders to back the plan. He did not expect this to be much of an issue once they saw the cash flow projections. The second weighed more heavily on Paul: what in the heck did any of them know about running a car dealership?

Chapter 19

There was nothing sexier than these sleek, beautiful monsters of steel as they glistened in the car showroom. The gleaming paint, the spotless chrome, the smell of the interior; you could imagine how these beauties would perform on the road. Cal rolled down the driver's side window and nonchalantly placed his left elbow on the door. He draped his right hand over the top of the steering wheel of the brand new 1966, Marina Turquois, Pontiac GTO. At fourteen years old, driving age was only a couple short years away, but that still a seemed forever to him. In any case, he had already picked his car; and this was it.

As a freshman in high school, Cal's life was pretty simple. It revolved around only three things: baseball, girls, and, of course, cars. He was a frustration to his dad and he knew it. Dad wanted to alter his priorities to include school and church. Cal had normally discounted his Dad's continuous badgering as proof that good old Dad had no idea what it was like to be young.

Things were now coming to a head. The ultimatum had been thrown down this past week; either get the grades moving north or baseball was gone and the promised car would become a distant dream. The baseball threat was a joke. Dad loved the idea of his son being a baseball star. The car threat was probably real and infinitely more important to Cal at this moment. This had been the dance between dad and son for years: Dad pushing priorities with incentives, then with threats, and then ultimately backing down as soon as Cal made even the most modest move in the desired direction. Cal had become a very good dancer, but the dance was boring.

Actually, Cal thought his grades were fine; a solid B average. It was just that Dad had been a straight A student and expected him to deliver the same; but then grades were only part of the disappointment for dear old Dad. Cal would never be the basketball player Dad had been. Genetics had just not been agreeable. At six foot two, Dad towered over Cal's five foot five frame. Although it did not look as if Cal was ever going to be tall, by fourteen he had developed what his Dad had referred to as a thick body. He was muscled beyond his years and had sprinters speed.

Even though basketball was never going to be Cal's forte, Cal would be every bit the athlete his dad had been. As a freshman, he had already locked down the catcher's position on the varsity baseball team. He was not only the first freshman to make the varsity, to be a starter was a huge accomplishment and honor. It was something even his famous dad had not achieved. That said, Dad's name was the only two-time name on the school's "Most Valuable Player" trophy that graced the Fort Collins High School honors cabinet. Cal had dreams of changing that.

Church was another thing. It meant getting up at seven in the morning on Sunday, dressing up in a tie, and spending all morning with his mother in the old, stone, First Methodist Church downtown. Dad only attended during the holidays. He seemed to always have an excuse to miss the weekly service, and it normally revolved around something that needed to be done at the office. In Cal's mind, Dad's badgering about church was hypocritical. If Dad found other things more important than church, how could he possibly insist that he make church a priority.

It wasn't so much that he disliked going to church; he actually enjoyed the sermons and the music; Sunday school, not so much. Most of his friends from school attended other churches or none at all, so the Sunday school was lonely; and the lessons were particularly boring and juvenile; taught either by old farts that had not talked with a teenager in decades or young parents that were much better prepared to relate to babies in diapers than they were with the modern adolescent. The worst part of the young volunteer teachers, they wanted to act like they were teenagers themselves. It was sad.

Cal pulled his left arm off the window sill to grab the steering wheel and moved his right hand to the gear shifter. He pushed down on the clutch with his left foot and ran through the shift pattern, imagining the torque pushing him into the back of the bucket seat. This "four on the floor" beast would really get up go. At least that is what Uncle Bill had told him. Dad had dropped Cal off at the dealership after school today so he and his Uncle could take out one of the GTO's for a spin. Uncle Bill had promised to drive out east of town to the newly completed interstate freeway so they could let the car fly. Cal was excited. On the country roads leading to the highway, he anticipated his Uncle would bend the law a little and let him hop behind the steering wheel to try out this beast for himself. This was a time for the muscle car; Ford had the Mustang and Fairlane, Chevy had the Chevelle, Plymouth had the GSX, Dodge had the Charger, but nothing rivaled the GTO. Someday, this would be his.

He loved the way the cars looked in the showroom. Everything in this place shown like sunlight. From the glossy grey asbestos tile floor to the glossy white painted cinderblock and glass walls to the ever-important cars. Today, three cars graced the floor; their black tires looking like black licorice, glistening under the intense fluorescent lighting. Their vivid paint colors: Midnight Blue, Riviera Red, and, obviously, his favorite, the Marina Turquois; powerful colors accentuated by the lack of color surrounding them.

Looking through the windshield, Cal could see Uncle Bill and Virginia talking business. Even though he had been looking forward to the GTO drive all day, he was content sitting in the cars in the showroom. He loved them; the smell of the vinyl interiors, the shiny dashboards, the feel of the steering wheel in one hand, the shifter knob in the other. The car was a God, full of power. The showroom was full of light, like heaven.

Cal reached down to begin adjusting his seat so that he might more easily reach the wheel when he heard a tapping on the driver's side window and almost instantaneously the click of the door opening. It was not Uncle Bill, but rather one of their salesmen and he looked nervous.

"Cal, your uncle asked me to watch over you for a while. Virginia just collapsed, and he has called an ambulance."

Cal, glanced back the office where he had just watched his Uncle and Virginia in discussion. Now, through the glass wall, all he could see was Uncle Bill's back as he knelt next to Virginia's prostrate body. He could see Virginia's prone legs, but the rest of her was shielded from view by his Uncle's wide body. Cal could tell the woman lying in the floor was Virginia by her shoes. He could not recall a time when he had seen Virginia not wearing a pair of brown leather pumps. In his eyes, the shoes defined her: classy, consistent, and practical. She must have dozens of them in her closet, varying subtly only in shade and decorative embellishment. Uncle Bill was holding her hand.

* * *

Lyle laid his Virginia to rest on a typically beautiful fall day in Fort Collins. Paul's father sat at Lyle's right, Paul's mother to his left. His mother's hands lightly grasping Lyles in hers. The four of them had been together for decades, longer than any of them had the right to hope for. They were as close as siblings; not by blood, but by circumstance. They had shared the stress of the Great Depression and had prevailed; only as a result of the gifts and support they had given each other. They had never had to make promises since they knew they would always be there for one another; any promises would have been redundant.

Wet trails traced down Lyles cheeks. He wept. Not for Virginia's death; he had no doubt she was in a better place now. He wept at being separated from her for the first time in more than 50 years. He felt alone. Separation was a funny thing. He could be on a job away from Virginia for days and never miss her, knowing she would be waiting for him upon his return. Now his heart was tearing at the loss; and it had the feeling of perpetual separation had started the moment William had told him what had happened to his Virginia. He was now lost, not knowing what to do, a flag without wind.

Paul and his family, along with William stood behind the trio as the coffin was slowly lowered into the ground. Cal held his little Randall's hand. Cal was a grown-up to Randall, and he needed the comfort of his big brother. Around the Simmons clan gathered the entire corporate family of PW Simmons. Virginia was certainly loved by more than Lyle.

Chapter 20

Uncle Bill and I were interrupted by Mark, "You two have a visitor and she's a lot better looking than Tim or me." Mark led Mom up the steps to our "private" dining room.

"Mom, shouldn't you be with Dad?" I must have looked incredulous because Mom started to laugh.

"Randall, it is okay. Honest. Bob is there and he takes great care of your Dad. He'll give us a call if anything changes. If it does, we can be home in less than 15 minutes. I don't know what your Uncle told you about the Mattsons, but I needed to come here to tell you a little about that time." Then to Mark, "You know I love this place, Mark. It's a shame that I could not get my son or brother to invite me to lunch here. It's not often I get to go to an eclectic place like *The Cut Above* on someone else's dime. Mark, you just make sure that old fart, William, picks up the tab for me, okay?" She winked at Mark as he turned to walk back down the steps.

Mom plowed on, looking directly at me. "You know your Granddad sacrificed almost everything he had for his family and Lyle and Virginia. The Great Depression was hard on them and harder than any of us alive today can comprehend. In one respect, it made your Granddad one of the most generous people I have ever known and yet, in another, it led to him doing one of the worse things I could imagine by not giving that money back to the Mattsons.

"Your Dad got caught up in that. Having some spare money was a new experience for him. Even to this day, I suspect he would try to justify actions by saying he was just trying to take care of his family. Let's face it, at that time he was just overwhelmed with greed and selfishness. I think it happens to everyone at some time or another. At that time, he was faced with an opportunity to give some of it back; not because he owed it, but just because it was the right thing to do. He made the wrong decision back then. He never thought," then nodding to William, "that his brother would be the one that would have to make things right.

"William, you will never know how much Paul and I are thankful you did what you did." She paused as if she were replaying the time in her mind. "Paul never made that mistake again, and I don't think Lattimore, your Granddad," she looked to me "ever got over the shame. He never showed his face in the office again. He was so disappointed in himself. You know I think that for the rest of your Granddad's life contrition greeted him in the morning and kissed him goodnight when he laid down to sleep. I still feel sorry for him."

"It's okay, Mom, I get it and everything is good now, right?"

"I just thought you needed to hear how your Dad changed back then. You never got to see why your Dad did some of the things he did." Then smiling at Uncle Bill, "I think William might have some context that would be good for you to hear about your Dad, that's all."

With this, instead of turning the conversation over to Uncle Bill she embarked on a conversation about a time and people I had no recollection of.

* * *

Adam and Sheila Hendrick with their three young kids strapped into the back of their Dodge Polaris station wagon pulled into Fort Collins for the first time. This was an adventure. None of them had ever been to Colorado, and compared to their active lives in Palo Alto, a growing and affluent community just south of San Francisco, California, this was the real wild west. They had decided to take the risk of leaving the high energy and pace of the city that was fast becoming the center of the technology development in the entire country for an opportunity to leapfrog their peers by being part of their company's first management team outside of the region a prominent newspaper writer had recently tagged as the Silicon Valley. For Adam, the move meant a move into middle management, a new title, a small bump in pay, and a lot of risk. In the longer term, Adam was hoping that the move would also mean some serious money, prestige, and perhaps a return to the Bay Area in a few years as a Vice President.

For now, however, the title and challenge would need to be enough.

For Sheila, the move held other promise. Her family had outgrown their small apartment in Palo Alto, and she had no pretense to believe their income would keep up with the rapidly rising real estate costs. Having a comfortable home in which to raise her family would mean hours of commuting for Adam every day. In effect, a big house would come with a life in which she would raise the kids on her own. Fort Collins provided the promise of breaking the dilemma. Homes were affordable and the commute was comparatively nonexistent. Out here a ten-minute drive was long. Of course, there would be cold weather and snow, but that was part of the charm. Everything was exciting and exhilarating; a new beginning.

In order to avoid having to dig into their meager saving, Adam and Sheila had decided to drive cross-country, staying in inexpensive motels, pocketing whatever they could from the small relocation stipend that had been provided to them from the company to pay for food, gas, and hotels. Once in Fort Collins, the company had also agreed to pay for two months of temporary accommodations. Whatever they saved would be set aside to pay for the incidental costs that would undoubtedly surprise them with their first home purchase.

Adam could not help but chuckle when he glanced at his wife's face as they pulled into town in the early evening. As they exited the freeway, the young family had a short drive directly west to get to heart of Fort Collins. The sun was just disappearing behind a jet-black silhouette of mountains; the bright light of day giving way to an amazing panorama of red-orange in the western sky to a deep purple to the east behind them. The effect was breathtaking. In this instant, he knew leaving here to return to San Francisco probably was not in the cards. He could see Sheila was mesmerized and hooked.

"Adam, I love it. I never realized that moving to the country would come with this. It will be like our own special art gallery, presented to us by God every night. This is gorgeous. We need a house facing that," Sheila said staring at the sunset.

"It is nice, and we should be able to afford a great house here. Something we would never be able to buy back home; I mean in Palo Alto." Adam corrected himself, realizing that Palo Alto was no longer home. Then upon stopping at the first traffic light heading into town, "Welcome to home."

The company had already arranged for the Hendrick family to stay at a fresh, new hotel close by the University. Until they could find a house, they would cram themselves into two adjoining rooms with a small kitchenette. Adam pulled up to the hotel entrance, but rather than pulling into the parking lot to check in, Adam decided to drive on. "Let's drive around a little to get our bearings while the kids are sleeping."

Sheila made no reply, instead just looked out the side window taking in all that she could about this new small town that would now be home.

Adam turned south onto what was apparently the town's main thoroughfare toward what would eventually be their company's newest manufacturing site and the first outside of the bay area. "Let's look to see what the houses look like close to the plant. Wouldn't it be nice not to have to fight traffic to and from work? Hell, you and I might actually get to see each other occasionally."

With the kids still soundly dreaming in the back of the car, Adam and Sheila began to weave north and south through small neighborhoods. They were thrilled by both the lack of traffic and the quaintness of the communities. "Thrilled" might sound like an overstatement, but for the Hendrick family, the lack of traffic would give them back three hours in the car every day. It was as if they had taken all that was good from where they left and pulled all the cars and congestion away. No, commuting would not be an issue. It was wonderful, and Adam was beginning to forget quickly about any ideas of returning to Palo Alto in a few years. Maybe this was the place to raise his family.

The meandering car ride had brought them to an older section of town with majestic trees and dignified, large homes. "Stop, Adam, look at this home." She pointed at a house with a *Klein Realty* for sale sign planted in its front yard. "It would be perfect; slow street, nice trees, close to the schools for the kids and I think it is vacant. Pull over and let's take a look to see what we can see in the moonlight."

This was the start of Adam's introduction to Paul Simmons.

* * *

"Seriously? You found a place already. Where is it?"

Adam described the house and location to one of his new friends, a local contractor that was working on their new company facility. The contractor had lived in Fort Collins his entire life and Adam wanted his inputs on real estate in town.

"Adam, that place is the old Simmons home. It has been vacant for a few months; ever since the wife passed away. Old man Simmons kicked off a couple of years ago. You will love the place. Their two boys inherited the place and have pretty much rebuilt it from the inside out. By the way, you will likely be dealing with Joe Klein to buy the place. He has been a friend and associate of the Simmons family for years, so be careful, but he will be easier to deal with than the oldest boy, Paul Simmons.

"You know he has a reputation for being pretty hard to deal with, plus, you don't want to piss him off. He is kind of a big shot in town. He is actually developing that." The contractor pointed across the field to a stretch of buildings that would eventually become a large indoor shopping mall. "Plus, he owns the Chevy, Buick, and Pontiac dealerships in town. Shit, if you upset him, you'll have to commute from Denver."

Adam thought this old construction worker was pulling his leg. "Okay, he can't really be that scary. I can handle my own in negotiations. Besides, he if he wants to sell the place, he'll deal just like anybody else."

"Yeah, sure." The contractor smiled. "Tell me how your offer goes, okay? Oh, and be clear with your offer contingencies. He is pretty hard core with earnest money. Rumor has it that years ago, he had a customer that got laid off from his job and couldn't afford to complete the deal to buy one of the Simmons's homes, but since he had signed a contract, Paul

Simmons said 'fuck you' and had the guy thrown out of their office. He wouldn't give him a penny back and the guy killed himself. Hell, Simmons never even sent a letter of condolence. He's pretty tough. My recommendation; if you want the house, don't haggle too much; you'll just piss him off."

Adam felt the acid rising in his stomach. He had no idea what he had gotten into. His wife had fallen in love with the place their first night into town and had become even more infatuated after a brief walkthrough the house this morning. The price was well outside their budget, but Adam had expressed his confidence to Sheila that they could make a low-ball offer and get the place. It was now starting to look as though he had made a promise he was going to have trouble keeping. Sheila was going to be so disappointed. She had already picked the rooms for the kids, and after dropping him off to work, she was planning to drive around to check out the schools close to the house.

"Look, I'll just go over to this Simmons guy's office and introduce myself. How can he turn down this face?" Adam smiled.

"My recommendation, take your wife. Her face is hell of a lot better looking."

After the conversation, Adam decided that it would be best to skip work this afternoon and steal a ride from one of his co-workers to drop him off at the realtor's office. He could walk to their motel from *Klein Realty*.

* * *

The car ride was only a few miles, but for Adam it seemed to take forever. His imagination was running through scenario after scenario of dealing with Simmons. He wanted to understand if Joe Klein would be their ally in working with the Simmons. He needed his realtor to be in his camp to come up with a reasonable offer. The crusty contractor already had him thinking he had better scrap his low-ball offer strategy.

Adam had called Joe Klein to make sure he would be available that afternoon and to give him a heads-up regarding what he wanted to talk about. He was surprised at Joe's casual transparency on the call. He fully admitted he and the Simmons family had been friends and business associates for years. Although Klein acknowledged he had a close relation with Paul Simmons, he felt confident that he could adequately represent Adam and Sheila, but would completely understand if they wanted to work with a different realty office to develop the offer. Adam decided to stay with Joe.

Adam's co-worker, a fellow engineer that had also recently relocated to Fort Collins, pulled into the drive and stopped short of the office entrance. "You want me to wait?"

Adam politely thanked him for the ride, but declined the offer to wait. "I'll see you in the morning. Hopefully, we will have submitted an offer by then."

Adam got out the car and walked to the office entrance as his ride rolled out of the parking lot. Instead of entering, Adam decided to take a moment to collect his thoughts on what he wanted to discuss with Joe. Neither he nor Sheila had been a home buyer before. All he knew was this was the largest purchase they had ever made.

"You okay, Adam?" Joe Klein startled Adam. "You look positively lost. I was watching you from inside and beginning to think you changed your mind or perhaps are waiting for your wife and kids. Sheila, right?" Joe opened the door to the realty and shepherded Adam inside. "At least come inside out of the heat to wait."

"Of course, but no need to wait for Sheila. I just thought I should have a talk with you about an offer on the Simmons's place."

"Well, come on in my office then."

As Adam entered Joe's office he was surprised to find he and Joe were not alone. "Adam, meet Paul Simmons. He was just here to touch base on a couple things related to one of their developments for which we represent his company PW Simmons, I thought you would at least like to say hello."

Paul got up from his chair and stuck out his right hand to shake. "Good to meet you, Adam. Joe says you and your family might be interested in Mom and Dad's house. My brother and I would love to see a family in the place, so I won't hold you up from your conversations. Good luck."

Paul waved to Joe over his shoulder as he exited the office. "Joe, see you tomorrow. Okay?" and then disappeared behind the closing door.

Joe turned to Adam, "So you want to talk offer. Just so you know, I will present whatever you want, but I doubt Paul or William, that's Paul's brother, will be very receptive to offers below asking price."

"That was what I was afraid of, but Sheila is so in love with the house I wanted to at least give it a try. Don' t you think fifty thousand dollars is pretty steep? I mean the house is big and the location is great, but that is almost twice the price of the average home in town. I was hoping to offer maybe forty-five thousand and even at that, it is going to be a dicey to see if we can qualify for the financing." Adam paused for feedback from Joe.

"Look, I think it would be smart to start looking at other homes, perhaps closer to your new plant. PW Simmons is building some great homes in a development just north of your facility and they are right in your price range." Joe, got up to pull a home brochure from his file cabinet.

"Can we at least try on the offer?" Adam asked. "I was thinking we could offer something like forty-five thousand."

Joe turned back to Adam, a man with beer budget, a good

beer, yes, but still beer, and a champagne taste. "I'll tell you what, let's get your wife over here and pull together an offer sheet. You will need to give me a check for $900 to accompany the offer. I will present it to Paul and William tomorrow. Okay?"

* * *

Adam was glad he would be walking home this afternoon. He had so many things cluttering his mind, he could not focus. The walk would give him time to collect his thoughts. Top of mind was needing to make an appointment with his credit union to see if they would even consider financing him for the purchase. He could imagine the manager looking at him sadly and just shaking his head to inform him the loan just was not going to happen. He had already considered asking Sheila's parents for help with the down payment. He was too proud to ask his own folks. It was going to be tough enough just coming up with $900 in earnest money to accompany the offer let alone an additional thirty-six hundred bucks to make up the balance of the 10% down payment.

It was hard not to get his hopes up even though he really had no reason to expect that they would be able to pull this off. Sheila did not have a job and what little savings they did have was tied up in company stock. They had not even begun to think about the incremental money they would need to come up with for closing costs. Maybe it would be better to punt on buying the Simmons house and focus their efforts on a more practical and affordable new home close to the plant. They were beautiful homes, but not what his bride had her heart set on; and he did not want to disappoint her, at least not if he didn't need to.

Chapter 21

ADAM HAD EXTENDED his walk to take in the downtown after dropping by their hotel. Sheila and the kids had not been in the hotel room; he could only assume they were checking out the area around the home of her dreams for schools, churches, shopping, and doctors. She was doing most of the heavy lifting to make this transition work.

His walk had taken him all the way to downtown, not more than a couple blocks from the house they were intending to buy; and more importantly close to the offices of PW Simmons. The walk had emboldened him to drop in unannounced and what? Plead his case for why the Simmons should accept an offer that had yet to be made? Try to make Paul or William Simmons to realize their price was too high? As he stood by the PW Simmons entrance he realized how stupid he was being, but he walked in anyway and asked the receptionist if Paul or William was in.

The receptionist smiled with that receptionist-only type of smile, the one that made it perfectly clear that they were really the boss because they effectively controlled the keys of the kingdom. Adam was prepared for the deflating questions; either 'Do you have an appointment?' or 'Is Mister Simmons expecting you?' At that he would politely have to respond "No" and he would then be informed that Mister Simmons is busy, but if he would leave his name and number, she would make sure he got the message. Adam would have walked this entire way for nothing. Maybe it would be good if the receptionist merely blew him off; he really did not know what to say to Simmons anyway. He suspected, Joe Klein would be incensed if he knew that he was here to speak to Mister Simmons.

The receptionist surprised Paul. "Sure, Paul is in the back. I think he is just getting ready to leave early today, so you almost missed him. William normally does not come in to this office, but you should normally be able to reach him at the Simmons Auto Mall during the day. Let me see if I can steal a few minutes with Paul for you. By the way, what is your name?" The receptionist, hopped out of her chair and knocked on a door leading into a glass walled conference room. Inside Adam could see the gentleman he had met a couple hours earlier at Klein Realty along with an older fellow. The older fellow was obviously comfortable; he had his legs propped up on the conference table and his hands were clasped behind his head as he and Paul were in what appeared to be a jovial conversation.

Paul and Lyle heard the receptionist knock and promptly invited her in. "What's up, Kathy?"

"You have a young fellow out there that would like to speak with you or your brother. I thought you might want to see him before heading off to Cal's ball game."

Paul looked out through the window and spied Adam. "Oh, I think that he is the fellow that wants to buy Mom and Dad's home. Tell you what, Kathy, send him on in. It shouldn't take too long." Then to Lyle, "Lyle, tell Sam I am on my way so save me a seat right behind home plate. This game should be a good one. Win this one and we're off to Denver in a couple of days for the Championship."

Lyle pulled himself to his feet "Paul, don't be late. It hurts Cal when his daddy doesn't show in time for the games." Lyle walked out the door ahead of Kathy and gave a look of apprehension towards Adam as he walked by.

The receptionist motioned to Adam to come on back to the conference room. As Adam walked into the room she suggested "We can reschedule if you need to. Paul has to leave soon."

"Thanks, Kathy. What can I do for you, Adam, right?"

"Thank you for seeing me, Mister Simmons. I just happened to be walking downtown and wanted to come in and introduce myself more formally and perhaps talk with you about your parent's home. My wife, Sheila, loves it, but I am not sure that we will be able to afford it. In any case, I was going to make an offer tomorrow and I did not want to offend you with an amount that was too low. It's just that it is all I think we will be able to afford."

Paul, looked at his watch, knowing he needed to leave soon to make baseball games opening pitch. Looking back to Adam, "I really don't know why you came here, Adam. This is really something you need to leave to Joe Klein. I don't want to talk with you about offers. You understand? That is why we listed it with him. Now, so as not to make this meeting a waste of time for either of us, let me tell you a little about the house." Paul loved talking homes, especially when the work his company had completed had given them new life. In this case, Simmons Company had taken on the challenge of almost completely rebuilding the house from inside out. Electrical wiring and plumbing had been replaced. The old fuse box had been replaced by modern circuit breakers. The Kitchen and bathrooms had all been remodeled with the modern cabinets, fixtures, and appliances. The place was now a show home. They had maintained the quaint structural aspects of the place while giving the home new life. Paul and William had sunk way too much into the home, but this was a labor of love. A gift to his dead parents and to the town.

By the time Paul had provided Adam an overview of everything they had completed on the house, Adam was convinced even more of the value; and that they would never be able to afford it. The Simmons surely would not bend on the offer.

Paul looked to his watch again. "Shit, you held me way too long. I have to leave now."

Paul gathered his coat and left the drawings on the table. As he opened the door to leave, he called to the receptionist, "Kathy, would you show Mister Hendrick out. I am way late." Paul was out the door before Adam could thank him for his time.

"I'm sorry. It probably was not a good time for a meeting, Mister Hendrick. If you need to reschedule some more time with Mister Simmons, I'll be glad to set something up for you." Kathy offered.

"Thank you, but I don't think it will be necessary. I think I upset him enough already." Adam walked home.

The following day, Adam was surprised to get a call at the motel before heading off to work. "Joe Klein, here. Can I meet with you and Sheila to finalize the offer paperwork? I finished it up yesterday evening and was hoping to touch base with Paul at his son's ball game to butter him up, but he did not get there until the third inning and he did not look too happy, so I passed on discussing it with him. I can go over the offer with him today after you review what I have. You will need to bring a check for the $900, too. If you want, I can swing by now and meet with you both at your motel. That would be a lot easier than you having to roust the kids over to my office."

"Uh, sure. That would be fine." Then putting his hand over the receiver to mute his conversation with his wife, "Sheila, this is Joe Klein. He has the paperwork for our offer on the house. I told him we could only afford forty-five K. You okay with that as an offer?"

"Sure, I guess, but can we really afford it?" she asked.

Back into the phone, "Joe, I think it would be great to have you come by here. Can we talk about financing; too, before we submit the offer?" Adam knew that Joe had a lot of experience regarding mortgages and it was time to make sure they were not getting in over their heads on the deal.

* * *

Sheila had a fresh pot of coffee waiting in the hotel room by the time Joe knocked on the door. The room was loud with the sound of playing children even though their kids were sequestered in the adjoining room. The hotel walls provided little to no sound insulation.

Adam and Sheila had cleared a section on the small kitchen table to provide Joe some room to go over the offer and to take a look at the family's finances to see if there was really any hope of getting the financing to make the offer work, assuming the Simmons accepted the proposal.

"Look, the benefit you have is that you have some great employment history, plus, your financial ratios all work. I think the financing will go through as long as you can come up with the down payment. Even with that your monthly cost is going to be a little higher than you expected since you are going to have to pay some incremental costs for private mortgage insurance." Joe pulled out a table that outlined the monthly payment schedule for various mortgage amounts based on the current interest rates. In addition, he reviewed the maximum ratio of monthly payments to their family income that the bank would be looking for in order to approve the loan. They would be fine, although tight. The monthly payment would be about a hundred dollars higher than they had been spending on rent at their previous home.

Then moving on to the offer. Joe Klein reiterated that he was extremely skeptical that the Simmons would even consider the offer. He became even more skeptical upon learning that Adam had showed up at the PW Simmons office the previous evening to discuss the home. "Not to be rude, Adam, but you did not help yourself by pulling that stunt. Paul, was late to his own son's high school playoff game because of you and he wasn't too happy. Just let me take it from here if you really want the house. One more stunt like last night and I think you will need to write-off the house and probably look to get a different realtor. Understand?"

"Understood."

Sheila looked to her husband and then back to Joe. "Is Mister Simmons upset at Adam? I mean should we give up now?"

Joe started to laugh and belted out "Not on your life. We need to get you guys into a house. Hotels are tough enough for one or two people, but a family of five. No way. I have an appointment with Paul and William already set up for lunch to present the offer. You have the check for the earnest money?"

Sheila pulled out her purse and their checkbook and wrote out a check for the required dollar amount. "We have money in the account to cover this and my Mom and Dad have agreed to give us the rest of the down payment, but that might take a few weeks. Will that be soon enough?"

"Well that depends, when will you want to move in?"

Adam and Sheila began to feel a new sense of optimism that the house purchase would actually happen and the timing was great. What little furniture they had was already on its way from California. They had planned for the furniture to go into storage for at least one month and likely two. Closing quickly on the house might allow them to avoid the second month of storage fees on this end of the trip. Every dollar helped.

"Look, assuming you have been straight with me on all of your finances and your parents' gift of the down payment, I have one additional thing we might be able to do to make this a little easier on you two." Joe pulled out another set of papers.

"I won't show this to Paul or William unless the offer gets accepted, but this is a temporary lease agreement to let you move in before the closing. Believe it or not, William and Paul actually have hearts and I think that if we provide a reasonable rent proposal, they'd be willing to let you occupy early. Your kids would sure like that. You would give up the pool, but you could have your furniture delivered directly to the house and you could stop living out of suitcases and boxes."

Adam, Sheila, and Joe Klein agreed on a $400 monthly rent amount. Although the amount was more than they would likely spend for their mortgage payment, it would be less than the amount allocated for their temporary living. It would be significantly more comfortable and let them save money; sounded like a pretty good deal.

Joe left a little over an hour after he arrived, committing to give them a call that evening with the Simmons's response.

* * *

Adam knocked on the hotel door with his forehead; his arms full with two bags of groceries and a large box of Pampers he had picked up on the way home. After the meeting with Klein, he had taken the car to the office to get some work done.

Stopping by the grocery store on the way home was a duty that came with having the car.

Although Sheila would normally have dropped Adam at

work so she could keep the car, today she had planned to let the kids play in the hotel pool a while and then they would walk to the library. It would make for a full afternoon. The pool always wiped the kids out. They would go to sleep early tonight. She and Adam would have the evening to themselves, except for the call from Joe.

Sheila opened the door for Adam.

"Has Joe Klein called yet?" were the first words out of Adam's mouth.

"Well, I love you, too," Sheila smiled, "and, no, Joe hasn't called yet. Hopefully, no news is good news. I mean if the Simmons said no, it is pretty easy to call to tell us the deal is kaput."

Adam sat his bags down next to the sink. "Maybe they have a counter offer and Joe is pulling it together. That would be okay, as long as it isn't too expensive. I hope I didn't screw it up by going over the PW Simmons office. You should have seen Mister Simmons when he left. He seemed pretty agitated. Sounds like he hadn't even cooled off by the time he had gotten to his son's baseball game."

There was a loud knock at the door. Looking out the peep hole, Adam could see Paul Simmons and another man, a bigger, taller version of Paul, waiting in the hall.

Adam whispered, "Shit, Sheila. Its Mister Simmons and another fellow. I'll bet it is his brother; and they do not look happy."

"Well, let them in. Let's see what they want."

Adam opened the door, but before he could get a word out of greeting, Paul Simmons took control. "Hello Adam. This is my brother William. Can we come in? We need to have a serious talk."

The request was more of an order than a question when coming from Paul. He was several inches taller than Adam and outweighed him by at least forty pounds and his brother was even larger. Adam moved to the side to let the imposing figures enter.

"So, you must be Sheila. Where are the kids?" William asked.

"Ben and Bernice are playing in the tub and our oldest, Lyle, is in the other room watching TV." Sheila responded.

"Lyle, nice name," William replied.

"Look, if you don't mind, can we get down to business?" Paul interrupted.

Sheila was taken back by the elder Simmons apparent directness, almost to the point of being rude. Small talk was obviously not this man's strong suit, but then again, she did not want a conflict with him, so she motioned the men to her kitchen table and asked them if they would like some coffee or tea.

"Thank you, but that will not be necessary, but one of you might want to tell me what the hell this is." Paul held up the temporary occupancy lease they had signed for Joe Klein earlier this very morning.

Adam was taken back, "Well, yes, it, uh, uh it was just a temporary agreement to let us move into the house before we could close; but if it is inappropriate . . . or if the rent is not enough, that is okay. We will stay here. I am sorry that it has upset you."

Paul looked to William with a stern face and slowly began to laugh. "My god, boy, we're joking. There is no way a family should be living out of boxes if they don't have to." He tore up the lease and threw it on the table. "You move in tomorrow. Now don't piss us off by not getting your financing straight." Paul and William stood up.

William reached into his pocket and fished out a couple keys to the home and tossed one to Adam the other to Sheila. "We'll let ourselves out. Touch base with Joe to schedule closing."

After the door shut, Adam looked to Sheila. "What was that?"

"You got me, but I think we have a new home." Sheila threw her arms around Adam, burying her face in his neck and started to cry.

Chapter 22

"Your Dad and Uncle Bill thought they were so funny the way they stormed the Hendrick's hotel room. I'm surprised the Hendricks didn't pack up and leave town for good. I mean what businessmen act that way; and to think Joe thought it was funny, too. I will never understand men." Mom could barely keep from laughing.

I actually knew the Hendrick family pretty well. Their oldest boy, Lyle was only a few years younger than me and eventually joined our firm, PW Simmons several years ago. In effect, selling my grandparent's house for a little below market was an investment Dad and Uncle Bill made a few decades ago that was still paying dividends.

My Uncle Bill added, "Randall, your Mom has no sense of humor. Let's grab a quick lunch, I think it is time we got back home to see your Dad."

After we promised to come back for dinner, Mark bagged up four sandwiches for us to eat at the house. Tonight, he had arranged staffing so that he and Tim could join us.

* * *.

I carried one of the boxes of Simmons' history back into Dad's room. On its lid, rode two plates with sandwiches, one for me and one for the nurse, along with two cans of Coke. I figured digging through the box of pictures and files would help pass the time as I kept Dad company; or perhaps, he was keeping me company. Bob, got up from the padded chair as I walked in, sacrificing the comfortable seat for my benefit.

"Don't worry, Bob. Stay there, I can sit here in the folded chair next to the dresser drawers."

"You sure, it's no problem."

"No, seriously, stay there. Over here I can flip on the lamp without bothering Dad. How is he doing?"

"Why not ask him yourself?"

I raised my eyes to Bob as if to say 'and he is okay?' Bob nodded back. Dad was awake again.

"Dad, how are you? I'm sorry I wasn't here this morning. Uncle Bill, Mom and I went over to *The Cut Above*. We figured you wouldn't mind."

"That's good, Randall. Can I have a sip of water? I am so thirsty."

I looked to Bob and he nodded that it was okay. I pulled Dad up gently with my left arm as Bob pushed the controller to raise the bed. Dad was so light. I was shocked at how his body had diminished. I held the cup to his parched lips and he sucked thirstily.

"Son, now the only thing that would make that better would be a little scotch to go with it." Dad smiled. "You should have been here earlier. Bob and I got to talk a little bit about my friends that are waiting for me. I suspect I might be seeing them full time pretty soon.

"I talked with Cal, he is so strong and still playing ball. He says hi and that he misses you. He wanted me to tell you he is sorry for leaving you so alone." Dad started to drift back into his staring look.

Bob touched my arm "Randall let's lower the bed again. I

think your Dad is done for a little while. Let's stay here though. Maybe he'll come back again."

I got the message; perhaps Dad would not come back again. Perhaps he was starting his journey to be with his friends of the past.

I sat down, kicked my legs up on the edge of the bed and pulled out a stack of pictures and folders from the middle of the box. I flipped through the stack until I got to a picture of my brother Cal. Cal was a full decade older than me. He was more of a second father than a brother. He took me under his wing. When I was little, I remember him always holding out his hand for me to grab and walking slowly so that I might keep up. He didn't even mind me wanting to hang with him when he was in high school; even going so far as to talk his high school baseball coach into letting me be the team's batboy for their home games. My heart soared when I was with Cal. That same feeling was coming back as I looked at his picture now.

I flipped the picture over to see in Mom's neat writing

Cal Simmons, Fort Collins High, 1970

The picture was one I was very familiar with. It had graced our fireplace mantel for years. It was a color photo that showed my brother in his Fort Collins High School Lambkins purple and gold uniform. He was casually holding a bat low with both hands, the bat barrel just leaning against his right shoulder, almost touching his ear. On his face, he had a slight smile that only hinted at the love he had for the game. I had also been a Lambkin, and I still get ribbed when I mention our team's name to friends, back home. The lamb just did not throw fear into one's mind when our team took the field, but my brother's bat sure did.

* * *

"Come on Randall, hop up here, you can ride with me." Cal grabbed his little brother's hands to pull him up to the high first step getting on the bus. This was going to be Randall's first bus ride and making it even more exciting, it was to take a long trip to his big brother's championship game.

As he walked down the aisle to the rear of the bus, Cal's friends all took their turns mussing his hair. Cal had told him this was for good luck, since he had two roles for the team: first their batboy and secondly, he was their good luck charm. They had won every game in which Randall had performed his duties as batboy; their only loss all season being an away game against a team in Denver prior to the start of their league season. It had been their first game of the season. Randall had not been at that game.

Today's game would be rematch with the same school; for the AAA State Championship. Making the game even more exciting, the game was going to be played in Mile High Stadium, a huge complex that served as the home for both the state's pro football team and a minor-league baseball team. The stadium could hold everybody in Fort Collins and still have a lot of room left over. Cal had promised Randall he could run in the outfield prior to the game.

Originally, Randall's parents were to bring him down in a separate car, but Cal had pestered his coach and begged his parents for permission to have Randall ride with the team. His justification was it was the Lambkins first visit to the championship game and it was only right to have the whole team experience it; and Randall was part of the team. The team had all promised to be polite and take care of the seven-year-old. It also did not hurt that the team's star player was the primary instigator.

Cal had had a great year as the Lambkin's starting catcher. Not only had he thrown out the vast majority of runners trying to steal on him, he had rewritten the record books for almost every category of offence. His 18 home runs, his .565 batting average, and 45 runs batted in this season along with his career mark of 43 home runs were all records. He was being billed as the most feared hitter in the state. For this game the Denver Post had placed his picture on the front page of their sports section. The coach certainly wanted to keep Cal happy. He represented their best shot at upsetting the number one ranked team in the state.

Today they would face a team that had three stars that were being billed as future pro ball players. The first player was a center fielder that ran like the wind, Marvin Brown. He had led their respective league in stolen bases, doubles, and triples, plus he could pretty much run down any fly ball in the center part of the outfield. The word was that if you wanted to get a hit to center, you better hit the ball on the ground through the infield or smack the ball over the fence. Marvin had a gun for an arm, too.

The other two stars were bookend, twin-brother pitchers, one lefty, one righty. They were known as the M&M brothers; Micky and Mark Madsen. They both were rumored to throw the ball over 90 miles an hour. Micky, the left hander also had a great curve ball; Mark brought a hard slider. Between the two of them, they had rewritten the record books for strikeouts and earned run average. Both pitchers averaged more than two strikeouts per inning. The only good thing for the Lambkins was that only one of the Madsen brothers could play at a time, but it was likely they would get to see both of them pitch before the day was done.

Cal had only faced Micky in their first game and he had to admit, Micky was impressive. Cal had struck out, popped up, and finally had struck a well hit liner to the alley between right and center for a double. He had only gotten to bat three times. Micky had seen to that by striking out 16 batters over seven innings. Cal and the rest of the Lambkins were looking forward to improving on their performance. Given that it looked like half the town was coming to watch, they wanted to prove they were the better team; they were taking no prisoners today.

The bus ride was long and quiet. Even at his young age, little Randall could tell the team was anxious and nervous. To him, it was scary for his brother to be stepping into the batter's box to face the M&M brothers. Randall was always amazed at how Cal could seem to hit any ball the pitchers threw at him, but now his brother had told him the guys that they would face today threw so hard it would make the other pitchers look slow. That was real scary for Randall. Randall's eyes could not even follow the pitch in their normal games. He could not imagine how fast the Madsen brothers must throw. He hoped his brother would not get hit. He did not want Cal to get hurt.

Chapter 23

Today the crowd was huge, at least by high school baseball standards. Still, in spite of being the largest number of people Cal had ever played in front of, the stadium still had plenty of empty seats. The feeling of first walking out onto the field was disconcerting; shocking the senses with vibrant colors, concentrated aromas, and never-ending echoes. The aromas were penetrating; the overwhelming smell of chlorophyll intensified by the green of the sod; the acrid musky odor of dirt accentuated by the red of the infield. More shocking to the senses was the quiet down on the playing field. It was as if the stadium sucked up all the sound of the fans and had just left the crack of the bat and the staccato pops of the baseball hitting mitts. The pops reminded Cal of a rifle shots. It was funny how the crowd was muffled, but the game sounds seemed amplified. It made Mark Madsen's fastball even more intimidating as he warmed up to throw the first pitch. Cal would bat second for the Lambkins and he was intent on making the Madsen brothers; and more importantly, the uppity fans from the larger Denver school, know that the Lambkins were gentle in name only.

Directly behind home plate sat a number of pro scouts. They were obvious by the notebooks they held in their laps, the stopwatches that hung from their necks and the radar guns that sat on the wall in front them. They were here mainly to get another good look at the Madsen brothers. It was rumored that they would both be drafted in the amateur draft in a few weeks. This would be as good an opportunity as Cal would ever get to show that he had what it took to make it in the big leagues.

Mark Madsen made short work of the Lambkins first batter. His first pitch was hard and inside and had the batter bailing out of the batter's box even though the ball was only a few inches inside. Madsen had accomplished what he wanted. The batter was unnerved; more accurately, he was afraid. The next three pitches were grooved down the middle of the plate, but the batter only managed one weak swing on strike three. The batter walked back to the dugout to take a seat.

As he passed Cal he only said "Man he is fast."

Cal took his place in the box. Mark had not pitched in their first game of the season, but Cal was prepared for what he knew Mark would be bringing.

Wanting to impress the scouts, Mark Madsen had no intentions of letting the upstart catcher from a small town stuck in the middle of corn fields get a hit. He started him out with a hard slider on the outside part of the plate. Cal was late on his swing; just catching a part of the ball and fouling it off into the ground. The second pitch came in hard, inside, high. It was the Madsen's way of telling the hitter who was boss. Cal did not move; letting the pitch pass just below his elbows and barely missing his chest. This was Cal's way of telling the pitcher he would not be intimated. The third pitch was another fastball, low and over the inside corner of the plate. Cal turned on the pitch lacing a hard liner down the left field line and just short-hopping the left outfield wall. Cal cruised into second base with a standup double. Cal one, Madsen zero. The scouts all put down their radar guns and began to scribble notes in their scorebooks.

By the time Cal had come to bat a second time, the Lambkins were trailing 2-0. They had failed to get Cal home in the first inning, and as Cal dug his cleats into the batter's box to lead off the 4th inning, the team was already beginning to feel defeated. Mark started off Cal the same way he had in the first, with a hard slider. This time, Cal was ready and made solid contact sending the pitch into the seats behind center field, leaving the Denver team's star center fielder, Marvin Brown, at the wall standing to watch the ball sail over his head. Cal two, Madsen zero.

It was a mammoth shot and obviously shook Mark Madsen. He proceeded to walk the next two Lambkins and when a wild pitch allowed the runners to advance to second and third bases, the coach for the Denver team called time out to bring in the other Madsen brother. It was not how Mark Madsen wanted to finish his last high school game.

Micky Madsen started out well with a strikeout, but a weak grounder from the next hitter allowed the runner from third to score, knotting up the game at two runs apiece. After the weak grounder, Micky strung together five straight strike outs before facing Cal to lead off the 6th inning. Micky wanted to make it six straight strikeouts and started Cal out with his best pitch, a curve ball intending to get Cal guessing so that he could put him away with fastballs. Cal recognized the pitch right out of Micky's hand and launched it deep into the seats behind left field. Cal three, Madsen zero and the Lambkins took the lead in the game, 3-2.

The Denver team pulled ahead to win with two runs in the 7th inning, but Cal had shown off his talent. Not only had he gone three for three against two of the best pitchers in the state, he had also shown off his arm; throwing out the speedy Marvin

Brown twice. The first came in the 1st inning as Marvin had taken a large lead off first. Cal had picked him off without even giving the runner a chance to try to steal second. The next time came as Marvin attempted to steal second in the 3rd inning. Respecting Cal's quick release, Marvin had taken a smaller lead this time. The smaller lead tipped the advantage to Cal as he fired a bullet to second, snuffing out the attempted theft of second by a full step. Cal had proven himself. After the throw to second he turned to the backstop to see the scouts smiling and shaking their heads in amazement. Cal could almost see himself now in the major leagues. He smiled and pulled the catcher's mask back over his face. Who needs straight A's in school?

* * *

The June amateur baseball draft did not disappoint. He had been picked in sixth round by a team from San Diego; drafted higher than any of the star ball players he had faced a just a few short weeks earlier. Not only was it surprising to be drafted so highly, it also meant that Cal might be able to negotiate a small signing bonus. These early rounds were typically reserved for talented players coming out of power house programs in southern California, Texas, or Florida; places where baseball was played year-round. In the southern states, baseball was a way of life. In Colorado, baseball season was short; limited to spring and summer. Even spring was questionable since winter would often reassert itself as late as early June with snow flurries. This year, Cal had confounded the system and he would start in the pro instructional league as soon as he signed his contract.

He had yet to discuss his decision to sign with the pro team and forego college for the time being. He was not looking forward to the discussion. Although he knew Dad would privately beam with pride at his accomplishment, it would not be as much as he would have had the news been that he had been accepted into college. In Dad's opinion, a college education was critical now more than ever. The world had advanced and to be educated was to be successful. Baseball was nothing more than a game that was meant to be left behind as his son moved from adolescence into adulthood. A career in baseball was nothing more than a child's dream; and one that could fizzle away in a blink of the eye, just long enough time for a collision at home plate to steal away the physical talent God had given.

Dad did not get it. This was Cal's big chance to make it big, to play on TV, to be famous. It was his destiny and he planned on realizing it no matter what his Dad said. It was hard to take Dad's insistence on college seriously, considering that he had never bothered going back to school himself. It certainly had not hurt him and his career. PW Simmons was doing great. Besides, Cal could tell his Dad was actually excited about the prospects of him becoming a pro ball player in spite of his protestations. Hell, he had even sent Arlin down to San Diego, his future baseball home, to look at land just north of the city for a potential housing development sight.

The land included what Dad thought would be almost 2,000 acres of prime real estate positioned to grow rapidly in value over the next decade. Today the area was largely undeveloped and yet bordered wonderful beaches to the west and orange groves to the east. It would be PW Simmons's largest investment to-date and one that would stress their finances and management capabilities, but in Dad's opinion, it was a paradise and a huge opportunity; even though he had never visited the site. Dad had justified the acquisition by saying they could not just build in Fort Collins forever; they needed to expand.

Cal could not remember his Dad talking of expansion before this summer. Amazingly, since the draft, not only had expansion become the prime focus, but San Diego had become the chosen place for the expansion. The idea that PW Simmons would consider buying development land more than twelve hundred miles away from their current operations was validation of his Dad's excitement. His mouth said no, but his wallet was yelling go, go, go.

Yes, even though Dad was going to fight him for passing on college, he knew it was the right thing to do. His Dad would make the same choice if he had had the opportunity to play pro baseball.

Chapter 24

I FLIPPED OVER A couple more pictures, looking for one that I had cherished forever. It was just an old color snapshot from Mom's little Kodak Instamatic. In it she had captured Cal and me walking to the bus for the return ride to Fort Collins after the state championship game, a day more than three decades ago. I guess the picture would not look like much to anyone else; just a faded color print of an older boy in a dirty baseball uniform looking down at the little brother's hand he was holding. I had been dressed in a miniature version of Cal's uniform, even down to same number 5, as we walked into to the sunset. When Mom had gotten the pictures back from the developer she had almost thrown this picture into the trash can, saying that the sun's glare had ruined it. True, the sun had ruined the contrast and color; and its brilliance had resulted in a harsh white flare that surrounded Cal's head. For me the picture was perfect. Cal was holding my hand and his face shown like a God. Not finding the picture, I decided to make a note to remind myself to ask Mom about it. I had hoped to take it home with me as a reminder of my brother.

    I gathered up the pictures and folders from my lap and

placed them on the floor next to the box, pulling Dad's blue book from my pocket.

Dearest, Cal, I pushed, you pushed back. Maybe I needed to pull a little. I am so sorry I let you down.

Love, Dad

* * *

This was bullshit, Cal thought to himself. Drafted in June to his life's dream; to be drafted again two months later was a nightmare. Winning the lottery was supposed to be a good thing; that is, unless it was the U. S. Selective Service that ran the lottery. Cal had won the lottery and lost big time. He would need to hang up his cleats for the time being and hope that some team would still remember him in a couple of years. He had kicked himself knowing that had he gone to college he would have been able to get a postponement and with the growing public outrage over the war, he suspected he might have been able to avoid donning the green fatigues altogether. Deferment was not an option now. The list for potential deferments was long, but being a pro-ball player was not among them.

He had left directly from the instructional league to report without ever returning home. He had no desire to hear dear old Dad and his "I told you so" voice drive home how important college was. He now wished he had taken those extra couple days out of his baseball schedule to spend them with his family. In fact, he was now convinced that had he solicited his father's help perhaps he might have avoided Vietnam. He might have been able to serve out his 23 months of service state-side, or even better, Germany.

Unlike previous US wars, Vietnam was an unrelenting

pressure cooker. In this war, the GI would see more combat in their first couple months than the WWII veteran would have experienced over the entire war. Here, battle was continuous, filled with almost daily skirmishes that could kill you. Cal quickly realized how many of his compatriots might never get the chance to see family again. He hoped he would not be among that unlucky population. Combining the pressure with youth, the average soldier was only 21, fully five years younger than had fought on previous wars; drugs and a lack of discipline was rampant. Cal was lucky to have avoided the lack of discipline by being accepted into the Rangers 75th infantry regiment. Unlucky for Cal was the fact that the 75th was one of the few regiments still engaged in heavy fighting as President Nixon was trying to find a way to personally save face while pulling troops out of the region. The war had become a huge cluster fuck and it was as if everyone in the world knew it except for the 75th. They continued to salute and fight. Today they were on another one of their long-range patrols into enemy territory.

As his patrol marched quietly through the jungle he pondered how he would describe patrol to his family when he got home. In one sense, the term ironic came to mind in that the silence led to boredom and at the same time a heightened sense of attention. One would think the boredom of the hours long hike would numb one's thought, and yet the stress in knowing that at any moment the peace could be shattered by staccato of guns firing and the all-too familiar thwip-thwip as the bullets cut the air was both exhilarating and fatiguing. The problem with the term irony was, as his English teacher had stressed, irony should be used typically to provide humor, and there was no humor in what they were doing today. No, perhaps sardonic was a better term. The quiet was a sardonic foreboding of what was to come.

The beloved huey copters had landed for the briefest of

moment, just long enough to drop their cargo of soldiers in the waist-high grass, leaving them stranded miles from any semblance of safety. This was just another day at the office, although this "office" was hot, humid, and filled with bugs and spiders as large as one's hand. The hueys would magically show up again several hours later at an agreed rendezvous point and return them to camp; hopefully, with all GI's intact. Sometimes this was true, but normally not.

The smells of the jungle were odd, not something Cal could get used to. Although the vegetation was intense, no smell of chlorophyll filled the air. Instead, the nose was accosted by a putrid odor of mud combined with rotting plants, not unlike the compost pile his dad had maintained in their backyard back home. The stink combined with the heat and humidity made each step labored and they had another twenty thousand or so more to go before today's patrol would be done. Their destination to the north was just an X on a folded map referencing a non-descript hill number. A number that would be forgotten tomorrow. The ground represented by the X would be littered with NVA, North Vietnamese Army, casualties.

The goal today involved engaging Charlie on their turf, a well-established set of tunnels that served as a base to ambush South Vietnamese soldiers, GIs, civilians, pretty much anything that walked on two legs. The Americans' job, meet vicious with vicious and kill anything that moved. It had been their mode of operation since he had arrived.

Eradicating Charlie from the tunnels was Cal's specialty. He had volunteered as a tunnel rat upon joining his platoon. He was made for the job; short of stature, but strong as a bull, great vision, adept with his hands, and capable of moving quickly from a squat position. Half a year ago, he had hoped his physical abilities would serve to make him rich, now they served to kill quickly and effectively. He hated killing, but at least in the dark of the tunnels he never had to see the faces of the men or women as he took their lives. For his buddies above ground, they would live with those faces forever.

Their sergeant stopped and quietly knelt down, motioning for the rest of the platoon to do likewise. He could see the hill that represented their objective. Not really much of a hill, just a small rise that barely lifted the green canopy of low trees and grass. They assumed that they remained undetected, surprise would be on the side of the Americans.

Thwip-thwip-phthit. The "phthit" a sound that signaled that one of the bullets had found its mark. The sergeant, collapsed forward into the grass; a body that had instantly lost its animation. Sarg was dead before he hit the ground. Cal poked his head just high enough to draw fire and to determine from where the shots were originating. He saw three quick flashes from a tuft of elephant grass followed by the loud, tell-tale snap-snap-snap of the AK-47. He fired a quick burst into the grass, not expecting to kill, but to drive the Charlie back under ground. Hell, the elephant grass was so tough, he wasn't even sure the bullets would make it through. He made mental note of the grass location. He would return to this location in search of an entrance to the tunnels.

Undeterred by the loss of their sergeant, the team moved quickly to enact their attack plan that had been established back at camp. Everyone knew their duty and the mission progressed unabated. Eight of their team progressed to the west with the intent of setting up a horizontal firing line on a series of huts that was well behind the tunnels. Cal's portion of the team would spread in a line to the south and slowly progress as far as the first tunnel entrance. The firing line would occur along an "L" shaped pattern; the intent was to overwhelm with machine-gun fire. Cal would move into the tunnels to drive Charlie above ground into the deadly fire. The objective: no prisoners.

The entire action was expected to take no more than 30 minutes, after which the team would move quickly approximately two miles east to their pre-arranged evac site - a break in the jungle just large enough for the two hueys to land, one at a time, and rescue the platoon.

The team moved quickly into their places and the action began with the launching of several grenades from the vertical portion of the "L." All hell broke loose in an all-out fire-fight.

Cal had already dropped his M16, useless in the tight quarters below ground, and holstered an additional 45 cal. pistol. He dropped a hand grenade through a small camouflaged trap door in the jungle floor just behind the elephant grass from which he had originally spotted the muzzle flashes. This was the access that had provided the Charlie sniper the shot that had turned Sarg into their first and, hopefully, only casualty. Immediately after the grenade explosion, Cal dove in through the small opening, not waiting for the dust to settle. Surprise and speed were everything in flushing the tunnel.

In his left hand, Cal carried his K-bar, a vicious-looking, and equally effective knife; in his right a semi-automatic .45 pistol. A flashlight was clipped to his belt, but Cal had rarely used this tool. He felt that the risk of marking himself as a target was much higher than any benefit the short beam of light provided. Also, clipped to his belt, Cal carried two hand grenades. He hated using the grenades below ground due to the concussion, but they had saved his life more than once. In a small satchel strapped to his side, he carried a small timed detonator attached to a block of C4 explosive.

Cal's strong thighs of a catcher allowed him to move with a quickness and speed that belied his size in the narrow, low tunnels. The tunnels had been designed to accommodate a significantly smaller human than Cal even though he was only

5'8" tall. He moved with his legs spread wide to avoid the small traps that would have been dug into the floor of the tunnel to slow or stop intruders. The traps, though primitive, were extremely effective; typically, a set of punji stakes set into a hole with their barbed, razor sharp points poised no more than a foot below the tunnel floor. A misstep and the tunnel rat's leg would be impaled by no fewer than a half dozen stakes, leaving him helpless until Charlie came to finish him off. For Cal, the hand grenades would at least guarantee that Charlie would at least have to sacrifice himself in the process.

Cal waited briefly to orient himself in the darkness before moving off. His objective was twofold: to push Charlie above ground and to find and destroy a store of ammunition that was critical to the North Vietnamese in their raids along the Ho Chi Minh Trail.

The tunnels were a series of drops and curves. Each drop would take him a step closer to the munitions dump. He would set the C4 charge to take out the dump, knowing the blast would likely take out the entire tunnel and all of its occupants, both man and animal, through the actual blast, cave in, or sheer concussion. For Cal, once the charge was set, he would have two minutes to get out. The challenge would be kill as many occupants on the way down so he did not need to fight on the way out; there would be no time.

He moved noiselessly and quickly through the dark, his left forearm serving as his guide as he followed the tunnel downward, mentally making note of each turn so as not to get confused in his rise from this hell. He stopped once, twice to listen for signs of Charlie. This second time he heard breathing directly in from of him. Hell, he had almost run right into his nemesis, invisible in the blackness. Cal, fired once high, once low; heard the cry and fall. He proceeded trampling over the victim on the ground, stopping only long enough to run the

K-bar across the fallen soldier's neck to ensure the kill was complete. There could be no surprises on the way out.

Cal smelled water and felt the tunnel wall become slippery. He slowed. The wet meant he was likely approaching the water source for the entire system, a well that would be accessed by a vertical shaft. To fall into the shaft would mean a slow death by drowning. Cal pulled out his flashlight for a brief flash of light to spot what would be well shaft extending downward to water and upward to the surface. He jumped across and continued his journey. The musty dirt smell returned, and he left the mold odor behind.

He heard noise and saw dim, indirect light ahead. A couple more steps and he could see a hole in the floor of the tunnel dropping to another level from which the excited voices were emanating. Although he understood nothing of what was being yelled, he suspected he had found the dump. It would only be moments before he would encounter Charlie, hand-to-hand, as they rallied to bring ammo to the surface to repel the Americans. The first came toward Cal carrying a light in one hand and using his other to balance a wooden crate full of loaded bullet clips to the surface. He had almost run into Cal before realizing that his enemy was there. Cal shot him and jumped into the munitions dump, just a squat room, no more than 10 by 12 feet filled with AK 47s, bullets, clips, hand grenades, RPGs, and two North Vietnamese. Cal dispatched them with two quick shots. In the close quarters shots were both effective and deafening. Cal knelt to set the charge.

He pulled his flashlight and turned it on. There would be no time to be concerned about being a target on the way out. If he got caught up in a battle below ground after the charge was set, he was dead anyway. He started the timer and ran. He moved quickly, jumping the dead munitions carrier that lay at the entrance to the room, up to the next level and jumping the slimy well. Almost to his first kill, Cal made a mistake. He had not noticed the punji stake pit on the way down; his spread legs had straddled the trap without ever being aware of its presence. On the way up, moving quickly, he ran with his legs straight below him, using the glare of the flashlight to point out risks. Even with the flashlight he did not notice the small drop in the tunnel floor until it was too late. His foot broke through a thin grass matte that had been covered with dirt as camouflage. His leg did not stop until it hit the bottom of a two and half foot-deep hole lined with jagged, barbed sticks that easily punctured through pants, boots, and skin. The top row of stakes was embedded into the hole's wall pointing downward to prevent the leg from being pulled out. Cal was as good as dead.

Above ground the battle was dying as quickly as it had started. The machine gun fire of the well-trained Rangers had decimated the rag-tag Viet Cong soldiers. They were now mopping up; making sure the dying were dead. They now awaited Cal to come up from the darkness, having finished his task; expecting him to surface at any moment. They heard two sounds. First, a muffled blast from close to the surface, was accompanied by a cloud of dust evacuating from the hole that Cal had entered no more than ten minutes earlier. The second explosion, larger and deeper followed quickly by smaller blasts accompanied by a series of dust clouds coming from here-to-fore unknown places where tunnels punctured the surface either as firing posts or ventilation shafts. The tunnel was now dead. Cal had not made it out; casualty number two.

Chapter 25

I don't think I ever got over losing my brother. At nine years old, I understood he was dead, but I could not understand why. At baseball games, I still catch myself concentrating on the catcher's play conjuring up in my mind how Cal would have blocked that ball better, would have thrown that runner out, or would have hit that pitch over the wall. In my imagination, Cal lives on and probably always will.

I think he does in Dad' mind, too. Dad's eyes opened and he saw the book in my hand. "So where are you in my little book, Randall?"

I was taken back by Dad's question. "Dad, you're awake. Sorry I didn't notice."

Dad tilted his head to look back to the book as if emphasizing his question.

"Oh, um, just thinking about your note to Cal."

Dad Smiled. "He is okay, now. I was just talking with him. We even got the chance to play a little catch. My gawd, he throws so hard." Then Dad drifted off.

Mom tapped on the door and came into the room. I am not sure why she felt compelled to knock before entering, but I think she was beginning to think of this as my private time with Dad, a time that she was reluctant to encroach on.

"Randall, you have been in here for a couple hours. You want to take your dear old Mom out for a walk; or perhaps a brief car ride down to the shopping mall."

I'm not sure, Mom. I'd hate to miss it if Dad wakes up again."

To this, Bob, piped in "Randall, I don't think you need to worry about your Dad waking up, at least for the next couple of hours. I just gave him a couple drops for his pain, so I think he'll be out for a while. Go ahead with your Mom. Your uncle and I will be here and we will call you if there are any changes."

"Alright, Mom. Let's go, and I'll drive. You want to ride in the Mustang or your car?"

"Let's try out that fancy, fast rental of yours. I'm not so old, like your uncle, that I can't bend myself into that car." She smiled knowing full well she was only half the size of Uncle Bill.

Our first direction was south toward the mall although I have no idea why Mom was thinking of shopping at a time like this. As we drove south, Mom tapped me on the arm and motioned me to take a turn fully two blocks early and we progressed through a section of older homes, then into the parking lot of a small, established set of professional buildings. It was a mall of a different type than I had expected. She motioned to a slot in front of a relatively non-descript, low brick building. It was a visit I was ill prepared for. The sign to the right of the front door, *Wright's Mortuary*.

"Mom, why are we here?"

"Randall, I need to make a couple of decisions and I have been putting them off for weeks. Don't you think it is about time I made them?"

"Well, sure. I guess so, but haven't you and Dad already figured out what you want to do when you die?"

Mom laughed and then started to cry. I had no idea what to do, so I sat there, not offering consolation, understanding, or comfort. I was incapable of handling my own feelings. I was a cad; hopeless and helpless. Mom sniffled, collected herself as she always had and looked to me, "Let's go in. They are waiting for us." She opened the door and headed in without looking back.

I sat there a moment longer than I should. I had never been in a mortuary before and entering now meant I had to acknowledge Dad was leaving soon. I was not prepared. Big tough Randall couldn't handle it and yet, my little frail Mom approached the challenge with a bravery I did not possess. I was proud of her, ashamed of myself. I opened my car door and went in.

Inside was not what I had expected. Of course, I really did not have any expectations. It was the first time I had ever stepped into a mortuary. There were four small padded arm chairs situated around a small coffee table. On the table sat a Bible, a Koran, and Book of Mormon. Next to the books was a box of tissues and an ashtray. Apparently, the local ordinance that prohibited smoking in business establishments did not apply here; or at least Mister Wright was not going to enforce them. On one wall was mounted a large television. The set was turned off and as near as I could tell its likely use was limited to demonstrating the services of Wright Mortuary. Opposite the television was the entrance to a small, quaint funeral parlor, just large enough to accommodate groups of twenty or less, along with a casket. Behind a receptionist desk was a hallway and a door that appeared to be the entrance to a small conference area. I could see a portion of the conference table through the open door.

As I entered, Mom was already in whispered conversation with the receptionist, almost as if it would be disrespectful to actually carry on a conversation at normal volume. I sat down in the closest of the four chairs. Everything was hushed, at least until Mister Wright entered through the hallway from some hidden office protected by the receptionist's desk. He walked over to greet us.

"Sam, why don't you come on back so we might discuss Paul. Your son is welcome to join us, if you would like." I stood up and followed them both into the small conference room.

The room was plain, but yet showed an excellent taste. The art on the wall, although minimalist, was original. The wall color, a grayish tan, had had just the slightest degree of gloss. Opposite the entrance door, the windows ran from floor to ceiling. Opaque vertical blinds, the same shade as the wall, lined the windows and provided for complete darkness if desired. The carpet, a rich gray berber. The mood of the room was set; somber, but not hopeless. The table was a rich, dark mahogany, the chairs were matching wood with black leather seat pans. In the center of the table, a tray with both coffee, tea, and cookies had been set. Next to the tray, another box of tissues.

Mom sat down facing the windows. Mister Wright poured a cup of tea for her and placed it on the table to Mom's left. "Randall, coffee or tea?" he asked of me.

I elected to pass on the beverage and sat down next to Mom and awaited Mister Wright to start.

I had to give Mister Wright credit. I have never seen an individual be so kind and respectful and, at the same, be so efficient. First, he ran through a number of options for Dad's ultimate disposal. Disposal is my term, not Mister Wright's. Instead he used language that suggested transition. He made sure not to diminish any comment or question and Mom's every decision was "excellent."

He ran us through a series of questions that opened or closed options. One of Mom's first calls involved burial or cremation. He made sure she was aware of both the financial and emotional ramifications of the selection. Dad had been clear that cremation was his choice, but Mom was seriously having difficulty moving in that direction. She could not bear the idea of her husband of more than fifty years being burned to ash. Mister Wright appeared to understand. His empathy and experience allowed Mom to come to grips with ethical, religious, and emotional concerns at her own pace.

Ultimately, Mom decided that Dad wanted cremation and, therefore, it was the only right decision. Cremation made any discussion of open casket moot; thank God. I was already having difficulty imagining talking about my Dad at his funeral, seeing his dead face would have made it impossible.

Mister Wright led Mom and I through a series of other necessary decisions including the service structure, the timing, and participants. Dad did not want a public memorial service, preferring something that could be held quietly in the Wright funeral parlor. Here, Mom also wanted to honor Dad's wish, but Wright suggested the Simmons family had lived in the town for so long and had such an impact on the community, she might be surprised at the number of people that would want to pay their respects. Perhaps she should plan on a memorial service at their church where the room would provide for a larger group. Mom relented, but made me promise not to mention this to Dad.

Mister Wright reserved the last part of the meeting to walk Mom and me through what to expect when Dad died. He provided us each a card with a phone number. No matter what time, this phone number would be answered and that would start the process going for Wright's staff. His team would come to Mom's house, they would quietly and respectfully wrap the body and take it from the home. He had set up another team to arrive the following day to work with the hospice group to remove the bed Dad would have died in. He then proceeded to go through a checklist of items Mom would need to address over the next several weeks; items such as contacting social security, getting extra copies of the death certificate, contacting her insurance companies, cancelling credit cards along with contacting her attorney for any matters involving their trust. The list was long. I made a note to myself to do what I could to make this part of life easier on my wife when I passed, assuming I died before her.

On the way home Mom was silent and stared out the passenger-side window. I assumed she did not want to talk, until Mom interrupted the silence by suggesting we head instead back to *The Cut Above* as a celebration of Dad's life.

"You okay with inviting Uncle Bill, too, Mom."

"Of course, I think it only appropriate to have Bill with us." This was the first and only time I ever heard Mom refer to Uncle Bill as Bill instead of William.

* * *

Uncle Bill was waiting on the front porch reading the newspaper when we pulled up in front of home. He looked over the top of the paper as we walked up the walkway.

"Hi, Sam. Randall. How did everything go?" It was obvious that Uncle Bill had been aware of the true purpose to the ride when we left.

"Fine, William. I am just going to freshen up a bit and take a little sofa nap before dinner. We are all going out tonight." Mom opened the screen door and passed through, quickly disappearing from sight as soon as the screen shut.

"Seriously, Randall, how did she hold up? She has been putting this off for weeks. She kept telling me she wanted to wait until you got here." He folded the paper and laid it on a small table next to a half-finished beer. "I really did not want to go, so thanks, you know, for going with her. She needed the support."

"It was nothing, really. I just sat there. Mom took care of everything with Mister Wright."

Uncle Bill chuckled, "You know I have known Wright for years and have never called him by his first name. It always just seemed appropriate to call him Mister Wright. I guess I never wanted to offend the guy that was going to send me off to eternity."

He stood up. "Okay, let's get ready for dinner. I'll call to see if we can get our special table and see if we can finally get Mark and Tim to join us. I am actually starting to think they don't want to be seen with us." He smiled and pulled his mobile phone from his pocket to call. Once the phone started to ring, he pulled the phone from his ear, "What time you want head over?"

Chapter 26

I PULLED OUT DAD's blue book while waiting for Mom to get ready for dinner. Uncle Bill had gone home to take a quick shower and planned on meeting us at the restaurant. I had some time alone with Dad's little blue book. I flipped backwards to the section for Johnny Jackson. Johnny Jackson had come into my life about the time that Cal left.

Randall and Johnny, I am glad you found each other. You both needed a friend. I am sorry I have nothing of value to give either of you. Please take care of each other. Maybe, this can make up a little for when I failed you. Randall, my apologies in advance. My heart is broken.

Love,

Dad

* * *

There was a knock at the door, but nobody got up to answer it. I was only nine and felt as though my world had been turned upside down. My best friend was gone forever. Nothing could make up for the loss of Cal. He was special still, a hero in town and in my heart.

My Father was quiet and disconnected. He never hugged me anymore. My friends looked at me as though something was wrong with me, but I know they just don't know what to say to me. They all knew Cal and could not come to grips with the fact that he was gone, either. I just needed someone to talk with. I was so alone.

The knock came at the door again and again nobody answered. The house was quiet. Dad was in the kitchen drinking coffee and shuffling through a stack of papers. I think he was working on something for the business. Since Cal's death, Dad preferred to work from home. Uncle Bill would swing by the home mid-morning every day, to briefly talk with Dad about the business and then head back to work. Apparently, he didn't have much time for me either.

Mom was at the stove cooking, silent, her back to Dad, me, and the world.

The knock came a third time. "You want me to get the door?" I asked. There was no response so I got up from the floor where I had been laying reading the newspaper comics and went to door and opened it. I was confronted by a big black man, dark as licorice. He smiled. I backed from the door. This was my introduction to Johnny Jackson.

"He-e-e-llo, i-is P-p-paul S-s-s-i-mons here?" he stammered.

"Dad, you need to come out here." I called, all too loud.

The big black man looked at me with inquisitive eyes that showed an intelligence, peace and thoughtfulness that was contradicted by his speech.

Dad stepped up beside me and placed his hand on my shoulder. "Yes?" Then he stopped, stammered and cried. "Johnny, you came. Welcome. Please come in." He grabbed the black man by the arm and walked him into our home.

I looked on the porch and saw a small, beaten suitcase. I picked it up; it was light. I followed Dad and Johnny into the house. Johnny moved into Cal's room that day.

Johnny had been a friend of Dad's in the Korean War. Dad never had talked much about the war or the people he knew from the war. In fact, I think that Johnny's name was the only name I had ever heard Dad mention from his time overseas; and even then, it was brief. I could only gather that something bad had happened to Johnny and Dad had had something to do with it. Dad had mentioned that someday he wanted to make amends to Johnny. At the time, I had not known that Johnny was black and that he and Dad were friends. Even at nine years of age, I could tell that Johnny was troubled. He couldn't get more than a couple words out at a time without stammering and stuttering. It was exhausting listening to him and Dad talk that afternoon and into the night, but I sat there and listened; the whole time just being happy to be included in that small part of Dad's life. I pretended I was one of the guys, just like Cal would have been.

Dad had arranged for Johnny to work at the dealership serving as a "lot boy." He would keep the cars clean and sparkling. Dad had tried to talk him into working in the office, but Johnny had declined saying that with his stammering, he would slow the work down to a snail's pace. He just could not communicate effectively anymore. He preferred something where he could work alone, besides he just could not cope well with stress. Dad just nodded and Johnny would start the next day at the Simmons dealership.

I asked Dad if I could go to the lot and work with Johnny on his first day. I still don't know why I asked. Maybe I just wanted to be a part of something again, to have a friend.

Dad said. "You know, I think that might be a good thing to do. Be ready by seven, Randall, we will head to the car lot early tomorrow. I want to surprise your Uncle Bill with his newest employee."

I suspected he would surprise Uncle Bill just by showing up at work.

* * *

Johnny, that's what I called him. Dad originally insisted I address him as "Mister Jackson," but Johnny would have none of it. He would frown and say something like "M-mi-ster J-j-jackson di-di-sappeared long a-a-go. I- I'm j-just J-j-johnny."

After a while, Dad relinquished and Mister Jackson became just Johnny to me. Johnny's stammering started to lose its hold on the man about the same time. It was if a great weight had been removed from his back by the move to informality and he could now talk freely. No stress.

For me, it was as if I got my brother back. Not that Johnny was a baseball star, or great looking, or popular, but he was happy to take me with him wherever he went, and he talked with me, not to me. He even tried to play catch with the baseball in our backyard. It was something I had done with Cal almost every day before he, well never mind.

Johnny wasn't much good with the baseball and I really don't think he cared much for the sport, but he seemed to enjoy our time in the backyard. If he didn't, he sure pretended well. We would throw for hours; from the time he would get back from work until dinner most days. When we were not playing catch, he would take me downtown to a little diner to buy me an ice cream cone or a donut. Unfortunately for my sports career, I like sweets even more than baseball and I never developed Cal's hard body.

That is not to say I was not a good ball player; I was. I just was not driven by it. My baseball prowess peaked sometime around 12 or 13 years of age. While my friends focused on developing their adolescent bodies into bone draped with muscle, I chose to study. Unlike Cal, I could not remember getting anything but A's for school grades. School and learning seemed to come easy and I was proud of it.

In high school, I developed all new friendships. It was not as if I had a falling out with my friends from childhood, it was just a function of growing up. We developed different interests. They remained interested in sports, I became interested in calculus and Shakespeare. Although we still sat together in the high school café for lunch, I was there as grandfathered member of their clique, condoned, but not really embraced. That was fine since it allowed me to sit next to the cheerleaders; girls were a common interest I maintained with my boyhood friends.

I think Johnny gave me back a family, too. Being greeted by his smiling face every morning overwhelmed any sorrows Dad and Mom wanted to bring to the breakfast table. Having Johnny in the house filled a void in our hearts and gave us someone to care for, someone who needed caring for, but yet who provided care for us in ways we could not describe. Today I think Johnny was a gift to my family that was given to us for healing. As a kid, Mom made me go to church on Sunday's, but I never thought much about God until Johnny showed up at our door. Someone or something knew we needed some help. I believe to this day it was God.

Chapter 27

Tonight, we sat around a dinner table set for six; Mom, Uncle Bill, Mark, Tim, me, and my Dad. Mark and Tim were already seated by the time we had arrived at the restaurant. Instead of greeting us at the door, they had their host shepherd us upstairs. A couple bottles of wine were already opened and Mark and Tim were debating what special appetizers they should order for the family to try. The sounds of Stan Getz and Joao Gilberto's *The Girl from Impanema* drifted up the stairs from the main restaurant. The song made us all smile; it was one of Dad's favorite.

Tim looked up as we entered the room. "Well, the third time will be a charm. We," he said nodding to Mark, "have the staff taking care of us tonight. We are celebrating your Dad tonight. That's his chair at the head."

I was touched by Mark and Tim's desire to honor my Dad, but I had to admit it felt wrong, given that Dad was sleeping in a bed not more than two miles from here. He was not dead, yet.

Mark must have noticed the distressed look on my face. "Randall, we meant no disrespect to your Dad or family by reserving a place for him at the table. It's just we owe him a lot and we felt he would be here in spirit even if not in body."

"I'm okay, Mark. I just haven't come to grips with him

dying." I sat down across the table from where Dad's place had been set. Mom and Uncle Bill sat to the right of the empty seat, Mark and Tim to the left.

Tim started. "You know this area of town wasn't always so nice."

I laughed. "No kidding. When I was in high school, I thought a big fire might be the best thing for the buildings on this street." This street was made up of small businesses that had long been usurped by newer, better, and cheaper stores in the malls south of town. It seemed to me that there were more dead storefronts with the telltale soaped up windows than there were open shops. I closed my eyes, trying to remember the way this area had been. "Even those shops that were open may as well not have been. I don't think they carried much inventory and the inventory they did have was so outdated I could not imagine anyone willing to pay for it. This street was a gathering of businesses either dead or dying. It certainly wasn't worth much. I never could understand why Dad and Uncle Bill were so committed to this area of town." I stopped, catching myself as if I had been talking badly about my Dad. Looking around today, there certainly had been something worth saving there.

* * *

Arlin walked into Paul's office. In his arms he held a stack of site plans and architectural drawings. Sitting on opposite side of the conference table, Paul and the company's CFO, Lanny Horton had been in an obviously animated discussion. Lanny sat back in his chair with his arms crossed across his chest.

Arlin asked, "Okay, you want to take a look at the site plan options now or do you want to continue to yell a little? You know we can hear you two through the door. You could be a little more quiet and professional."

Paul was not accustomed to being chastised by anyone, let

alone one of his employees, but in this case, he stayed quiet. Arlin was also an owner, albeit a minority owner, and was only concerned for the good of the company. The fact that he had taken the risk to reprimand them just was evidence at how out of line they had been.

"You're right, Arlin. Sorry. I'll apologize to the office staff after we meet and talk through the proposal." Then looking toward Lanny, "You want to join me in talking with the staff?"

"Sure, Paul. We need to get aligned on this and we sure as hell do not want to leave the team out there," he said motioning to the office through the window, "thinking we are in trouble."

"Great, then let's get started. Arlin, what have you pulled together for us?"

Arlin laid the stack of drawings on the corner of the table and pulled a large folio-sized folder from the top. He opened the folder and pulled a series of drawings starting with a series of building elevations encompassing three full blocks of Linden street, the blighted section of down-town that had been the topic of discussion earlier in the week. This area had been hit particularly hard over the last several years by the introduction of the modern shopping malls south of town. The shopping malls had brought with them a number large, beautiful stores to the community, stores that to visit, prior to the mall, required a family to drive the hour and half or so to Denver. Now they were available to everyone in town. The malls brought a perceived quality of life improvement for the residents of Fort Collins; that is if you excluded most of the small business owners that occupied commercial space or families that lived in the older sections of town.

In any case, the modern shopping mall was progress, and progress had meant a lot of money for PW Simmons Corporation. The company had been involved in numerous aspects of the mall development, including the construction of a number of large stores. The moral dilemma - as PW Simmons succeeded in developing business to the south of town, they had effectively cut off the life-blood, the commerce, from downtown. Paul had always wanted his company to be an asset to Fort Collins, but he was slowly coming to realize, his success was killing the downtown. He had asked Arlin to pull together the proposal for the redevelopment of one of the worst hit sections, Linden Street. This had remained a polarizing topic for the past week and had spawned the loud conversation between Paul and Lanny.

Lanny had been unable to imagine a way that the firm could afford to bite off another big investment at this time. Years ago, the company had taken on some large debt with the acquisition of the large plot for future development down in San Diego that had yet to pay off. They had used up a significant portion of the company's cash and line of credit to hire additional staff and develop the preliminary proposals required before they could even consider breaking ground in California. It had put incredible stress on their finances and it looked as though it was going to be some time before the newest PW Simmons development could generate any positive cash flow. It was Lanny's job to make sure the company did not get into the cash bind they now found themselves in and he was feeling the pressure. He certainly could not condone making the financial stress worse by embarking on what he thought was a hair-brained, high-risk, low-return investment trying to engender a revitalization of down-town. After all, PW Simmons was a business, and the business's objective was not benevolence.

The battle lines had been drawn: the emotional obligation Paul felt to rectify the damage he felt he had in some way caused, pulling money from the downtown businesses and flowing it into the suburbs contrasted by Lanny's pragmatism posturing that PW Simmons just did not have the financial wherewithal to pull off one additional investment at this time. In Lanny's opinion, the short cash crunch caused by any redevelopment of downtown would not only sink the company, it was based on the folly that the downtown could actually be recovered. What could possibly make this downtown area attractive and safe enough to motivate new business and, more importantly, stimulate new customers to return? Hell, this portion of town wasn't particularly vibrant even before the introduction of the new malls and new housing expansion south of town. Combine that with the lack of down-town parking in the land of the car guaranteed the project to be a big bust. Although Lanny deeply respected Paul, this whole idea seemed more hope and prayer than sound business.

In spite of his skepticism, Lanny knew he owed Arlin and Paul the courtesy to hear the proposal and yet he was paid and obligated to fight for the fiscal health of the company. He certainly wanted to avoid any internal battle within the firm's ownership. It would be a battle that could tear the business apart. The options would be terrible: go bankrupt or destroy the company at its very roots. No, the only good result would come from reviewing Arlin's proposal and, through questioning, allow Paul to realize the folly prior to wasting any more money on the idea.

Arlin started in with the proposal, not by showing drawings of what the redevelopment could look like when complete, but rather by starting with discussion of business objectives and assumptions to ensure business alignment prior to jumping into a sales pitch. Lanny had to give Arlin credit; he was attempting to take as much emotion as possible out of the review.

The conversation actually initially progressed well through this phase. All three concurred the investment would need to have a high likelihood of generating positive cash flow quickly. The rub was the definition of "quickly." Paul said the right things regarding cash flow, but Lanny suspected he was not realistic regarding the budget to pull off the major project. Lanny was concerned that Paul would seduce himself into believing the redevelopment would miraculously work in spite of facts. For Lanny, the cash flow crunch meant the project would need to achieve break even within the investment's first year. It was a conservative investment strategy he was championing until their California real estate investment could start to pay off. Although he pretended he was open to ideas that looked to provide significant upside, he had already nixed a number of potential programs over the past year as function of risk. Now, he could not see the downtown reinvestment as something that could provide any of the upside the company needed. It was critical to align on the importance of cash flow neutrality before jumping into the actual project presentation so as not to become overpowered by pure speculation.

Lanny felt he had already learned the hard way the folly of becoming too enamored with "potential." The land they had purchased in California had looked so exciting. Almost two thousand acres of prime real estate just waiting for a developer to come along and build homes on it. At least that is how Paul had initially positioned it. They had pulled together projections that looked too good to be true. Ultimately, they now appeared to have been based more on hope than reality. The original projections were what he now referred to as financial modelling masturbation; sounding and feeling good, but far from real. Although he was hopeful the project returns might still materialize, it would take years for them to get through the miles of red tape and start generating some profits. Linden Street starting to sound the same way; lots of potential and devoid of any sound logic. Lanny wanted to make sure objectivity was represented in the discussion.

The second portion of Arlin's presentation centered on

demographics. He was sensitive to ensuring his proposal was not just pretty pictures of what the downtown could be, but was based in a pragmatic view of what types of people might be attracted to a downtown venue and what would be required to stimulate their interest and ongoing patronage. Arlin presented a number of market studies and actual data from other cities that had been successful to some degree on revitalizing sections of their communities. The studies outlined the types of commerce and people that might be excited and willing to locate businesses or shop in a revitalized area down-town. It was central to any proposal that PW Simmons might consider.

Within an hour, the three had agreed on a number of items. First, it was true there had been a major shift in demographics for the city; it was becoming younger and more affluent. Second, the affluence had resulted in people looking for, and willing to pay for, higher quality and differentiated products. The quality needs had been addressed by the introduction of some major, national, upscale stores that came with the shopping malls. The need for some type true differentiation and uniqueness, however, had largely been unaddressed. The young, affluent customers wanted to have product and shopping experiences that were new all the time. For the most part this still meant a long drive to the big city, Denver or the eclectic smaller community of Boulder. In either case, it meant dollars flowing out of Fort Collins. The third item of agreement, the impact on PW Simmons cash, essentially meant any investment would need to limited and likely would require help and participation from the city, itself.

To avoid getting too bogged down in a conversation centered only on financials, Arlin jumped into the third part of the discussion, an open-ended conversation centered on answering what could the downtown be "famous" for? What result would make PW Simmons proud? This question had not been one that either Paul nor Lanny had discussed before, but it was exactly the one they needed to agree on before even thinking about spending a dime on the project. For Paul, it defined how his family's name would be remembered. For Lanny, it provided an opportunity to be part of something bigger than just the company; it was something that could excite him enough to get on board the project. The question opened up possibilities rather than closing down options based on individual predispositions. Lanny and Paul became animated as they took turns jotting ideas on the conference room's white board. The animation reflected none of the anger that had polluted the room no more than an hour earlier. Instead, animosity and frustration had been replaced by the energetic synergy of sharing of ideas; one building on another.

Arlin was excited to see this conversation outlining a vision of what Linden Street could be sparking the creativity of both Paul and Lanny. One could feel the energy in the conference room grow, the potential was apparent. They began to coalesce on a set of attributes for any successful redevelopment effort. The most important "a-hah" for the team was that the redevelopment needed to take reliance on the car out of the picture. Walking and strolling had to be part of the plan and would be integral in delivering an experience that could not be had in the conventional covered shopping malls of the suburbs. Granted, the whole value premise behind the covered mall was to enable customers to walk from shop to shop without ever having to hop back into a car or brave nasty weather, but the purpose was singularly shopping. It was efficient, but not necessarily fun; it reflected a stagnant experience. The redevelopment needed to provide for a high degree of experience flexibility so as to always remain fresh for the consumer.

Business risk could be addressed through project diversification. The area to be redeveloped would include a broad range of occupants including stylish boutiques, art galleries, professional offices, stylish apartments, live music, and trendy restaurants and nightclubs. In order to be exciting, the look needed to be ever-changing with stimulating additions. The redevelopment needed to combine an active street scene with quality indoor venues; a place to see and be seen without necessarily breaking the bank. Okay it sounded good, but how to make it work?

Arlin pointed to his first drawing. It was a street view except all the cars were gone. Instead the street had been turned into a park spotted with raised planters, trees, cobblestone walkways, sculptures, fountains, and a new breed of stores; all upgraded with a common exterior look starting with large awnings and fancy doors. Gone from the buildings were the utilitarian stainless-steel doors and plain plate glass windows that had seemed modern in the fifties, but today looked only cheap and dated. The had been replaced by stylish wood panel doors and casement windows. The look was comfortable and inviting. The post-modern blonde brick was gone, too, replaced by a recovered red brick of an earlier generation, providing a calling back to a simpler, safer time. The look was to provide a destination for young and old alike.

Lanny's excitement faded and his pragmatism resurfaced. "Looks nice, Arlin, but how does this fit with what actually exists on Linden Street today? You know we cannot afford to tear down and start from scratch?"

Chapter 28

On paper, the Linden Street transformation being laid out by Arlin appeared magical. The existing buildings lining the street along the proposed three block redevelopment were going to experience a major overhaul. Although the majority of the decades-old buildings would maintain their overall appearance, they would need to experience modest external visual retrofits to enable each building to maintain their uniqueness while creating a continuity for the entire street mall. Major construction overhauls were focused on two large, post-modern architectural building atrocities that at one time had been symbols of post-war affluence and efficiency. Today, these were only dated, tired, plain and ugly. Although replacing the uniform yellow-blonde brick on the two large buildings and adding some exterior retrofits to add a little interest would just be too expensive, Arlin reflected a white-washed painting treatment to mask the old color and drab conformity of the post-war construction. The white-washed buildings provided a nice contrast with the rest of the colors and textures on the street; red-hued, aged brick structures of buffs, burnt oranges, burgundies and browns. The smooth white provided a striking diversity from the other, more ornate structures lining the street.

Tying together the eclectic mixture of rich brick colors and textures was a consistent application of dark, forest green awnings. The awnings served three primary critical purposes. First, they provided shade and cover, both to comfort the walker-by and the protect the product on display from the harsh Fort Collins summer sun. The second contribution of the awnings was cosmetically tying the look of the entire street together. They provided a degree of commonality as one walked from store to store. The last and most important purpose of the awnings served was providing a subtle pallet for signage. No longer were the businesses demarked by a mishmash of post-modern, painted, florescent, and polyester signs, some attractive, some garish, some trashy, and all, outdated. Instead, business names were now a common cream white embellished on a sea of green; with only modest differences in font and design. It was not that other forms of signage had been removed completely; however, only the non-standard signs remaining added to a classy, retro impression, and uniqueness of the entire street mall. Arlin had envisioned a number of examples of large, porcelain painted tin and colorful neon signage extending above street level hearkening one back to an earlier time; perhaps to a time when Route 66 was still the main thoroughfare connecting the country's east and west.

Another post-modern architectural casualty were the practical, boring brushed aluminum and stainless steel window and door frames. These had all been replaced by wood and masonry, providing each mall visitor with a sense of opulence and adding quaintness the shopping experience.

What had once been a wide, sterile road for car traffic and street parking had also gone through a significant transformation. The black-gray asphalt was gone. The cracked and damage sidewalks were gone. The traffic lights were gone. The curbs were gone. Replacing these remnants of a tired, second rate commercial segment of town all centered around the almighty automobile was a broad walking boulevard of a mosaic of red brick and smooth concrete. Interspersed along the boulevard were raised planters, trees, and a large, trapezoidal reflecting pond, punctuated by a large bronze sculpture of a hawk just taking flight over the large curled horns of a ram resting on a boulder, at its center. The modern pool, although a striking anachronism to the retro feel and look of the rest of the mall, added to something Arlin referred to as the feng shui, binding the mall life around the ambient sound of trickling water and the vision of a slice of nature caught forever in bronze.

At one end of the outdoor mall, a new building had been added, effectively closing off one end of the mall and extending into the cross street. An antique brick façade belied the modern construction that dwelt underneath, provided the same look and feel as the rest of the buildings making up the mall. Behind the façade was a dual-purpose structure for both parking and upscale apartments. The intent was to provide easy access to the downtown mall while contributing some needed diversification to the project. The residential aspect was critical. It not only contributed an incremental and lucrative revenue stream, it provided an opportunity to develop a sense of community around the project, one in which the resident could shop, work, and play without ever getting into the car. The luxury apartment residents also benefited the commercial tenants by creating a local population of relatively affluent workers, clients, and customers.

Appended to the base of the parking structure, facing and extending into the mall, Arlin had created a modern, single-story glass and brick facility to house multiple restaurants or pubs. The intent was to provide a destination far beyond shopping, pulling in people from the entire region to an eclectic night experience. It was a striking deviation from the rest of the architecture on the street.

Arlin pulled a second series of drawings from his stack and jumped into his ideas on the building interiors. All of the old buildings were to get a significant retrofit to their interiors as part of the process. Although the majority of building skeletons were in reasonable shape, their internal organs were a mess and woefully outdated. This had been Lanny's primary area of concern, financially. Gutting internal walls, remodeling the long neglected upper levels, replacing wiring, plumbing and the heating and ventilation systems was going to cost a fortune. This was even before considering unanticipated cost over-runs that would invariably surface once walls were torn out and environmental or bio hazards like asbestos or mold were found.

For interior renovation, Arlin had taken the novel approach to clear all the street level building interiors down to exposed brick. Conduit, plumbing, and air vents would remain open to view, enhancing the rustic appeal of the buildings and providing a stark contrast to the pristine, sterile, large shopping centers south of town. The benefits to the PW Simmons Corporation were obvious, significantly lowering the cost of the initial renovation while maximizing flexibility for future retrofits as new tenants occupied space. Interior walls had been limited to the rear portion of each building to provide for alley access, restrooms, warehouse, and needed administrative space. Ceilings were a challenge for Arlin. Although he had wanted to maintain the rustic nature of an unfinished ceiling, total exposure of the second-floor ceiling joists also meant no sound insulation. As a compromise, he had spec'd in acoustic batting material that would be inserted between floor joists above all vents and lighting.

The look was appealing, different, and timeless. Instead of drywall and paint that could easily get dinged and damaged,

Arlin's interiors were almost indestructible and yet provided an almost organic feel. Even better, the walls would remain fresh through tasteful application of art rather than repainting.

Another of Arlin's innovations eliminated the need for each building having its own individual stairway access to upper floors. Today the upstairs floors were accessed by dark, steep, stairwells. They were a hazard by modern building codes and, in effect, severely limited the value of all square footage above the street level. These floors had fallen into disrepair and essentially represented wasted or underutilized square footage. Even in the rare cases where the square footage was occupied, the ability to generate any significant income was lost as a result of poor maintenance, foot traffic, and access. Arlin not only wanted to make these floors more integral to the entire downtown experience, he wanted the redevelopment to radically increase the value of the heretofore wasted square footage. Given all of the buildings in the mall had three to four levels, the amount of potentially marketable additional square footage was huge.

In tackling this challenge, Arlin had taken the novel approach of linking the formerly separate and distinct buildings together. He eliminated the individual, narrow, dark stairways that currently originated at narrow, orphaned, locked, street-level doors stuck in between major shops. They were dingy and dangerous looking; certainly, uninviting for the casual passerby. Instead, Arlin had taken the daring approach to carve out a glass walled atrium stealing square footage from the middle of each block's building structures on each side of the mall. Within each atrium, he had included two elevators and steps leading to the floors above. Access to the square footage on the second through fourth floors had been enabled by extending a continuous passageway along the rear of the buildings, cutting through what were now exterior brick walls and providing an unimpeded access to all the buildings on one side of the street. Although expensive, Arlin's approach opened the upstairs to a multitude of potential uses: offices, apartments, light warehousing in support of the businesses at street level, or even eclectic shops and art galleries that had no need for the significant floor space provided below them. It certainly opened these floors to a completely new level of rent potential. Keeping the hallway to the rear of the buildings maximized window views to the mall below. Keeping the atrium enclosed provided for year-round access even in the most unfriendly weather.

It was a completely reinvented three city blocks.

* * *

The outdoor mall design was not without its shortcomings. Arlin had not even begun to tackle budget, financing, property acquisition, or ongoing property management requirements. He had moved so quickly from the discussion on cash flow to one of vision for the downtown, Lanny and Paul doubted Arlin had done much homework as to the potential cost implications of his design. If he had, it was likely he had already realized it was too expensive. More importantly, he had not even touched on how they might open the discussion with the city on closing down the street for three city blocks or the interruption of traffic on the cross streets. In general, he thought the city would be glad to dump their responsibility for the street maintenance. Public pushback might be another manner altogether. Although Lanny loved the picture Arlin had painted for them, he was even more a skeptic of the business proposition than he had been a few hours earlier.

Paul sat quietly as Arlin wrapped up his presentation and sat down. After a pause, Paul asked if he could make some comments before he or Lanny jumped in with questions or asked for clarification on Arlin's vision of downtown. Surprising to Lanny, Paul's comments took a very practical direction, providing a sobering shift from the Arlin's exuberance.

"Arlin, I appreciate you taking on the challenge to recast Linden Street into something special. It is wonderful to see what Linden Street could be. Thanks." He grasped his hands together and brought his elbows up onto the conference table. "Now let's start thinking about it from the perspective of what we can realistically afford and what we might be able to pitch to the city. I know our friend, Lanny, would want us to now look at this from a purely business perspective.

"Lanny, Arlin, I suspect you would agree pulling something like this together would require a huge commitment in time, people, and money to pull off. It also would mean taking it to the citizens of this city for a vote for both changing Linden Street use and to get some serious public funding. No way are we going to get this off the ground without support from the planning commission, the city council, and then a vote by the community. Let's look at what we can cut to make this something that still provides some value, but trims the bucks in a big way." He smiled, "I wouldn't be surprised if this would take every dollar we have ever earned in this company and some. Let's see what we can do with a budget we might realistically cobble together with the bank. OK?"

Paul stuck his head out of the conference room and asked the receptionist to order three lunches to be delivered by a local deli so that they could remain engaged in the discussion. As they began to debate aspects of the redevelopment that would need to be discarded without destroying the entire project, a much more limited, but practical plan coalesced. By the end of the day they aligned on an overall plan centered around the establishment of an outdoor street mall; meaning the City Council and a city vote would likely still be required, but they had cut the likely up-front cost to PW Simmons by more than

80%; gone was the parking structure and restaurant facility, as were the glassed-in atriums and the related investment to connect the individual buildings. In this way, it was no longer needed to acquire all the buildings on each block of the redevelopment. Instead, PW Simmons could limit real estate acquisitions to those that made the most economic sense. Lastly, the original three-block plan had shrunk to two blocks to minimize the anticipated pushback from the city as a result of impacted on car traffic flow. In spite of the severe cuts in required costs, Lanny still expressed serious reservations on the entire project in that it would consume significant resources from their team before the first shovel hit dirt. The plan would require prolonged review, negotiation, and approval processes involving the PW Simmons leadership team, the city planning commission, the city council, and, ultimately, the voter.

Chapter 29

THE FIRST CHALLENGE was money; and for a relatively small company like PW Simmons, it was a lot of money, money they did not have. Compounding the problem, the prospects from the bank were not great; that is, unless they were prepared to pay a huge rate of interest. Interest rates had skyrocketed through the roof over the past four years. It was already putting a big squeeze on the company's profits and its ability to grow. Taking out a loan to finance the project would make even breakeven difficult, meaning it would have to pencil out as one of their most profitable business ventures, before interest.

The second challenge to hit the project came with a preliminary review with the city's planning commission. The company's real-estate expert, Joe Klein, had wanted to get a read on what obstacles they might be facing with the proposed redefined use of Linden Street. The entire project centered on the elimination of automobile traffic. In addition, Joe had wanted to see if the city might consider using their eminent domain or condemnation authority to facilitate the redevelopment. He did not want to embark upon purchasing any properties unless the city was prepared to take control of problem buildings, buildings whose owners were unwilling or unable to reinvest in the structure, through eminent domain by condemning the property. Purchasing the property in this section of town would be a risky endeavor, especially if only a few of the properties were to be renovated. The company would not begin the process of buying the real-estate if the entire project could be held up by one or two recalcitrant owners that desired to use the redevelopment as means to extort high selling prices for their properties.

Although the members of the commission appeared to be interested and amenable, all politely nodding their heads in understanding during the presentation, one member, a Phil Barton, questioned the wisdom of investing in this particular section of town. Phil Barton had been a dominant member of the committee for years and when he escalated opposition to the proposal the rest of the committee listened. As Barton moved from being initially lukewarm on the project to becoming almost virulent at the suggestion of the city using eminent domain, it became painfully clear Barton would be a problem. He aggressively established his position on any government intervention that took private property, regardless of the public good could not be entertained. He would not easily be moved from his rebellious position.

Cynically, Paul thought Barton's push back was less based in an ethical position and was more of a squeeze to get something out of PW Simmons, essentially a negotiation play for a quid pro quo. His intuition was quickly validated when Barton suggested his opinion could be possibly altered if PW Simmons would consider a commercial development just north of the proposed site. He might even support the use of eminent domain given the property he suggested alternatively for redevelopment was so underdeveloped and the impact would be less significant on existing owners. Conveniently, this redefined property just happened to border on a section of undeveloped agricultural land that had been owned by Barton's family for decades. Currently, Barton's land was only valuable for growing corn. After redirecting the redevelopment per his request, Barton's farmland would increase in value over night more than tenfold. Paul was unwilling to bend to Barton's request and actually went on to suggest during the meeting that Barton was using his government position of power to enrich himself. As such, it was not something PW Simmons could overlook and support.

Barton, feigning offence, went on the attack, first suggesting he had been misunderstood then quickly moved on to threats; reminding Paul how the planning commission could make things pretty difficult for his company. Barton's tone suggested he was the only voice on the committee that really mattered, obviously isolating and agitating the rest of the commission members. While Barton talked, Paul held him in his stare. Barton, on the other hand, deflected his eyes downward to the pages of the proposal that lay on the table in front of him. He would hide behind the power of the committee's processes to get his way.

* * *

Over the short car ride back to the office, Paul was regretting his comments during the meeting. He had let his anger get the better of him. He had dismissed a recommendation from the commission, accused the senior member of the commission of being unethical, and pretty much impugned the integrity of the entire process; not a good thing given that they would continue to need the support of the planning commission for not only the Linden Street development, but for any future developments. He had made a bad enemy today. Making matters worse was the fact that the section of town suggested by Barton for redevelopment might not actually have been such a bad alternative, although it would never have the panache offered on Linden Street. Paul was questioning himself as to whether his actions had been driven by the obvious ethical issues presented by Barton or as strictly an emotional response from being pushed away from his proposal. Paul hated to be questioned and had never been good at hearing a "no" answer. He had grown accustomed to getting his way. In any case, the issues would be addressed back at the office before any serious commitment.

With the blow-up between Paul and Barton, Lanny and Arlin had been placed in the position of attempting to salvage the meeting. They suggested PW Simmons would take Barton's request under consideration, but prior to moving forward with internal discussions, they wanted to understand if the Linden Street project had any chance of getting the Planning Board and Council approval. This was critical in that the proposal required the city converting the use of two city blocks of existing streets in addition to supporting the interruption of the diagonal traffic flow for two additional streets. In the proposal, the city would maintain ownership for the street and its maintenance as a common area.

Again, the conversation broke down quickly. The fact that this section of town had fallen into significant decay and had little hope of pulling out of the blight; the fact that the city revenues associated with the product sales tax and property tax had all but dried up for this entire section of town; the fact that the tax revenues were not sufficient to even remotely pay for the city services of fire, police, and maintenance, had done little to keep the board from balking at the proposal. The notion that they would be on the hook for the common area given that the private companies would stand to make serious profits off the city investment had resulted in serious discord. They were adamant that PW Simmons should provide the ongoing funding for the street maintenance and improvements. This potentially could alter the already tight economics of the entire project. Not only had they failed to placate Barton, they ended up creating another area of conflict.

* * *

After the pushback from the Planning Commission, the entire PW Simmons management team needed to align on how to proceed. William and Paul Simmons, Joe Klein, Arlin, Lanny, and the elder Lyle Jones sat around the conference table discussing the value and wisdom of a downtown redevelopment effort. Although the areas south of town had grown prosperous with heavy investments from new companies and existing company expansions, it was true the heart of Fort Collins had become old, stale, and depleted. It seemed the only viable businesses remaining in the downtown were banks, bars, dusty boutiques and some professional buildings for dentists, attorneys, and real-estate agents. Vibrant retail had all but disappeared.

For weeks, Paul had been championing a redevelopment effort to revitalize at least one section of the downtown; culminating with the blow up with Barton in front of the city's Planning Commission. A pragmatist would have begun looking for other options for investment in that the likelihood this project would ever get approval was dubious. Paul would not give up.

Even if the city's approval could be gained, the project came with huge financial risk for the company. Downtown had become a pariah for majority of people living and working in Fort Collins. To create a pull for people to come back into the downtown meant the company would not only have to rejuvenate a number of buildings just to make them safe and viable places for commerce; it meant creating something chic and trendy. For most of the PW Simmons management team, it meant awakening the community to new possibilities. The project was beginning to sound like the unbounded dreams of an unrealistic politician seeking election; not the serious business plan for a responsible business owner.

Lanny Horton was of the mind to scuttle the project. His perspective had been a constant from the onset of discussions. In his opinion the project would stress the already tight finances of the business. Plus, after Paul's run in with Phil Barton, he doubted they could ever gain the support of the powerful city planning commission for any real meaningful changes to downtown. Today, even though the area was blighted and moving from bad to worse, it did not require much from the city to maintain basic city services. It was apparent the planning commission would prefer to continue "kicking the can down the street" for some future generation to fix. The preliminary discussions with the city planning commission had been a dismal failure.

Opposing Lanny, Paul, Arlin, and William remained ardently supportive of pushing forward with some type of serious investment for the city's downtown, specifically focused at the Linden Street. For Paul, he felt it necessary to give something back to the town. Arlin had become a huge proponent of a downtown redevelopment, not for any altruistic, or business notion, but because it provided him an empty canvas to show off his architectural talents. William supported the project because, well, Paul wanted it.

Surprisingly Lyle and Joe Klein had remained noncommittal throughout the discussions. Joe was confident they could win the support of the city council and voters if they pushed with the issue. Realistically, the city was addicted to the increased revenues coming from sales and real estate taxes; it was difficult for him to believe it would walk away from something that could help fill the city coffers and enable an ever-increasing budget. He recognized the company still needed to come up with some serious financing. If not for the financing challenge, he was squarely in the camp of continuing.

Lyle brought a unique perspective to the discussion. Looking to Paul and William, he started, "You know, when Virginia, your Dad, Lattimore, and I were just kids, this section of town was pretty nice. The street was marked less by car traffic and more by people strolling sidewalks, enjoying the day. It was always less busy than the business on College, just one block west, but it was just as important for the neighborhood. As a kid, before the depression hit, I can remember walking there to buy candy after school." He vaguely pointed at the drawings that had been laid out on the conference table. Then with more specificity he put his index finger on the picture of a corner building on the west side of Linden Street. "It was called Arnold's Market back then. Markets were a lot different before the war," then as if slipping back to an earlier, simpler time, Lyle closed his eyes. "I can still see and smell the little market. When I opened the door, I was instantly bombed by beautiful and intense aromas that were concentrated in the small shop.

"I can remember almost as if it were yesterday, the gleaming hardwood floors, the shelves and counters that lined each wall, the way you had to walk through his entire shop to get to his main counter at the rear of the store. Arnold would have a selection of brewed coffees to taste as you first entered the store. Behind the coffee were shelves filled with the various coffee choices so that you could taste a free sample before buying a selection. It's funny, decades before Starbucks, Old Man Arnold already saw the value in coffee, he just never understood that if he put out tables he could actually charge people for the privilege of taking a cup in his shop. He used to tell me that the coffee was his advertising. He said the aroma was what kept people coming in. He said people would line up to smell and taste and invariably snag a can from the shelf, and meander to the counter, picking up other foods along the way.

"Along the opposite wall, directly across from the coffee, Arnold had the shelves stocked with breads and pastries.; not a huge selection, mind you, his store was just too small. The whole place couldn't have been more than a thousand square feet. I doubt if it was more than fifty to sixty feet long and it couldn't have been any more than 15 feet wide. The pastry selection was just enough to entice the customer to grab something to take home for dinner, to have with their coffee, or to nibble on as they walked from store to store. He was ahead of his time, but he could not compete with the big grocery chains that were coming to town over the next several years. He had four counters lining each side of his store, each being maybe ten feet long. Each counter was essentially a mini-store concentrated on one type of food or dry good. One would be coffee, one for tinned meats, one for canned vegetables, one for soaps, one for dry beans, and; well you get the point. The problem, the big grocery stores had whole aisles filled with choice for each one of Old-Man Arnold's counters. The biggest difference was the butcher section. For Arnold, his whole butcher section was probably less than five feet wide and shared space with the cash register and main counter. Arnold would pull meat from his counters, wrap it in brown paper, then bag the rest of the groceries, and then take the money from the customer, all on the same counter space. Probably not the most hygienic, at least by today's standards. He did not have a chance to survive against the modern grocery store; but he was vital to this neighborhood.

"I can remember how Virginia and I would walk up to the glass counter in the rear of the shop to lay down our couple of pennies for candy. Old-Man Arnold would dig out a couple candies from a jar he kept behind the counter. He told us he had kept these candies especially for Virginia and me, they were a special treat for us. Even today I can remember popping a hard caramel or a fruity jaw breaker in my mouth. Those treats would keep us slurping all the way home.

"You know, Virginia and I had a special relationship. We knew from our earliest time together our friendship would blossom to love. Of course, back then we argued and fought a lot; all kids do, but we were inseparable. By the time we were ten, I could not imagine a day without seeing my Virginia; and I think she thought the same way about me. Old-Man Arnold, I think, sensed it too. When we would walk up to the counter to buy our candy, he would address us a mister and missus. We laughed then, but we knew it would only be a matter of time until we grew up and could make the salutations real.

"Time passed quickly enough. Virginia and I got married right out of high school. Lattimore was my best man, my best friend, and I considered him my brother. I still do." Lyle paused as he nodded to Paul and William. "Most people don't know it, but both my family and Virginia's family were pretty poor. My dad passed away when I was still in elementary school and Virginia never knew her father. Paul, old-man Arnold never knew it, but your dad was the one that always gave us the pennies to buy our candy. Virginia and I didn't have any money. Your dad had shared with us his entire life. He was a lifelong friend and I was never able to thank him enough.

"When Black Tuesday came, what little money Virginia and I had been able to earn dried up. We lost our jobs. Mister Arnold was still running his shop back then, but he was certainly getting pressure from a bigger and newer grocery store just a block away on College Boulevard. He made sure Virginia and I had food to eat. He would wave us in and give us a bag with a loaf of bread and some canned food. He knew we could not pay; he would just shrug and say that we could pay him later.

Then the next day he would see us walking and he would repeat the process; saying, we could pay him tomorrow. You see, for Mister Arnold, tomorrow would never come and he knew it. He knew that Virginia and I had no money.

"Lattimore saved us and so did Mister Arnold. When your dad opened the awning shop, he gave us a job, even though there was hardly enough business to take care of his own family. Lattimore was godsend.

Mister Arnold's shop went out of business long before the economy rebounded. I heard he died shortly after he closed up shop. I am not sure if the death of his business led to his own death, but I suspect so. He was a kind person that took pleasure in taking care of his brothers and sisters in the community even though he didn't have much to give. That's the way it was back then. You know, in some small way, I think his death was the start of Linden Street's prolonged death march; and it is still dying.

"Virginia and I never got to pay Mister Arnold back for his generosity and God knows I will be forever in debt to the Simmons family. Now I think I have the opportunity to finally make good on some of that debt by helping that part of town. My Virginia is gone now and I don't think I have too much longer before I join her. I certainly will not have the time to spend the wealth this business has given me. I would like to make a go at fixing up this street even if we need to do it slower and without the help of the city. Whatever savings I have I am going to give back to this business to get this started. I think that is what Virginia would want me to do." The room fell silent. Each captivated by our imagination as to what life had been like in that little section of Linden street based on Lyle's recollections.

Lanny finally broke the silence. He breathed a big sigh, pushed himself back in his chair and said, "Well, shit, Lyle, if you are willing to give up your own money to get this going, I guess I can support it, too." He looked at everyone around the table, picked up his glass of water, held it up as if in a toast, "To Arnold's," then as almost a second thought, "and fuck that Barton prick!"

Chapter 30

Mom held up her glass of wine for the first toast of what was going to be many over the dinner tonight. She made a brief thanks to Lyle for getting Linden Street started again. For me, it was nice to hear about Lyles contribution to this project. Sure, for my entire life he had been important to me, but I had never developed a true appreciation for the man. He seemed to me to be a surrogate grandfather, but I never realized what had made him tick. Sometimes you are just too close to see who people really are. Lyle must have died shortly after the meeting kicking off Linden Street. I don't think he even got to see the first of the renovations even started, but I guess his hand and muscle turned every shovel of dirt.

Tim and Mark had been noticeably touched by the conversation. They had never met either of the senior members of the PW Simmons family, but they had always held them in reverence. Now they understood why.

Uncle Bill jumped in to continue the conversation. I was surprised that for this evening he had barely touched his glass of wine; only taking a sip during Mom's toast. Instead he had limited himself to drinking mineral water. I suspect it was not for a lack of desire, but because he wanted to stay engaged with the entire evening. I was proud of him.

"Randall, Lyle gave us some of the means and all the motivation to get the project started, but what a pain in the ass the Bartons were. If I recall, you were friends with Barton's kid, right?"

"Hardly." I answered

* * *

Pride makes us lie to our friends, our family, and to ourselves. I lied to you, Sam. Linden Street was never about the city. At first it was about me. I wanted to be remembered for doing something good. It was hard on us. You and Randall bore most of the brunt while I just plowed on. I know now, I was selfish. I am sorry.

By the time Dad's company began in earnest to create the Linden Street Mall, I had started High School. Yes, I was a third generation of proud Lambkins for the Simmons family. It was a proud, sad, and exciting feeling to walk into the school my first day as an actual student.

Proud in that the first thing I saw upon entering the main hall was a large glass trophy case in which the Simmons family was well represented. A picture of Dad in his old basketball uniform hung in the case at the far right, closest to the school's entry. It was hard to imagine my father as a high school basketball star. True, he was tall and still cut a formidable athletic physique, but he was old and had always been old to me. I could not imagine what school must have been like way back in the 40's. Dad's name was one of the first names emblazoned on the "Most Valuable Athlete" trophy that held a position of honor at the case's center. He was listed twice; once for 1942 and again in 1943.

Sad in that the second name I looked for was that of my brother, Cal. Cal also had a picture hanging in the case, but his picture was followed by the brief note "Taken too early from us." Cal's name also had been inscribed on the trophy; three times for 1968, 1969, and 1970.

Yes, the Simmons family was well represented already. It was a good thing because it was highly unlikely I was going to keep up the tradition. Sports were not going to be my thing. Yes, I still loved sports and I guess I was an okay athlete, but star potential? Hell, no. I must have been staring at Cal's picture for a several minutes, because I was startled back to reality by the gentle touch of a hand on my shoulder and quiet, "You had better get on to your class before your teacher marks you tardy. The bell rang a couple minutes ago." That was how my time at Fort Collins High started.

My first class was algebra, and I was, unfortunately, the last to walk into class. As I entered I could feel the eyes of my already seated classmates baring in on me. The teacher, an old man wearing a plaid, short-sleeve shirt that badly needed to see an iron, caught me by the arm and accusingly stated I was late and not to let it happen again. He then pointed me to one of the last two available desks in the room, both of them sitting right in front of his desk. Great! Not only was I late, I was now going to have to sit in the front of the room for the remainder of the term. I made a mental note to hurry to my next class in hope that I might find a more agreeable seat smack dab in the middle of the sea of desks. I did not like being visible.

I felt a flick on my shoulder. I turned to see a large, freckled, auburn haired boy smiling back at me. Not a kind or even funny smile, but one that said, 'you're a fuck and I am going to fuck with you from now on.' That was my first encounter with Billy Barton.

Billy was a mean-spirited cut-up; someone that thought he

was smart, important, and funny and wanted everyone to know it. Unfortunately, for him, he was neither as witty or bright as he thought he was. His importance was gotten vicariously through his equally dull and mean spirited father. He was from one of those families that you hated to admit existed, one that got their jollies out of bullying anyone they thought inferior. If I had been Cal, I probably would have stood up, popped him on his freckled nose and ended his mean games right then and there; but I wasn't Cal and never would be. I turned back around, faced the teacher and resigned myself to being pushed around by this jerk until he found someone even easier to pick on.

I don't know why I was so timid as a teenager. I was pretty good sized and well built in my own right, but I just didn't have that killer instinct necessary to throw the fear of God into anybody. I guess that is why I never was going to make it as a sports hero.

The first day in algebra was terrible. Although the subject matter was not going to be tough, I could not get focused on anything the teacher was saying. The teacher was trying to lay down the law for the term; I got it. I heard something about there being tests every Monday morning and something about all homework needing to be handed in as we walked into class, no exceptions, but outside of that, my mind wandered. By the time the bell rang for the next class, I was left not having a clue as to what our assignment was for the next day. I was lost and had to suffer through the embarrassment of staying after the class had emptied to ask the teacher for the assignment.

"So, Simmons, are you going to be trouble for me the whole term. I will not put up with it. Take a look at the syllabus I handed out at the start of class and you better get on to your next class or you will be late again."

My second class, English, was almost as embarrassing. Once again, I was the last to enter the room and was relegated to sitting in the only remaining seat at the front of the room; and once again, right in front of Billy Barton. Billy took the opportunity to jab me with his pencil and whispered to his friend seated beside him, "This is the same fuck that was late to Algebra. What a moron."

The only saving grace in English was that the teacher actually seemed to care about her students. She called out Billy, "Mister Barton, I would appreciate you not using profanities in this class. If you continue I am sure we can have you spend some time in the principal's office for the remainder of the period."

Billy, being the rude individual he was, responded, "So you want me to shut the fuck up? I may as well go to the principal now, then." He gathered his books and headed out of the classroom. As he walked by me, he made sure to bump me with his books. "Uh, sorry, Simmons," then he was gone out the door.

That was my first couple of hours at Fort Collins High School. Billy and I would have more than that one occasion to get to know each other better over the next several years. He was a prick. I cannot understand how someone like Cal could be taken and someone like Billy got to live on to terrorize.

* * *

Paul and William decided to tackle the planning commission on their own, taking a crack at presenting a revised proposal involving what they hoped would be the Linden Street redevelopment. They were seated on one side of a large conference table facing the five planning commissioners. They had taken their seats on other side of the table opposite of Paul and William, with Barton taking the center position. It was set up to be confrontational, a tactic that had been orchestrated by Barton and had been fully expected by Paul.

Barton started the discussion. "Well, let's hope now you

have a good response to our recommendation from last month, Mister Simmons." Barton ignored William, focusing his comments squarely at Paul.

"Actually, I think we do, Phil, and please call me Paul. Mister Simmons was reserved for our Dad." Paul again laid out copies of the plans for the Linden Street redevelopment for the entire commission, but in this case, PW Simmons had made some significant changes to reflect a much more modest endeavor.

"Before you start, Simmons, where is your proposal on the property I asked you to consider from our last meeting?"

Paul put on his most professional demeanor. "Well, Phil, we considered it and decided it was not going to work for us; so, we decline. Please note we have a deep commitment to the Linden Street area and still want to proceed, but we fully understand your desire to not use eminent domain to help us acquire the real estate, so we have adjusted our plans accordingly. It just means we will have to move significantly slower. At this time, we have no way to guarantee that existing owners will be willing to sell their property; at least at a price that would support our investment to retrofit the buildings and resell them to make a modest return. Once word gets out on the redevelopment, I would expect we will see at least a couple owners refuse to sell in an effort to extract top dollar for their properties. As such, some properties will likely be excluded from our investment so we are resigned to embark on the redevelopment one building at a time; that is, as long as you can support shutting off the car traffic and turning the street into a walking avenue."

Paul continued, "It is a shame; however, the property and sales tax bump the city would have gotten from our original proposal would have been substantial. If you take a look at the financial projections we prepared, you can see the delta." Paul handed out separate financial summaries to each member of the planning commission. He then sat down to provide them time to go over the tax revenue calculations.

All of the members of the planning commission, with the exception of Phil Barton, began looking at the financial projections, Paul had laid out before them. Phil merely stared, alternating his gaze between Paul and William. After only a brief few minutes of review, what appeared to be the eldest member of the commission, broke the silence. He had been quiet prior to this point, but it was clear he was speaking with some degree of authority and deference from the rest of the members.

"I think we may have been rash in our previous direction. Paul, William, would you mind excusing us for thirty minutes or so, so that we might discuss your proposal in private? I think it should not take too long, and we can send for you to come back in once we are done.

Chapter 31

TIM AND MARK had chosen a large selection of hors d'oeuvres as starters to be delivered to the table. I had to laugh when I realized how much food we were going to be eating tonight. "Mark, Tim, you guys are going to have to roll us out of here even before we get to the main course."

Tim smiled and responded humbly, "Randall, I wouldn't say that yet. Mark is doing a little recipe experimentation on us with the hors d'oeuvres. Who knows? I'm not convinced we'll make it to the entrees. He winked at Mark, knowing full well the food would be delicious. The broad selection of starters was their way of making the evening special and showing off, just a little.

"So, the old guy from the planning commission; I take it he swayed the rest of them to accept your proposal?" I asked as I stood up to snag a bottle of wine and refill my glass. I filled Mom's glass, too, then passed it around the table. Likewise, we started passing around the various foods that had just been delivered: escargot, calamari, goat cheese with an assortment of breads, fresh buffalo mozzarella on sliced melon and prosciutto, and, well, we were not going to go hungry tonight.

Uncle Bill had leaned back in his chair, stretched out his arms, and then linked his hands behind his head. "Well, not exactly all of it, but it was pretty humorous when we came back into the conference room; and it took a heck of a lot longer than thirty minutes. Daylight had turned to dusk, then to night by the time the old guy came to get us. He was smiling, so your Dad and I thought we were home free. By the time we entered the conference room the committee had shrunk by one. Barton was gone.'

* * *

The approvals for the development had taken the better part of a year to weave their way through the various city departments, but ultimately, PW Simmons had gained approval to move ahead with a significant portion of the proposal.

The request to extend the mall for a total of two uninterrupted blocks, was nixed due to concerns over car traffic. As a compromise, the north south traffic would effectively be limited to pedestrians only for the two blocks, but cross car traffic would bisect the walking mall; not perfect, but the team thought it workable. The most important aspect of the project was a breakthrough in the use of eminent domain for the project. Although limited to only the furthest southern block, the city council had agreed to acquire the buildings on this block and resell them to PW Simmons for redevelopment under the expectation and obligation that certain aspects of the development would be fulfilled. The approval also came with significant penalties, to effectively make up for lost tax revenues, if the overall project was delayed. The additional penalty provisions added huge financial risk for PW Simmons; however, it eliminated the need to negotiate the acquisition of each building of the project, a process that could take years.

In any case, it was good that it looked as if they would no longer have to deal with Phil Barton as part of the commission. His resignation had addressed a number of issues related to getting the project started, at least. Unfortunately, Barton had now become an even more significant impediment to the project, one that could likely kill the entire project.

Upon resigning from the committee, Phil Barton had aggressively moved to acquire two buildings in the targeted redevelopment area, one on each side of the street. He had little trouble finding a couple of motivated sellers. Being unaware of the potential redevelopment project, they were thrilled to dump their property. The acquisition gave Barton the opportunity, he hoped, to once again extort huge profits from PW Simmons, or the city. Quite frankly, he did not care where the money came from as long as it ended up in his pocket. The fact that he had effectively used insider knowledge to his benefit did not bother him in the least. Since he was no longer a member of the commission, he theoretically no longer had influence over the council, and any accusations of insider knowledge would be tough to prove. If it was not illegal, he did not give a shit if it was ethical or not.

Barton intended to assert his power through extortion. He had filed a lawsuit against the city to prevent them from using eminent domain and to block the transfer of properties to PW Simmons. Lanny joked that, like a mad dog, Barton was pissing all over the place to mark his territory. Although it was doubtful the lawsuit would prevail on legal grounds, it was clear it could hold up the progress for the foreseeable future. The suit could take years to meander through the system. It was clear that Barton was either going to make a mountain of dough out of his investment or everyone was going to fail. He was confident the Simmons family and the city would not want the project to fail. There was too much good to gain, both in tax revenues and the life of downtown.

PW Simmons now faced a dilemma. From one aspect, they were confident they could make the problem go away merely by offering to buy out Barton; however, this came with huge costs. Barton was going to likely require a massive premium for his properties. The premium would then likely re-establish the fair market values that would then be applied to the rest the properties as the city exercised eminent domain (a real problem). The second option was to let the suit run its course; letting the city deal with Barton and fund the battle. On the surface, this seemed to be the most prudent course of action; however, it came with a long leash that could leave PW Simmons obligated to move quickly with the redevelopment as soon as the suit was resolved. It could tie the hands of their company to a potential liability for years. This option was frightening in that it would effectively limit PW Simmons from alternative investments the entire time Barton's suit weaved through the courts.

Paul and William had holed up in their conference room all morning discussing how they should address Barton's lawsuit. They needed to come up with a way to blunt the effect Barton was having on their business.

Paul jokingly said, "You know it would be a hell of a lot easier if that son-of-bitch would just keel over from a heart attack."

William looked up from his notes without moving his head and responded "Well, we have had our experience with people dying over our company priorities before. Maybe he could just shoot himself, huh?"

Paul cringed. "Not funny, William. I was just kidding on the heart attack. I don't really wish the guy harm; well maybe a little, but not dying. Hell, a judge would end up feeling sorry for his family and they'd end up winning."

"Look, Paul, what would really be the problem if we just pulled back on owning all the properties anyway. We could still push the city to redo the street. We'd renegotiate the deal with the city and let the prick keep his two buildings. Sure, he will have won a small battle and he will make a bundle after the redevelopment starts, but at least we could still do some good for the city. I suspect we could still afford to buy a few of the most important buildings and renovate them."

"I doubt we could really afford much of anything. Interest rates are higher than we have ever seen and you know Barton is going to let it leak out about the development just to drive up the value of his buildings. So even though we should be able to go it alone, I just don't see how it could work. Eventually those buildings are going to end up costing us a hell of a lot more. Worse, we could be faced with metering out the renovations over years, delaying the payback, if there is any left over. I am not sure how we can make it work financially."

"How about we sell the car dealership and plow all of that into buying as many buildings as possible and passing on the rest?"

"William, you love that business and besides, we would not be selling at top dollar with this shitty economy. The car business pays a lot of bills. Yes, it's a nice idea, but our biggest challenge right now is the property I bought years ago, in San Diego when I thought Cal might actually end up playing baseball down there." Paul paused in silence, " I don't know what I was thinking back then. It seems like we are paying a small army to jump through hoops to get that housing project going and I don 't think it is going to get better anytime soon. God, if I could turn back the clock I would have never pushed us to get involved down there. I just seemed so good at the time."

William sat with his arms crossed across his chest. "I think it was a good idea then and I still think it will be a good investment for us; maybe our best investment. No, I would not sell that land now."

"Good thing, because I don't think it is worth a nickel more than we paid for it right now. In fact, I doubt we could get what we owe out of it. We are in never-never land there - heavily invested in it, but still needing to invest more before it is of any value. Today, if we sold it, we'd be wasting our total investment. Plus, we would need to lay off people. That's something we have never done before. I don't want to start now."

William was silent, "Look I think I am going to want to retire in a few years, so selling the car dealership really makes sense, unless you want to still run it after I'm gone. I know it is doing well for us, but I'll bet it is worth a hell of a lot more than we paid for it. It might buy us time to get this Linden Street thing off the ground and maybe even the San Diego tract, too."

"Well, maybe so, but it would be a hell of a lot easier to just cut our losses by pulling out of Linden Street. We could actually make Barton squirm. He'd be left with a couple of old buildings no one wants in a crappy section of town and a big mortgage." Paul smiled to himself thinking about sticking it to Barton.

William laughed. "Paul, you are so full of shit. As fun as it would be to hurt Barton, I know you want to do the Linden Street development. You need to do this; if not for the city, then for yourself. Let's quit kidding ourselves and make it happen; even if it is on a smaller scale. Maybe we could back out if we had not already pulled in Lyle's money, but now we have his legacy to remember. We owe it to him. We have to make it work. Hell, if we cash out of the car business, I can spend my last few years working managing the project. I can run the construction aspect of Linden Street and you handle the property management to make sure we actually have someone that is willing to put their businesses in the buildings once we're complete. Otherwise, we are all going to be looking for new jobs soon."

* * *

My freshman year in high school was not a fun time for me. It started out with my first day unwittingly making enemies of both teachers and the Barton kid and never seemed to get righted. I mean, I got great grades, never created trouble, but for some reason, teachers never seemed to like me. I was condoned, but never accepted. It sucked.

To make it worse my best friend in the world, Johnny Jackson passed away just before Christmas that year. He had met me after school at our favorite café. We had agreed to meet over a couple slices of pie and coffee, Johnny was buying, to discuss what it was like for him to serve in the army during the Korean War, the current subject in my American history course. I had made the mistake in class of bringing up the fact that my Dad and my best friend had both served in the war. The teacher latched onto this and decided to assign a new assignment for the class: interview someone that was directly affected by the war and write a paper of at least five hundred words about the impact to their life. It represented an additional class assignment and just before Christmas break. It served to make me even less popular with my classmates.

Johnny and I had just finished up our pie and I had bent over to pull my notebook and pen out of my backpack. As I placed the notebook on the table, I looked up to notice something wrong with Johnny; his eyes were open and were staring at something across the room. Well, not really staring, all the life was drained from them. They were sightless. It is hard to imagine that with just a briefest of glances, I could tell that Johnny was no longer with me. I guess eyes really hadn't changed much; still the same clear brown with just a hint of hazel, but the sparkle had disappeared. All the life had evaporated in a puff. I sat quietly, waiting for something, anything that could jump revived life into those eyes. It never happened and that is my last memory of being with Johnny: getting ready to fire some questions at him on a topic I suspect he never ever wanted to talk of.

* * *

Johnny's funeral was a quiet, sober, and small event. We were his only family and Dad had him buried in our family plot. I think it only made sense. He had lived with us for almost five years and had become a part of our family that would be dearly missed.

In retrospect, Johnny's passing gave me a much-needed push to grow up and start making a path unique only to me, pulling out of my self-made wake of frustration of trying to live up to the standards set by my Dad and Cal. I had to set my own course and not look back. It's not that I was not proud of my family, but I finally realized I needed to be my own person.

For me the challenge meant stepping away from my temerity to stand for up for something, for myself. My first opportunity came the very first day after returning to school from Christmas break. Billy Barton and his group of goons had monopolized their normal lunch table just inside the entrance to our cafeteria. I call them goons now because to me they were nothing more than bullies and thugs; probably always had been and probably always would be. I suspect they laid claim to this location just inside the cafeteria to harass the other students as they arrived for lunch. I was one of this group's normal targets and today would be no different, at least that is what Barton thought.

Barton pushed himself out from the table, sliding his chair into me as I walked by. Laughing and looking to his buds he commented half to intimidate me, all to impress his friends, "So your brown-tard friend finally kicked the bucket?" Bill Barton laughed once again, self-impressed at his supposed witticism. "Rumor has it you bored him to death with your Korea..." I really do not recall specifically what happened next other than I tackled the jerk. Apparently, after landing a number of punches and a head-butt for good measure two teachers had pulled me off Bill Barton. Years later one of those same teachers confided in me that they actually let me pummel the Barton kid longer than they should have just because the bully had it coming. His friends had just sat in silence, not a one willing to stand up to help their friend and leader.

I had the pleasure of sitting outside the principal's office for the remainder of the day waiting for my Mom and Dad to arrive for a conference that would end-up including the Dean of Boys, the Principal, my Dad and Mom, and the two teachers that broke up the short fight. Time ticked by in slow motion. Two hours may as well have been two days. At 2:30, Mom and Dad walked into the school's administration office. Dad's eyes were piercing through me. It was the first time I had ever been in trouble and I could tell from his look, he intended it to be the last. There was no forgiveness there, just anger and the presumption of guilt. I looked to Mom to get some support. She just slowly shook her head as if to say, "Don't say anything, yet."

My principal opened his door, noticing that my parents had arrived. "Mister and Missus Simmons, I am happy you could come on such short notice. We have to discuss a serious matter regarding Randall's conduct today over lunch break." He motioned us all to come into his office and shut the door after us.

Dad started even before the principal could sit down. "I want you to know fighting is not something we condone in our household, and we will deal with Randall appropriately. You can be assured of that." Then to me "Randall, I cannot believe you got into a fight and your principal tells me you started it. What were you thinking? I know; you weren't."

The principal interrupted. "Mister Simmons, I think there might be some extenuating circumstances. After talking with you on the phone, I discussed the matter with the two teachers that stopped the fight, and apparently, Billy Barton may have started the whole thing by pushing his chair into Randall. Anyway, I thought we owed it to Randall to hear his side of the story before I determine what actions the school needs to take."

"Billy Barton?" Dad looked at me and I nodded. His whole demeanor changed in an instant. One moment bristling and dominant, the next, the anger deflated, and he was elated. He understood.

After hearing me recount Billy's "brown-tard" comment, the principal had his secretary call in the Dean of Boys and the two teachers that had rescued Billy. After confirming my story, I thought I was home free. I probably would have been, too, except for the fact that I had broken Billy's nose. For me I would be suspended for three days from school. Billy would likewise be suspended and would be placed on probation; any more fighting or tormenting of me, and he would be expelled.

The walk from the school office to Mom and Dad's car was quiet, I could sense Dad wanted to say something but had decided it best to wait until we had the relative privacy of the car.

Dad smiled as he lowered himself into the driver seat. He looked at me in the rear-view mirror and said "Damn, Randall, good job. I wished I'd had the nerve you had today. I know Johnny appreciated what you did." He smiled again. Mom smiled and I smiled. High school was now fun.

Chapter 32

M**Y RUN-IN WITH** Billy Barton changed my relation with Dad. Prior to Billy Barton, ours had been a weak association, marked not by animosity, but by indifference. My father never seemed able to bring himself to be close to me. After Barton, we had something in common with one another, and it was good. Instead of spending afternoons with Johnny, I now spent them with Dad and Uncle Bill at the office. I was learning the business and at the same time getting to know my Dad for the first time. I truly got to see him in action not more than a month after the Barton incident of Fort Collins High. Now I got a front seat at the second Barton act here in Dad's office.

* * *

Watching through the glass wall of the conference room I could see Phil Barton, confidently sitting at one side of the long conference table; his feet crossed and propped up on the chair beside him. Dad sat at the end of the table facing him while Uncle Bill sat directly across the table from Barton. The conversation was to be the start of a negotiation for PW Simmons Corp to acquire Barton's two buildings on Linden Street and to get

Barton to cease his lawsuit that had thrown such a large wrench into the entire Linden Street redevelopment schedule.

Dad had been avoiding this negotiation for weeks, but now was faced with either buying Barton's properties for an unrealistically high price now or delay further and be faced with an even more insane asking price later. The only other likely alternative was to cancel the project with the city and move on to other investment opportunities. This later choice was particularly unpalatable in that it would waste more than a year of planning and approvals with the city.

Barton rocked back in his chair with his hands clasped behind his head. "So, Simmons, I was going to be nice on this negotiation, but my price went up once your little dick of a son attacked my boy last year. My attorney tells me I probably would not be successful at suing your ass for breaking my kid's nose, but I figure I'll get my money out of you one way or another."

Dad and Uncle Bill sat quietly as Phil Barton attempted to set the stage for the negotiation, positioning himself as the man of power, holding all the cards, and being magnanimous in just showing up at the office to discuss the potential of him selling his buildings. Uncle Bill could tell from Dad's fidgeting with his pen that he was having great difficulty in not jumping up to strangle the prick. He wondered how long it would be before Dad's fidgeting would break the pen, spewing ink over the table.

Uncle Bill interrupted Barton. "So, I get all your posturing, Phil, but let's cut to the chase. Paul and I know what you have tied up in those two dilapidated buildings so do not push too hard. What are you looking to get for your investment?"

Phil, smiled and pulled his brief case up to the table. He opened the case, but instead of pulling out his proposed price and terms, he pulled out a cigar and proceeded to light up in the closed conference room. Figuratively, he was using this opportunity to piss all over Dad's and Uncle Bill's turf. He then proceeded to throw out a number that was more than three times the amount for which had purchased the buildings not more than two months earlier. He puffed on his cigar a blew the smoke in Dad's direction.

Dad surprised everyone by starting to laugh. "Damn, Phil, that is stupid. I knew you had balls, but I hoped you also had brains. Now I realize you and your son have a lot in common: air between the ears. Here we were prepared to give you a generous offer for your properties.," he motioned to three folders he had stacked in front of him on the table, "but, you just attacked my sensibilities with your comments and just pissed me off."

Dad rose from his seat, gathered the folders and dumped them in the trash can. "I can see we have no room to work. If I am forced to cancel the project, then so be it. William, let's set up some time with the mayor to tell him what's going on. I'm sure he will be disappointed, but in the same respect, he will be glad to be able to put Barton's lawsuit to rest." Then facing Barton, "Barton, you may as well pull your attorney off the lawsuit. There is not going to be any imminent domain issues anymore. Oh, and, by the way, enjoy owning those two pieces of shit you call buildings. I am sure you will enjoy owning them every month the mortgage comes due." Dad turned to walk out of the conference room.

Barton's face took on a look of shock and he let his feet drop to the ground. "Heck, Paul, I was just joking. Get on back to the table. We can negotiate something that works for both of us. I'm sure."

Dad turned back to face Barton. "You know, Barton, my kid reminded me how important it is to stick up for what is right and, you know, I think I am going to do it. No deal."

Barton, stood up and faced Uncle Bill. "My God, William, talk some sense into your brother. This project has already cost you tons. To walk away now is crazy. It will end up costing you a small fortune. Look, let me just take a look at your offer and let me see if I can make it work."

Uncle Bill just smiled and motioned Barton to the door. "You know, Phil, I have never been prouder of my big brother than I am now. Good luck with your Linden Street real estate."

* * *

Sitting at one of Dad's employee's desks watching the three men through the conference room windows, imagining what was being said had been entertaining. Regardless of what was said in that room, it was clear that old man Barton had over-played his hand with Dad. When Dad had opened the conference room door and walked out nonchalantly with a calm, small grin, as if the world's weight had been taken off his shoulders, I knew he had won. What exactly had happened behind those glass windows I had not been sure of until tonight. I remember us walking down the steps together, his arm draped over my shoulder, leaving Uncle Bill behind with Mister Barton.

One thing Dad did share with me that day was that it was probably best to keep some distance between me and the Billy Barton kid, at least until he got done "bloodying Phil Barton's nose." That is what Dad had said; "bloodying Phil Barton's nose." I guess Dad was just saying it was time to take down another bully.

* * *

Uncle Bill laughed so hard he was almost in tears as he described Phil Barton begging to get them to pull the offer back out of the trash can. He went on to say that after my Dad had left, Phil had gone so far as to say he would be willing to part with the buildings if we would just take over the loans, he'd sacrifice his down-payment. It is amazing what a fourteen percent loan will do to a person. Those buildings that Barton had hoped were assets that would enable him to extort huge profits were now just mill stones. They were likely going to force him into bankruptcy. He was ruined.

"So, Uncle Bill, what finally happened with Barton? It was kind of like the Barton family faded away during my sophomore year of high school."

Chapter 33

William knocked on the door of Paul's office and walked in. "So, Paul, you think we have let Barton sweat long enough?"

"I don't know, has he filed for bankruptcy?" Paul smiled at William.

It had been two weeks since they had called Barton's bluff in their office. Since that time, Paul and William had met with a city's attorney to review options to renegotiate their agreements with the city. Interestingly, the attorney had informed them that their communications with Barton had gone quiet; neither he nor his attorney were returning phone calls. The city attorney had assumed they were looking for an additional means to introduce additional delays to the project.

Paul and William knew a more likely scenario was that Barton had realized he was in serious trouble, and he was no longer acting logically. He was now looking for some way, any way, to extricate himself from his unaffordable financial burden. Avoiding the city was just an attempt to put off the unavoidable. They had both seen people in this position before. As Barton's options dried up, he was now relying on nothing more than hope and prayer, not a powerful negotiating position.

William had come to the office today to meet with his brother and Barton. Paul and he had decided it was time to let Barton off the hook. No matter how enticing it would be to let Barton suffer, the brothers had agreed it was now time to save Barton, whether he deserved it or not. They had set this meeting up for today at four o'clock with Barton a week prior under the pretense of presenting him with a take it or leave it, final offer for both the buildings he owned on Linden. The purchase would be on their terms and there would be no negotiation, so they had suggested Barton bring legal representation if he needed, so that they might consummate the deal during the meeting. PW Simmons would have their attorney present along with a notary to sign the documents.

They had purposely set the meeting up for late in the afternoon to keep the discussion short and focused and to create just a little additional pressure. Although Paul and William had actually developed a pretty fair offer that should make Barton whole, they had thoroughly enjoyed themselves in making Barton think their offer would squeeze the life out of him. They could only imagine how their "take it or leave" language must have made Barton sweat over the past week.

Four o'clock came and went and no Phil Barton. It was a full fifteen minutes before the reception knocked on the conference room door and ushered Phil Barton in. In his right hand, he held a well-worn, soft leather brief case. In his left, he carried his overcoat. His face looked as if he had not slept and if he had, he had done so in the suit he was now wearing. His tie was loosened and his top shirt button was open. He was alone. He was obviously beaten.

Paul and William moved from exuberance to shame. They had pushed too hard.

Ignoring everyone in the conference room except Paul, Phil sat without being asked. "So, Paul, what do I need to do to get you to take these buildings off my hands? Look if you could just take over the loans, I have a little extra savings I might be able to provide to sweeten the deal. I just can't go into bankruptcy."

Paul stopped Phil from going any farther. "Look, we are not here to steal the property from you. We were prepared to give you a fair offer last time you were here, but you were the one that decided to take advantage of the situation." With that comment, Paul placed a contract in front of Barton. "You were rude and a prick, but William and I aren't. If you are serious about dumping the property, we'll give you what you have into it. It's more than the property is worth and you'll be doing a heck lot better than you have any right to expect. We are willing to overlook the crap you have put us through and hope you understand this is how William and I prefer to do business, not how we have to do business. Just know had this been twenty years ago, I'd have told you to go fuck yourself, and I would have gotten the property a hell of a lot cheaper from the bankruptcy trustee."

Phil Barton closed his eyes collapsed forward onto the table, leaning his head on his clasped hands. Hiding his face, he began to sob. Between his sobs, they heard him say, "Thank you. Thank you, Thank you."

William motioned to Paul without speaking and both brothers silently got up and left the conference room, leaving Phil Barton along with their shocked lawyer and the notary.

Soon the sobbing sound dissipated and Phil Barton opened the door of the conference room to leave. "Paul, William, thank you again. I signed the papers. Just send over copies when you are done." He turned away and started to leave.

Paul called after him, "One last thing, Phil, we're done now. No more trying to wreck our projects and keep your kid away from Randall. Understood?"

Phil turned back to Paul "Understood."

After Phil had left the office, Paul and William returned to the conference room and their attorney and notary.

"Any surprises?" Paul asked. He looked first to the attorney, then to the notary.

They shook their heads. The attorney slid the signed agreement across the table to William. To Paul, he nodded to the chair next to the seat that had been occupied by Barton, "Mister Barton seems to have forgotten his briefcase. You want me to drop it by his house for you?"

Paul let out a deep breath. "No, you have earned your pay today already. Thanks. Thanks to both of you."

After they left, Paul and William were left alone in the conference room with the agreement and Barton's briefcase.

"Paul, I'm glad we have that behind us. I think we may have pushed it a little too far with Barton."

"I think you're right and I sure am glad it is over. Hand me Barton's case, would you?"

William picked the case up noting it was heavier than it looked. "Shit, Paul, what the heck as Barton carrying in here?" He looked to Paul, "You mind if I take a look?"

"Be my guest. He shouldn't have left it here anyway."

William opened the case on the table exposing a large, loaded 357 magnum revolver along with a half empty box of shells and a note to Barton's wife that merely said, 'Betty, I'm sorry. Take the insurance money and don't think of me again.'

Chapter 34

"Well, somewhere along the way your Daddy went from being a hard-core business driver to a guy that was pretty much all heart. He let Barton sweat for a few months, but ended up giving him a lot more than he needed for the properties. By that time, we had sold the dealership, so we could pay the mortgages off. Barton was crazy in the first place to buy those properties at such a high interest rate. The interest alone had to be sucking him dry. By the way, it was good Billy never bothered you again. I cannot imagine what your Dad would have done if the Bartons threatened you. I don't think he ever returned the brief case, I think he kept it and the note just as insurance to make sure Barton kept his word."

I was blown away. "I know Dad did not like Barton and I sure as hell hated his kid, but wasn't that a little extreme?"

"Don't ask me. Ask your Mom."

I looked to Mom, and she only smiled back. "Randall, you were the most important thing in Dad's life. Of course, he'd never have told you that. After losing Cal, he was always watching over you; trying to make sure you were safe. I think taking care of Billy Barton was more important to him than those stupid buildings."

Mark and Tim started to serve dinner by first opening up another couple bottles of wine. Mark quipped, "William you may as well have some wine now. These are a couple great bottles of wine you'll be missing. After dinner gets started I move to the cheap stuff."

I chuckled when Uncle Bill finally relinquished and held out his wine glass to be filled. "I can have just a little now that I have been talking so much. I need to provide a little lubrication after all that work." He laughed and asked Mark to pour a little more in his glass "just so I can catch up." Mark was happy to tip the wine bottle a little longer.

Mark talked as he poured. "Okay, while you dig into your meals, remember if you don't like something, it is Tim's fault. If you love it, it is my inspiration."

Tim was used to the ribbing. It was a banter that had marked their relation from their first time together. It kept the business happy and fun even when times had been rough. Tim took a brief look around the table and said, "Randall, what do you know about what your Mom and Dad did for the businesses here on the mall?"

Tim surprised me with the question, catching me between bites. "Well, I know they have always taken a lot of pride in what the mall has become."

* * *

Mark and Tim had stared up at the red brick building that they had hoped would eventually be their business. Mister Simmons had walked through the building with them, pointing out areas that could or could not be changed to accommodate their dreams. It had been exciting and the two young men had to try to control themselves so as not to look too enthusiastic. They did not want to tip their hand and lose any opportunities to negotiate a favorable deal from the developer.

Reality had set in as Mister Simmons started sharing his "ball-park" cost estimates to alter the facility to turn it into the restaurant Mark and Tim envisioned. These estimated costs were so much higher than they had been prepared for they had each begun to cut back on their expectations as the walkthrough had proceeded.

"Mister Simmons, I know we had outlined a pretty unique picture of what we were looking for. We really want the place to make a statement not only for the quality of the food and service, but we want the ambiance and environment to provide the clientele a reason for getting out of the house. We want the restaurant to speak to its uniqueness the first time a person walks through the front door. This place can certainly address that, but I am afraid it might be more than Mark and I can handle, you know, given this is our first restaurant. We just have to recognize our limitations, and I certainly don't want to waste your or your company's time if this building is just out of reach."

"Tim, thanks for your concern. I appreciate it. Oh, and please call me Paul. Mister was reserved for my Dad, and he's been dead for more than a decade. Look, for most of the buildings on this mall, we did some generic remodeling to bring them up to code and make them useful for general retail and sold them. For this corner building, we have decided to keep it in our real estate portfolio and make it the cornerstone for the entire mall. It needs to scream uniqueness and provide a cool experience that calls people back to mall time after time. When William and I looked at your vision for your restaurant, we liked it a lot. What you need to think about now is whether you really can pull it off. I want to invest in a business and owners that have the creativity and energy to do something exciting. I think the initial financing needs to take a back seat for now." Paul paused. "So, what do you think? Can you make this something you and I can be proud of? Can you make this a business that calls back repeat customers time, after time, after time?"

It was a question Mark and Tim had not confronted seriously. Sure, they thought they had a great business plan, but Paul had put it to them so directly, they now doubted their plan. They were struck speechless as they thought about why their plan would succeed.

Paul sensed their new-found indecision so he stopped the discussion. "Look, you two need to think about this some more. Meet me here tomorrow, same time, and I want to hear why you believe you have a great plan. I want to know why your restaurant is going to continue to be exciting to clientele. I want you to tell me why PW Simmons and I should bet on your success. I'll have a table set up inside for us to discuss your plans for the restaurant, so don't disappoint." At that Paul turned on his heel and walked to his car, leaving Mark and Tim staring after him.

He had called them on their plans. They needed to re-examine their belief in their plans to understand if they were really committed or if they had just seduced themselves into believing their own set of optimistic assumptions. They had not an idea as to how to proceed or what would convince Paul Simmons. Even if they could convince Paul, they still had the issue of money. The building cost dwarfed the investment they had built into their business plans.

* * *

Tim and Mark showed up early to the meeting. Tim was pushing a cart filled with a couple chafing dishes, a cutting board, and cooking utensils. Mark trailed carrying a satchel over his shoulder and pushing a second cart filled with wine, place setting for four, a portable gas stove and a couple bags filled with groceries. They came prepared for show and tell.

Paul, William, Arlin, and Lanny were already waiting inside, sitting around a table configured from an old door situated atop two saw horses, drinking coffee they had picked up along the way during the walk from their office. Tim and Mark were obviously surprised by having the PW Simmons management team in attendance for their pitch.

Paul stood up to welcome the two budding entrepreneurs and to introduce his partners. "I hope I did not throw a wrench into your presentation by inviting the whole team, but this is our most important building and everyone here has a vested interest in our selection for the lessee."

Mark smiled. "Paul, not a concern. It looks as though we brought just enough to take care of everyone, but I hope you don't mind if Tim and I do not join you for what I think will be a memorable lunch.

"We thought the best way to show off our plans is to make them more real. We want to show you why we think, no, we know we have what it takes to keep people wanting to come back. We want to be a destination for the mall. If you don't mind, I have also brought an outline as to how we think the place can change over time to make sure it always stays fresh and interesting for our clientele."

Paul, William, Arlin, and Lanny sat back and enjoyed the next couple hours as the two promising restauranteers jumped into action. It was obvious Tim represented the culinary creative genius and Mark provided the management horse power. It was equally obvious they not only supported each other, but they fed off each other's energy. Tim worked at a frenetic pace as he prepared dish after dish, while Mark provided a calming face to the four developers that belied the activity behind him. Mark provided knowledge and individual service,

Tim provided a unique food in both taste and presentation. They both combined to provide an exciting, memorable, and tremendous dining experience.

Between dishes, Mark and Tim would sit at the end of the table and call attention to specific aspects of the building they thought might enhance the dining experience. For them the old building provided a wonderful empty canvas just made to perfect the artwork that would be their restaurant.

After the meal, Mark and Tim laid out a stack of rough drawings that provided some insight as to their vision for the business. They had laid out a bold redesign of the building, removing the majority of the second floor to provide for a beautiful high, open beamed ceiling for the main dining area and smaller open loft for special dining occasions. They had penned in a broad central staircase leading to the upstairs area. Below the staircase, they had included a small but classy bar area. The design of the bar was important in that it was large enough to cater to the bistro clientele, but small enough not to cater to bar hoppers. They did not want their business to lose its place as a high-class restaurant. The kitchen was a novel concept; the grill areas were completely open to view, providing a unique experience, but one that came with huge challenges. The first challenge was that food preparation had to include showmanship and be 100% committed to cleanliness, both in practice and perception. Management would need to be vigilant. The second challenge was noise. If the ambient noise level rose too high, people could not talk, and the experience would deteriorate.

Paul was skeptical of the kitchen concept, but loved the majority of what he was seeing. Arlin was fascinated with the potential that had been unleashed for this tired, old building. He got up from the table and grabbed a couple of the drawings and began to walk and talk as he pointed to specific structures in the building to suggest alterations and improvements to Mark and Tim's plans. In real time, he was reinventing the interior of the building. Eventually, the whole group was following Arlin around as he outlined how the building's character could be maintained while synergistically delivering on Mark and Tim's dream.

After half an hour of exciting brainstorming, they returned to the table to share a bottle of a wine that Tim had told them he had been saving for the end of the meeting. "I hope we have had enough time away from the food to enjoy this. We think you will really like this." In reality, they had saved two bottles for the PW Simmons team: first, a 1970 Bordeaux from Chateau Mouton-Rothschild and second, a 1973 Cabernet Sauvignon from a relatively young winery out of Napa Valley called Stag's Leap.

As Mark poured he introduced the wines. "The Bordeaux is something Tim and I have been saving for a very special occasion, and we hope this is it. It should have a huge, concentrated taste. It might be a little dry for your taste, but with a great steak, wonderful. The Stag's Leap, might be a little less dry, but the taste just goes on and on. It is a surprisingly wonderful wine that we hope gives the Bordeaux a run for its money, but we are going to leave that up to you." Mark pulled out two glasses for each member of Paul's team. Smiling he said, "I think it is a good thing you will be walking back to the office."

Tim and Mark left Paul, Lanny, William, and Arlin to enjoy the wine and, hopefully, discuss what they saw and experienced today. After waiting for what seemed an eternity, but in reality no more than five to ten minutes, Tim broke the silence "So what do you think? Do Mark and I have what you need for the mall and this building? I know we kind of tripped over your questions yesterday, but now I think we have answered them. Yes, we have something that will make us all proud, and it will be an asset to the mall. We think you should bet on our success because we have talent, vision, and energy for this business. Plus, Mark and I complement each other so well; we cannot lose."

* * *

The discussion back in the PW Simmons's office after Mark and Tim's presentation became circular: acknowledging the creativity, but concern over the lack of experience; loving the talent and passion, but lacking the financial capability. All four men liked the idea of a high-end restaurant at the entrance to the mall, as long as it could keep itself contemporary and fashionable. It would provide a welcoming business that spoke to quality and instantaneously differentiated this experience from the shopping malls.

Ultimately, they agreed Mark and Tim were the right candidates for this piece of real estate. Their passion and talent would guarantee they had a showcase business to attract future businesses and customers. They also agreed that they absolutely wanted to maintain ownership of this particular piece of real estate as the cornerstone of the entire mall. They desired to lease the real estate and maintain tight control over the improvements to ensure the work complemented the entire mall. That said, the investment to take the skeleton of structure and create a functional and exciting restaurant would be huge, probably a lot bigger than their two prospective clients could afford, so they needed to come up with a means to provide the upfront capital.

William provided an opening to move the discussion forward. "Look, if we think these are the right guys, can we fund the interior investment and do it in agreement with Mark and Tim. We could up the rent to pay off the investment over time. I have to believe, getting that building occupied with a vibrant business is going to make leasing or selling the rest of the real estate a heck of a lot easier."

Lanny responded, "You are right, but we have earmarked our budgets already and we are pretty close to being tapped out. Paul, how much do you think Tim and Mark have available for investment? Maybe enough to take care of the kitchen at least?"

Paul shook his head. "I might have screwed up on this one. These guys have barely enough to take over an existing small restaurant. They don't have even close to what it would take to start a place like we discussed today. I probably shouldn't have showed them the building on Linden. It is at least twice the size they had originally looked for, but they are so passionate, just the kind of people we want running businesses on Linden. Lanny, they're kind of like us when we jumped into our first development. It scared the hell out of me.

"I actually thought those two guys would fall apart yesterday when we showed up in mass, but they took it in stride. Hell, if they failed, we would have just chalked it up to the business and the building being too much for them, outsizing their dreams, and their pocket book. Instead, I think they are right for it for everything except their pocketbook. Look, how about Sam and I loan the company the money to complete the retrofit."

"Paul, are you serious?" asked William. "It's a lot of money and you have a kid getting set for college. Maybe you and Sam need to talk about this."

"We have. Last night. And she said that if I thought it was a good thing, we will pull out some of our savings to make it happen." Then he smiled, "Randall doesn't know it yet, but it looks like he will be working to pay his own way through college. Just kidding, I think we'll be fine."

"Okay," said Lanny, "then I think we need to get Arlin's team into there to finish the design, assuming Tim and Mark are ready to sign on the line for the lease."

Chapter 35

TIM PUSHED BACK from the table and stretched. "My God, I am good. I don't think I could have improved on that dinner. You agree?" he said, fishing for complements.

Mark shook his head "Folks please ignore him. If you complement the meal, I will have to listen to his bragging and his cooking secrets all night. Randall, just so you know, your Dad made our business happen. He was, and still is, our patron saint; but not just ours, but for a lot of the businesses here on the mall. Back then when we started, interest rates were so high, and the economy was terrible. I can't tell you how many of our neighbors could not pay their bills and ended up going out of business. It was a bad time that lasted the whole time you were away at college. I am so glad your Mom and Dad saved this place."

Mark looked at my Mom and mouthed, "Thank you."

* * *

Paul leaned back in his chair. The office was quiet now since it was after seven at night. All the lights were out except for his desk lamp. He had just laid off one of his company's employees, a young, budding architect that had joined their firm this past year. This had been her first job out of school, and she had been such an energetic addition to the office. Laying her off had been one of the hardest things he had done in his life. It was like saying goodbye to his kid.

She had taken the news like a pro, sitting stoically, taking in the words without responding. He had thought everything was okay until he heard her sobbing as she cleaned out her desk. He felt ashamed. He stayed in his office until she had left and only then had he opened his office door. He had decided to inform her of his decision late in the day so that most of the rest of the staff would have already left.

He had known he needed to cut costs for some time now. In general, their business was doing okay, but they were facing a noticeable slowdown in the local economy. High interest rates had put a major hurt on their home sales. Their most recent development was selling out at only half the rate they had planned, forcing them to reduce their construction teams. Rental incomes were probably doing even worse. He was facing a number of commercial properties that were behind in their rent. Of these businesses that had fallen behind, a number were small retailers that would never catch up. These were just barely holding on now, deciding daily who should be paid next, trying to stretch their limited dollars as best possible to provide an opportunity for some type of miraculous recovery. They were slowly shrinking their inventory to pay utilities or the employees' salaries. Many of his small retail tenants had already laid off their sales staff, hoping that they could work even more hours to somehow make up for the short staff. They would just slowly die, of course, their owners facing bankruptcy.

Tonight, before heading home, he would be visiting one of these dying businesses. This business was particularly troublesome. The tenant had been running a successful and profitable upscale retail business for years. He had recently expanded his business to a second site, and everything was going good; maybe too good. The expansion had forced him to take out a small business bank loan that had adjusted with rising interest rates, resulting in rising costs each quarter. The killer had been the ultimate slow-down in the economy. His product, high-end stereo gear, had been in demand when the economy was ginning, became an unaffordable luxury now. The owner had called him up this morning and had informed Paul he was leaving the shop's keys on the counter. The building was now turned back over to PW Simmons. He had seen businesses die before; just not at the rate he was currently seeing.

For PW Simmons, this had been the first layoff for their office staff; however, Lanny had already warned Paul more would likely be required. It was going to be a trying time. The good news; they could finally see the end of the bureaucratic tunnel that had been holding up their development in California. If they could outlast the current economic downturn, they had a very rosy future. One might think this would make the layoffs easier, knowing it was preparing the company for future success, but for Paul, it made it even more difficult. It just meant PW Simmons was going to survive, but a lot of people that had made the company a success would not.

He took comfort in the darkened office. He did not want to go home to face Sam, now. He knew that she would say she understood, but he knew she would also be ashamed. Ashamed that her husband had failed. Every person laid off was just another mark of shame.

* * *

Mark and Tim were waiting outside the PW Simmons entrance as Paul came into work. He could tell from their look they were concerned. Paul had taken the two under his wing almost as his and Sam's adopted kids. They had been great tenants, at least until the past few months, and they had showed all the creativity and passion he had seen in them the first time they met. The past few months had been a struggle, however. They had fallen behind in their rent. Today they were fully a month late and he had called them in to discuss what was going on.

After a brief hello the three walked together up the steps to the PW Simmons place of business. Without stopping to say hello to any of the staff already present, Paul ushered Mark and Tim into his private office. "So, guys, have a seat." He motioned to the two chairs facing his desk. Instead of taking his place behind his desk, Paul instead pulled over a third chair from the corner and sat down.

Mark started before Paul could even tell them why he had asked them to his office. "Look, Paul, I know we're behind and we are working with the bank to secure a small loan to get us through. Business has really slowed down these past few months on the mall. Can you give us a couple more months to get our funding together?"

"Thanks, Mark, but stop right there. Tell me how borrowing money at 14% is going to help you when what you are really dealing with is a drop off in business? I'm not here to badger you on being late with the rent, even though that is unacceptable. I brought you here to discuss what you are going to do to stimulate the business level. Borrowing money at a high interest rate is merely going to dig the hole you are in deeper, unless you have a plan for those dollars that result in increased traffic.

"For me, I think I need you to be successful for the success of the entire mall. Everyone in the mall is suffering, and you are one of the mall's cornerstones. I need you to be successful. One month's rent is the least of my concerns. What I need from you is to consider expanding your operating hours to include breakfast."

Mark looked to Tim then shook his head and responded, "Paul, Tim and I think that makes a lot of sense, too. It would give us some more revenue with a lot less food costs. Plus, we even thought we might be able to put some café tables out in the mall to extend the seating area, but it costs us money to get the staff and menus in place. Money that we just don't have right now. We really don't know what to do."

Tim added, "Even if we do add the breakfast, it is going to take some time for it to catch on."

Paul interrupted, "Look, Sam and I are going to give you a personal loan. Part of it goes to bringing you up to date on your rent, okay? The rest goes to breakfast, right?"

"PW Simmons is going to throw in funds to advertise the mall and kick off a series of outdoor exhibitions; you know, live music and artists. It will be a waste if the businesses are not prepared to take advantage of it. You will have free customers if you can pull it off."

Mark looked to Paul and asked, "Paul, this is an amazing offer, but why? I mean, why are you giving us a personal loan to make it work? It is so risky."

"Look, last night I had to go home and tell Sam I laid off my first employee; my first ever. I never want to do that again. Sam agrees. So, you better not let me down."

Chapter 36

THE TABLE WAS quiet. I looked to Mom and she stared down at her plate. She finally offered, "I think Dad's laying off that young lady almost killed him. All he said when he got home was 'I don't want to do this anymore.' I knew things were bad then. He never talked about work at home and I never knew things were so bad. I did then. You know, we had made a wonderful life out of this business. I guess it was time to give something back, even if it was just to make it easy for your Dad to live with the decisions he needed to make. Plus, he actually liked these two guys." She said nodded to Mark and Tim, "So do I."

Uncle Bill was beginning to dose. He had certainly caught up with the wine as the conversation had dwindled so I suggested it was time we headed home. "Thanks for telling me a little about Dad. After we moved the business to San Diego, I really hadn't had the time. Oh, that's bullshit, I haven't made the time to get home to see my family. Now, I realize how much I have missed by not being here. Thanks."

* * *

Sitting by Dad's bed I pulled out his little blue journal. I once again pulled off the rubber-band that bound it closed. The band broke. No problem, I'd snag another from one of the drawers in the kitchen. The only light in the room come from the small bureau lamp next to my chair. I had chosen this small lamp in hope it would let me read a little more while not interrupting Dad's peaceful sleep. I could hear Dad's shallow breath, rhythmically reminding me Dad was still with me.

Near the back of the journal, Dad had written a note to me.

Randall -

I remember when you sprouted and when everything you experienced was new and exciting.
Perhaps it still is that way, but not so much . . .
At least in the way when you first felt the wind cool you or the sun warm you.

You brought smiles with your smile, melted our hearts when you bent our way
When you first took a step, we saw, not a baby, but a young boy
And our minds set off in wild imagination of the man to come

I am sure now you have grown as a tree in the forest, strong and flexing
Busy spreading branches, reaching out to places never touched
Reaching beyond anything my older branches could ever imbue.

My branches used to be the same, reaching out further each day.
Achieving heights well beyond those which my parents enjoyed
Stretching for the heavens with hubris, seemingly, to some . . .

Only to realize so many years later the importance of the rest of the trees in the forest.
They provided shade when I was the sapling
They shielded me from the winds that threatened to tear my branches.
They gave me water to quench my thirst while keeping the rains from washing away the soil.

Now you are just beginning a new phase of growth;
Your branches will get stronger, albeit less flexible,
Your leaves will become thicker, so that you might provide shade to others.
Your roots will go deeper, so that you are less reliant on rain.

You are a man.

Be strong, but not so strong that you ignore new thoughts.
Strength is not something you have,

But something you give to others through your compassion and care.
Strength without flexibility is useless.

Providing cover and guidance to others is hard.
It is risky and has to come out of love,
But, a little cover goes a long way.
A sapling never grows if it can't see and feel the sun.

As your roots grow deeper, don't forget the importance of rain.
Roots without water are useless;
We dry and whither without.
Stay with God, he is our water and sustenance.

If my tree is still around when you read this
My branches will have fewer leaves than I desire
And my branches will have become less flexible,
Less capable to shield young trees from the wind,

But my roots will be strong for you
If I am gone, remember me as I once was.
I hope I was good for you, providing shade and protection,
But, also room to grow into your own wonderful tree
 . . . and always remembering the water

. . . and if I wasn't good, hopefully, I made a good fire.

For Randall, something I could never say

Dad

I was numb. Dad and I had slowly developed a relation, but one that I had always thought of as being almost entirely professional. I know it sounds funny now, but Dad and I never really talked of anything even remotely smelling of emotions; but we would talk for hours about our business. Up until this past year, he had remained my primary resource when I felt like consulting with someone on a business decision we were facing with PW Simmons. I felt guilty reading Dad's poem; I have no doubt he meant this as something I would only see after he had passed from my life. That said, I don't think he can ever pass from my life really.

I got up from my chair, needing to give myself a break before returning to the book. I was shocked that my eyes had begun to mist, something that I was unaccustomed to. In the living room, Dad had kept his old stereo intact, an esoteric assortment from a by gone era. The pride and joy of his stereo was the large, tube McIntosh amplifier and preamplifier that he swore provided a superior sound to anything on the market today. In reality, I had to agree with him. They were beautiful both in sound and in looks. I can remember laying on the floor at night listening to these beasts pump out the music. I would flip out all the lights so the only illumination would that that came from the tubes. They were gorgeous. They oozed class. Beside the amplifier, Dad still had his old turntable, a huge monster from Thorens.

I thought it comical that his old turntable and vinyl records had once again become popular and valuable; not just as collector items, but for real audiophiles. I have no doubt his hundreds of old records still stacked by his stereo system would be just one more of Dad's investments that paid off. I suspect they were already worth more than he paid for them. For me, I dumped all of my vinyl albums years ago.

Idly looking through his albums, looking for what? Who knows. I guess I would know it when I saw it. It had been years since I had last flipped through Dad's records. It was like stepping back in time, a time when I was still back in college. I had always been surprised at the range of music Dad had. His tastes ranged from the driving rock that I had enjoyed as a high school student to orchestral pieces that included both classical and dissonant composers and his favorite, jazz. His jazz collection was extensive but he had had his favorites. Like my uncle, Dad had always been mesmerized by the smooth, bossa nova of Stan Getz. His favorite was now in my hands. It was a record from the early 60's that Getz had recorded with a Brazilian guitarist by the name of Joao Gilberto. The album was merely titled *Getz/Gilberto* and I can remember Dad playing this evenings with all the lights turned off in the sitting room, closing his eyes to hear all the nuances of the music. I imagined the music carried Dad away to a place where worry was no more; no more business challenges, no more responsibilities, just the floating melodies of Getz and Gilberto. Dad's favorite song was a piece that had eventually became my favorite, too - "The Girl from Impanema."

I turned on the stereo, enjoying watching the tubes come to life with their green glow. Turning down the volume so as not to wake the house up, I placed the album on Dad's old turntable, dropping the stylus on Dad's favorite track. Instantaneously, I felt the warmth and beauty come through Dad's stereo speakers.

I returned to his room to sit with him a little longer and maybe enjoy our song together.

Dad's eyes were open and looking at me as I entered the room. He smiled, I swear it was a smile, and spoke. "Randall, thank you for putting that on. I needed that to take me on to my next home." He stopped to let his words sink in.

"Randall, it is time." He held out his feeble arm and motioned to his pain killing opiate.

"Dad, are you hurting?"

Dad nodded yes.

I opened the bottle and removed the dropper and placed a small droplet under Dad's tongue. Dad looked to me and motioned again to the bottle.

* * *

Dad's eyes are still open. They are glassy and lifeless now, but I know he is not really gone. He is just done with the pain. Now, I think he is talking with Johnny, Granddad, Lyle, and Orley, figuring out how to get to San Diego.

I turned out the bureau lamp and went to bed.

Author's Note

Although the town of Fort Collins is real as are the many places and historical figures referenced in in this book, it is important to note *Countenance of Man* is purely a work of fiction. The characters and situations are all make believe. True, Colorado A&M, Colorado State University, the Northern Hotel, the Linden Street Mall, College Boulevard are all real and are located in Fort Collins, the situations involving them in this book are all made up. In fact, I have to admit I had never even set foot in the Northern Hotel even after living in the town for more than a decade. Likewise, Fort Collins High is real and has a proud history dating back to 1890's; however, any references to the school in these pages are only part of a story.

Fort Collins represents a backdrop for one family's life and growth in these pages. The story might just as well have been situated in a number of wonderful towns dotting our country's heartland, but Fort Collins happened to be a town I was familiar with. So, it became home to the Simmons and their lives. Suffice it to say, that this is merely the story of a man rediscovering and appreciating his family roots.

Made in the USA
Columbia, SC
01 January 2023